"My legendary

Adam looked out to w̶̶̶̶̶̶ ̶̶̶̶̶̶ ̶̶̶̶̶̶ ̶̶̶̶ ̶̶̶̶̶̶ horizon. "The most intriguing woman I've met in years, and she's on her way to somewhere else."

Priss's small shoulder gave his a gentle bump. "It's only March. Nacho's not out of school till the end of June."

"We'd better get going, if we want to be back by dark." Adam stood, and reached a hand down to help her up. Her hand fit in his as if it belonged there.

She squeezed his hand. The look in her dark eyes lit the pilot flame in his chest, and the heat cranked up.

When his pâté sandwich tried to crawl up his throat, he swallowed it again. He'd *just* made up his mind to grab for the life he wanted....

Three months was not going to be near long enough.

Dear Reader,

I was so happy when, after *Her Road Home* (Harlequin Superromance, August 2013), Harlequin wanted more stories! I was missing the little Central Coast California tourist town of Widow's Grove and the townspeople.

The Reasons to Stay was born of my personal experience with cobbled-together families. You see, when I met my Alpha Dog twenty-eight years ago, he came with a bonus: sole custody of his two young children. Overnight, this clueless single girl became a wife and mother. Although none of this book is autobiographical, I hope I was able to convey some of the perpetual lostness I felt during that first year.

I hope you enjoy *The Reasons to Stay,* and watch for the cameo appearance of Sam and Jesse from the first book. Then watch for them all to turn up in the next book coming in 2015!

Laura Drake

P.S. I enjoy hearing from readers. You can contact me and sign up for my newsletter through my website, www.lauradrakebooks.com.

LAURA DRAKE

—

The Reasons to Stay

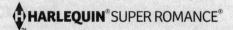
HARLEQUIN® SUPER ROMANCE®

Recycling programs
for this product may
not exist in your area.

ISBN-13: 978-0-373-60863-8

THE REASONS TO STAY

Copyright © 2014 by Laura Drake

All rights reserved. Except for use in any review, the reproduction or utilization of this work in whole or in part in any form by any electronic, mechanical or other means, now known or hereinafter invented, including xerography, photocopying and recording, or in any information storage or retrieval system, is forbidden without the written permission of the publisher, Harlequin Enterprises Limited, 225 Duncan Mill Road, Don Mills, Ontario, Canada M3B 3K9.

This is a work of fiction. Names, characters, places and incidents are either the product of the author's imagination or are used fictitiously, and any resemblance to actual persons, living or dead, business establishments, events or locales is entirely coincidental.

This edition published by arrangement with Harlequin Books S.A.

For questions and comments about the quality of this book, please contact us at CustomerService@Harlequin.com.

® and TM are trademarks of Harlequin Enterprises Limited or its corporate affiliates. Trademarks indicated with ® are registered in the United States Patent and Trademark Office, the Canadian Intellectual Property Office and in other countries.

H HARLEQUIN®

Printed in U.S.A.   www.Harlequin.com

ABOUT THE AUTHOR

Laura Drake is a city girl who never grew out of her tomboy ways, or a serious cowboy crush. She writes both women's fiction and romance stories. She rode a hundred thousand miles on the back of her husband's motorcycle, propping a book against him and reading on the boring stretches. Then she learned to ride her own motorcycle, and now owns two—Elvis, a 1985 BMW Mystic, and Sting, a 1999 BMW R1100. Since then, she's put in a hundred thousand miles riding the back roads, getting to know the small Western towns that are her books' settings. Her twenty-five-year aspirations came true this year when she officially became a Texan! She gave up the corporate CFO gig to write full-time. In the remaining waking hours, she's a wife, grandmother and motorcycle chick.

Books by Laura Drake

HARLEQUIN SUPERROMANCE

1870—HER ROAD HOME

Other titles by this author available in ebook format.

This book is dedicated to my long-suffering resilient children, Glenn and Kimarie. In spite of my well-meant, yet fumbling efforts, you've grown to be strong, wonderful people. I couldn't be prouder if I'd given birth to you.

I learned much more from you than you ever did me. Thank you.

CHAPTER ONE

BILLY JOEL IS full of crap. Not only the good die young.

The low gray clouds seemed to settle on Priss's shoulders as she walked between the graves, zipping her leather jacket against the chill air. Was it a sin to wear jeans to a funeral? Probably. But it was a long way from Boulder to Widow's Grove, and Mona had overheated in Phoenix. If she'd stopped to change clothes, Priss would have been alone in this graveyard.

As it was, there were only two other people in the cemetery on the right side of the winter-brown grass. They stood beside the subtly Astroturfed dirt pile.

She stopped a few feet short of the open grave. Her mother was down there. Shouldn't she feel something beyond tired? Hearing her heart thud in her ears, she listened for something else. Sadness, maybe, or loss? Regret?

A little late for that. Old wounds didn't always heal—the deepest ones festered.

By the time the hospital had tracked down Priss

and called, her mother was gone. Better that way really, for them both.

"Come, Ignacio. It's time to go." A meager woman stood at the foot of the grave, both her face and raincoat set in similar generic authoritarian lines.

Priss recognized a social worker when she saw one. Given her past, she should.

A kid stood beside her, head down, face obscured by a black hoodie pulled out of shape by fists crammed into the pocket across the front. Crotch-sagging jeans puddled atop untied tennis shoes that might have, in a former life, been white.

The woman touched his shoulder. The kid shrugged her off. One hand appeared from his pocket, and Priss got a flash of knuckles lettered with homemade tattoos before it disappeared beneath the hood.

She heard a muffled snuffle, and the boy swiped the sleeve across his face.

Priss felt a pinch in her chest, somewhere in the vicinity of her heart.

Shit.

The hood flew back and for the first time, she stared into the defiant eyes of her half brother. She stuffed her hands in the back pockets of her jeans. "I'm Priss, your—"

"I know who you are." Below the knit stocking

cap, his almost delicate eyebrows drew together over narrowed eyes.

His hostility slapped her hard. She took a step back.

The matron spoke up. "Well, *I* don't know who you are."

Priss looked her over. "Who are *you?*"

She sniffed and looked Priss over. "I am Ms. Barnes, children's social worker for Santa Barbara County. And you haven't answered my question." Her tone was haughty, but her glare was weak. She should ask the kid for lessons.

"I'm Priscilla Hart." She tipped her chin at the grave. "My mother's the one in the box."

The Barnes woman tsk-tsked and her lip curled, as if she'd encountered a turd in a church pew. It was a response Priss was used to. She'd always been what her mother called, "outspoken," but Priss didn't know how else to be.

Her opinions were like a deposit of crude oil, buried shallower than most people's. Others had regulators to control and filter to a civilized flow; hers were much more likely to spew. She never meant to hurt people's feelings, but mostly the nuances of refined talk escaped her. Dancing around the facts to be polite made her head hurt.

She'd take her facts straight up, thank you.

The social worker reached for the kid's shoulder

again but at his glare, dropped her hand. "Come, Ignacio. We'll get your things."

"My name is Nacho!" His shout rolled away through the empty graveyard.

The woman pursed her lips and pink spread from her cheeks to the rest of her face. "Well, then… come with me." She turned, took a few steps and waved her hands to encourage Nacho to follow her.

But the kid didn't move, just stood looking at his sister. His defiant eyes had taken on a shiny cast and his bottom lip wobbled. The tough guy morphed into a scared ten-year-old.

Oh, crap.

When Priss followed the social worker away from the grave, Nacho was right behind her. "Where are you taking him?"

"To pick up his clothing at his home."

Something old and lumbering stirred deep inside Priss. She was curious to see where her mother had lived. "I'm going with you." She said it to Nacho, but Ms. Barnes stopped and turned.

"I'll need some identification to prove you're re-lated to…" She shot a glance at Nacho. "Mr. Hart."

The kid rolled his eyes.

Priss restrained herself from doing the same, pulled her wallet from her jacket pocket and handed over her Colorado driver's license.

The social worker inspected it like a Stop-n-Go clerk checks a twenty then handed it back. "I suppose you are also next of kin. You can follow me in your car."

Deciding the clouds were window dressing for the funeral rather than rainmakers, Priss left Mona's top down and pulled out behind the county Chevy.

When they reached the outskirts of town, Priss took in the fussy Victorians perched on manicured lawns, looking down their patrician noses at the traffic in the street.

She rolled to a four-way stop in the middle of town. A tall flagpole with a limp flag graced the middle of the intersection. Up the cross street, buildings crowded each other for space, cute wooden signs declaring them B & Bs, antique shops, art galleries, coffeehouses.

Her mother sure hadn't lived in this part of town.

Following the county car, Priss took a left. Sure enough, the posh buildings were replaced by ranch houses, and after they crossed over a creek, single-wide trailers and ramshackle cracker-box houses lined the street. The stunted, skeletal trees did nothing to soften the dingy neighborhood.

After parking behind the Chevy, Priss cut the engine and waited as Mona went through the death throes the '81 Caddy had been named for. Priss had seen past the scaly black paint and the rust-dotted chrome to the Glory of Detroit in Mona's lines and under her hood. She'd bought Mona off a university student and since then had put every penny she could spare into restoring her.

Priss finger-combed her short stand-up black hair in the rearview mirror. The painful squeal of her car door cracked the quiet.

The squat one-story wooden building was set in a C, creating a courtyard full of weeds and wind-blown trash. It had probably been a Motor Lodge, back in the '60s. But that heyday was long past. Its boards were warped and wavy, a faded barn-red. The hand-lettered wooden sign out front advertised rooms for rent by the week.

The familiar weight of poverty and want settled over Priss like a foul-smelling wool blanket. As she stepped out of the car, a shudder of *déjà vu* ran through her, helping to shake off a taint of despair. It wasn't hers any longer.

But it is his.

Nacho stood on the cracked sidewalk, his face empty of emotion. When Ms. Barnes asked him a question, he dug in his pocket and handed over a key. She led the way to a door at the end of the derelict building.

Nacho walked in first, and Ms. Barnes followed, flipping on the light. She flinched slightly, but to her credit she didn't wrinkle her nose.

Priss stepped in behind them. It wasn't the bare lightbulb hanging from the ceiling that brought it all back, or the tired room it illuminated. It was the smell. The walls exhaled ghosts of damp rot, untold cartons of her mother's cigarettes and decades of starchy food, into her face.

Oh, yeah. She knew this place.

It was her past.

Priss glanced at the tinfoil-tipped rabbit ears on the TV, the sagging, sheet-covered couch, the dimestore painting of a rapturous bleeding Christ hanging over it. His suffering-crazed eyes had always frightened her—as if his hanging on the dirty wall was somehow *her* fault.

She shouldn't have been curious about this place—her mom changed locations a lot, but "home" remained the same. Widow's Grove was the final stop on Cora Hart's rutted road in search of happy.

Priss had bailed off that road ten years ago, when public school set her free with an emancipation proclamation they called a diploma.

The county lady walked across the warped linoleum to the kitchen area. "Just pack a few changes of clothes. We'll deal with the rest later." She pulled open a sagging cabinet and peered in.

Head down, Nacho strode to the doorless room on the right. Priss followed. A small, rumpled cot with dingy sheets took up one corner of the eight-by-eight room. Nacho pulled a backpack from under the bed and stuffed it with clothes from a stack of plastic storage bins. Priss had had that same dresser, growing up.

He glanced at the schoolbooks lying on the bed, then shot a sly look at Priss. She just shrugged. None of her concern if he left them behind. He pushed past her, stopped in the bathroom only long enough to pick up his toothbrush and jammed it in the outside pocket of the backpack.

Outside the bathroom door he reached for a small, ornate iron cross hanging on the wall beside his head. He lifted the cross off the hook, dropped it into the backpack and snapped the bag's flap closed. His eyes cut to her again. Sad, moist eyes.

She remembered that cross. According to her mother it had been passed down from her Spanish ancestors; it was her proudest possession. A gossamer wisp of nostalgia floated through Priss's chest before she could quash it.

Pushing away from the wall, she sauntered to the kitchen area feigning untouchable indifference. "What happens to all this stuff?"

Ms. Barnes handed Priss her business card. "Anything of value will be sold to reimburse the State for her medical care." Her pinched lips told Priss what she thought of that likelihood.

"Oh, I don't know. A museum might want the TV."

Nacho walked by her. "Museums don't pay for things, stupid."

She smiled. He sounded like her. "You've got a point there, kid."

He stopped in front of the social worker who stood washing her hands at the sink. "I could stay here. There's food, and I know how to cook."

"I'm not sure I'd call what's in that refrigerator food. You're ten years old. You cannot live by yourself."

"She could stay with me." The thumb he threw over his shoulder pointed at Priss.

She backed away. "Oh, no. Uh-uh. I've been there and done that. Couldn't afford the T-shirt." Alarm raced along her skin, chasing the goose bumps.

It didn't matter that she was grown, had a life of her own and some money in the bank. Her first instinct was that someone was going to force her to stay here. Forever.

Claustrophobia bloomed like squid's ink in her brain. In a panic she rushed out of the apartment. Outside in the clean air, she pulled in deep, grateful lungfuls, exhaling the past.

Her ears buzzed. Exhaustion or *déjà vu?* Maybe both.

Nacho barreled past her, stopped in the weeds and chest heaving, looked at her, his eyes full of betrayal. "Don't you think I know nobody wants me?" His fists clenched and unclenched at his sides.

The pain and animosity on the kid's face brought

it all back—a slap-in-the-face reminder of why she had never come back.

Ms. Barnes stepped out, pulling the door closed behind her. "Now, now, Ignacio. I understand that you've had an emotional day. But anger will not serve you well."

"My mom's dead. My dad's in prison. And this one—" he jerked a thumb at Priss "—is useless." He spit into the weeds. "Fine. Take me. I don't give a shit." He stalked to the car and stood with his back to them, shoulders square, head up.

Way to go, Mom. As usual, you bail and leave someone else to be responsible. Well, I didn't sign up for this. It's not my problem.

She strode to her car, got in, and peeled out, tires squealing as she made her way back to her life.

When the gunmetal-gray ocean rose in the horizon of her windshield, Priss realized she'd made a wrong turn. No surprise, since she couldn't recall the roads she'd taken to get here.

Idling at the corner of whatever and Pacific Coast Highway, she stared at the moody water until a driver honked behind her. Her mind still churning, she pulled across the road to an empty parking lot on the deserted beach.

Memories banged at the door she'd locked years ago and her head pounded with the hammering. Jesus, the smell in that apartment. She thought she'd forgotten it but when she stepped inside that hole it was *all* there, waiting for her.

She switched off the engine and Mona settled with a wheeze. Opening the door, she stepped into the wind. It was much colder here than inland. Her eyes watered, so she closed them and absorbed the astringent scent of timeless salt caverns at the bottom of the ocean. Zipping her leather jacket, she floundered through the loose sand to where the waves pounded the beach smooth, making walking easier. She walked, watching the little bubbles that rose with each wave's retreat.

She ached for the mindless drift of Colorado. Those days when Ryan was home and they'd make love in the long, languid mornings until her skin burned all over from passion and his beard stubble. Reading him the comics, tangled in the sheets and sunlight.

Ryan was fun-loving, and no more interested in ties than she. They fit.

She lifted her face to the wind. But Boulder hadn't really been like that in a while, had it? Certainly not the sex part, anyway. She couldn't exactly say when it happened, but things were off, somehow. Ryan was on the road more this spring, putting on skateboard tournaments, or filming them. And when they spoke over the phone he seemed distracted, distant.

Her temp office jobs felt mundane lately. And

when she wandered down to the bar with her friends, the laughter there sounded forced, almost fiercely jolly—as if a sparkly facade would make happiness sink in and become real.

A bit cynical maybe, but you've been to your mother's grave today. That's bound to stir the shit on the bottom of the tank.

But Priss was the one who demanded truth above all. She couldn't lie to herself. She *knew* what was wrong. Her perfect, shiny gold life was flaking away, revealing a cheap dime-store bauble underneath.

And that scared the crap out of her.

What if she'd run from her mother's world—the grinding poverty and the bogus rosy future of the next man at the bar—only to settle for an upscale version of the same life?

She crammed her icy fists into the pockets of her jacket. She had made sure not to get trapped by the chains that had held her mother captive. Priscilla Hart wasn't getting tied to anything: a man, kids or a dead-end job. Better to just fly above it all. Jettison weight and take in the good things that came to her.

That philosophy had served her well for ten years. The past stayed in the past, and the present…

If Colorado had lost its shine, there were lots of other places to explore. She turned her back to the ceaseless wind and let it push her to her car. Maybe it was time to hit the road and get out of Boulder. There were plenty of other chances just waiting for her to swoop in and claim them.

The comforting thought lasted until she slid into Mona, turned the key, and hit the button to raise the top. The cold had whipped past her flimsy barrier of skin and muscle to freeze-dry her bones.

Nacho.

He was a good-looking kid with his dark eyes, soft mouth, and the same widow's peak and cowlick their mother had. The same one Priss saw in her rearview mirror.

But his tawny skin was his father's. Priss knew, because she'd met the man. Her mom's shift from losers to married losers was the gas that fueled Priss's flight from the bad side of Vegas, from the "slut spawn" taunts of her classmates, from her mother's assurances that with *this* man things would be better.

And her mother's record for losers stood unbroken, since it seemed he was now in prison. She rolled up the windows and cranked the heat.

Nacho wouldn't have the luxury of driving away. She wondered where they had taken him.

Not your problem. He'll be fine. They'll take care of him.

Wherever they put him would be safer than being alone on the rough side of town at night, while his mother worked as a barmaid in an area likely even rougher.

"He's better off." She ignored the shiver that ran through her like ice water, and put the car in Reverse.

He'd stood there, waiting for her to make some kind of decision. A decision that told him he didn't matter any more than the trash blowing around their feet.

She knew that feeling. She'd lived that feeling.

After checking for oncoming traffic, she hit the gas and pulled onto the open road. It wasn't her job to save orphans. At eighteen, she'd left that fouled nest back in Vegas, spread her wings and flown, never looking back.

And she wasn't starting now. Her hands tightened on the steering wheel.

She drove south on PCH, planning to pick up Highway 15 out of L.A., driving on autopilot. The spectacular vistas of bluffs tumbling to meet the ocean barely registered.

Those eyes.

He'd looked right into her, seen that she knew. Knew about lying in the dark alone as your mom left for work. When she leaned over to give a kiss goodnight, he'd begged, just like Priss had begged.

Don't leave me. I'm afraid.

Yet she'd always left. And with the closing door, the shadows would shift. The space would change from something warm and safe to a place that hid bad things and held scary sounds, just on the other side of the flimsy walls. A kid's imagination was worse than reality. Most of the time.

Again she pictured him lying in the dark, alone. Night after night. For years. Waiting for Mom to come home, bringing the smell of cheap perfume and menthol "smokes" with her.

"God*damn* it!" She pulled off at a scenic over-look. Below, crashing waves drove the spray up a cliff face with the same relentless battering of her conscience.

She knew nothing about taking care of a kid. After all, her mother hadn't been a shining example. And she had no interest in learning.

But she also knew what could happen to a kid in foster care. She shuddered.

Why would you even consider this? It's not like you can save yourself retroactively.

Maybe not, but she might be able to save another kid. Her half brother.

"I am *not* my mother." She put the car in Park, picked up her phone and with shaking fingers, di-aled.

Shouting in the background. "Damn sketchy trick but he nailed that pop shove-it, didn't he? It's gonna make epic film. Hang on. Hello?"

"Hi, Ryan. I'm—"

"Hang on, babe, I can't hear you." The background noise faded, then a door banged.

"Okay, I'm outside, but it's like ten degrees. If I stay here long they'll use my balls to chill some loser's drink. How's it going?"

"Well, Mona broke down for a couple hours in Arizona, so I missed the funeral."

"Oh, hell, I'm sorry."

"It's okay. Hey, listen, when are you coming home?"

"We're filming at one more indoor park, in Albany. I'm planning on being back by next Tuesday. You'll be back by then, right?"

"Yeah, no problem. But Ryan?"

"Damned wind is brutal. Yeah?"

"Um. I ran into my half brother. He's like ten. They're putting him in foster care."

"That sucks. What's it got to do with you?"

"Well, I was thinking…what would you think if I brought him with me?"

"To Boulder?" His voice rose higher at the end than the question warranted. "Why would you want the baggage? You always said you were a free bird."

"I know. I am." She pulled at the roots of her hair as memories chewed at her with wolf-size bites. "Damn, Ryan, I told you what those places are like. Believe me, I don't want the hassle. But I'm not sure I can leave a kid to that."

"Um, Priss, I don't mean to sound all evil, but

I didn't sign up for that gig, you know? We got a good thing, just you and I." She heard his teeth chatter. "Listen, I've gotta go, or they're gonna find me freeze-dried like that guy in that Stephen King movie. But I gotta tell you, Priss, three's a crowd that I'm not interested in hanging with. See what I'm saying? I mean…"

She let her head fall on the back of the seat, suddenly weary down to her DNA. "Yeah, I hear you. Listen, I'll call you later, okay?"

He must have walked back into the bar, because Rihanna wailed in her ear. "Yeah. Later, babe."

Click.

Talking to Ryan only solidified what she'd almost known before the call. She was done with Boulder. But of the zillions of flight paths she had, was one of them taking custody of her half brother?

She hadn't realized until she stepped into that apartment how much the past weighted her. The fact that she hadn't made it ten miles out of town was proof that today her wings had been clipped.

"Shitshitshitshit!"

Leaning her head on the cool plastic of the steering wheel, she waited until her breath stopped hitching. Then she sat motionless for a long time, poised between past and present, between facts and emotions, between flight and landing.

Her stomach pitched with the rapid altitude change. Maybe doing this would be the last payment, the final stamp that said "paid in full" on the chit she owed her mother for giving Priss life.

Then she could fly off, unencumbered. Karma balanced.

But don't think you're forgiven, Mother, for leaving this mess for me to clean up.

She sat up, pulled the county social worker's card out of her back pocket and after staring at it for a while, called the phone number listed.

"MOTHER, BE LOGICAL." Adam Preston lifted a box of dishes and carried it to the hallway to add to the rest of his mother's carefully selected household goods. "If you'd look at this unemotionally, you'd see I'm right."

She stumped behind him, one wheel of her walker squeaking. "Don't you 'Mother' me. I'm allowed to be emotional. This is the house your father and I bought when we married. Leaving it isn't easy, you know."

Olivia Preston wouldn't let a little thing like recovering from a broken hip keep her from looking presentable—from her beauty-shopped silver hair to the soft loafers on her petite feet.

"That's my point. You don't have to leave. We could set you up in the downstairs bedroom, and have a ramp put in so you don't have to navigate the porch steps. And I can take the bedroom upstairs." Thank God his mother was healthy, but at seventy-nine, brittle bones and balance issues were an accident that hadn't waited to happen.

"Ruining the facade of this cottage with an ugly, old-lady ramp would be criminal." She straightened to all of her five feet. "And you are *not* moving in with me. How would it look to my potential daughters-in-law, you living with your mother?"

He wasn't touching that one. "Your friend Lily lives in that retirement place in Santa Maria. Why don't we look into it?"

"And leave Widow's Grove? I've lived here all my life. Besides, can you see me getting on one of those odious little buses to go for a rousing night of bingo?"

Not without a partial lobotomy, he couldn't. She'd been a professor of philosophy at UC Santa Barbara for thirty years. "But, Mom, above the store?" The only reason this was remotely possible was the elevator that survived the renovation when his father bought the two-story Ben Franklin dime store, back in the '60s.

"If I can't stay in the bedroom Tom and I shared, I'd rather be in our old apartment. That way I'll still have his memories around me."

His dad had died six years ago but you'd never know it, hearing his mother talk. He was proud of how she'd soldiered on afterward—not that there'd been any doubt. His mother was a strong woman. Maybe too strong. Because *this* was a crazy idea.

Adam had moved into one of the apartments over the family drugstore when he'd returned from college with his degree and pharmacist's license. "You'd be all alone up there."

"You'll be working right beneath me. Besides, if you hadn't broken that sweet little schoolteacher's heart she'd still be living in the apartment across the hall."

He dropped the box on the growing pile. "Mom, let's not start that again."

"Why else would she have left in the middle of the school year if not because of a broken heart? I hate to point it out, but you're not getting any younger and neither am I. I'd like to meet my grandchildren before I move on to whatever is next. But if you keep being so darned picky—"

"Mom. I didn't break her heart." He looked at the ceiling and blew out a breath. "She was gay, okay? She said that dating me made her sure that she wasn't interested in men. She moved to Carmel and in with her ex-girlfriend."

Mother winced. "Ouch."

"And thanks for reminding me of the lowest point in my love life, to date."

"Well, then, you need to pick yourself up and get on with your life, Adam." She patted his hand. "Jesse at the café gave me a couple of names of nice girls you can call."

He had to get out of here before his head exploded. "I've got to get to softball practice, Mom. I'll stop by on my way home with a load of my stuff." He walked out, shaking his head. His mother discussing his love life, or lack thereof, with the town matchmaker? How pathetic was he? He bounded down the stairs to his midsize sedan, the backseat loaded with bats, bases, and dirty laundry.

So maybe pharmacist wasn't on the "top ten sexiest careers" list. But he wasn't hideous looking. He was neat, led a quiet life, and—

And arguing your good points with yourself is even more pathetic.

Mom was wrong. He waved to Burt Hanks, who drove past, then unlocked the car and sank into it. But lately, the safe life he'd put on like a Teflon suit so many years ago had started to chafe—as if it were made of wet wool.

But just the same, the thought of stepping out of it made his stomach muscles clench to guard his guts.

CHAPTER TWO

A WEEK AFTER her mom's funeral, Priss walked down Hollister, Widow's Grove's main drag, trying not to sweat. It had been chilly when she left the hotel this morning, so she'd worn a turtleneck with her pencil skirt and heels. But the day had turned warm, especially downtown, where the buildings blocked the breeze.

She paused at the display window of Hollister Drugs, more to rest her feet than to window-shop. Toeing out of one shoe, she rubbed her toes on the back of the other calf while glancing at the merchandise.

It had taken some convincing but Ms. Barnes had finally agreed to a temporary custody hearing with the Family Services Court. She didn't seem to trust Priss or her intentions but didn't have much choice since Priss was Nacho's only unincarcerated kin.

The judge seemed wary as well, in spite of Priss dressing up and being on her best behavior. Though to be fair, her lack of a job and spiky hair probably had something to do with it. She hated looking so young. People often guessed her ten years younger than her twenty-nine years and assumed her maturity level matched her youthful face. They had no way of knowing that she'd gained her street smarts at a younger age than Nacho was now.

But the judge did grant Priss temporary custody, with strings. That meant home visits and interviews, and the judge had left the timeline open-ended. Priss would have to prove herself as a parent to Ms. Barnes's satisfaction before she and Nacho could leave Widow's Grove.

Priss had agreed to their terms. This would be as good a place as any to settle, at least in the short term. If she didn't like it down the road, she'd make a different choice. What worried her more was the fact that she hadn't a clue about how to be a parent. After all, she'd never been exposed to a good one.

But the worry about screwing up Nacho's psyche had to take a backseat. They had to eat in the meantime. She needed a job.

The lady at the temp agency had no openings for office workers. Turned out tourist towns weren't big on office management. And the few jobs they did have wouldn't support Priss, much less her *and* Nacho. She had to find something soon. The hotel was expensive, and Ms. Barnes wouldn't release Nacho into Priss's care until she had a job, and a proper place to live in. The apartments she'd looked at on the outskirts of town were way too expensive, and too far from Nacho's school.

So here she was, footsore and sweating, walking the streets looking for work. She'd stopped in The Gift of Words bookstore, a trendy clothing store for kids and an antique boutique. She'd never been a store clerk, but if it paid enough she'd find a way to become the best damned clerk they'd ever hired. But none of the shops needed help.

God, she was thirsty. She leaned in, cupping her hand around her eyes to see past the window's glare into the drugstore, but still couldn't make out much. Surely they sold cold soda. She slipped back into her shoe, stepped to the door and opened it.

Her heels tapped hollow on the wooden floor. A wall of blessedly cool air bathed her face, bringing with it the smell of coffee, French fries and old building. Two checkout counters faced her and beyond that, several shoppers wandered aisles that led to the pharmacy counter against the back wall.

But it was the area along the left wall that snagged her attention. An old soda-fountain counter stood on a black-and-white-checkerboard tiled area with a huge mirror behind it, reflecting stacked parfait glasses and sundae boats. Several of the frilly white wrought-iron tables were occupied by early lunchers. The whole area was bathed in light streaming through the huge front window, making it look like an oasis in the desert—or heaven.

Her feet led her without conscious direction around the tables and chairs, straight to the counter where she collapsed on the red vinyl stool farthest from the sun.

A girl stood behind the counter, flipping burgers and snapping gum.

"Could I have some water?"

Snap, snap, snap. "Okay, but you gotta order something. You know, something that costs money." She didn't move to get a glass.

Probably just out of high school, the girl wore a pink, sixties-throwback A-line dress, with a white frilled apron and a pink pillbox cap perched on hot-magenta shoulder-length hair. The rims of both ears were encrusted with stud earrings, and her lipstick and short nails were both painted black.

Rising irritation only made Priss hotter. "You're going to lecture me on manners?"

The girl rolled her eyes to the back of the store. "Hey, it's not me. I could give a crap. It's the boss's rule."

"Okay. After you bring me water…" She glanced to the menu board on the wall to her right. "How about a BLT and a diet coke."

"Coming up." The girl finally moved, albeit slowly.

When the ice water arrived, Priss drank half of it at once, then winced as the brain freeze hit. Her stomach growled at the smell of grilling bacon. She tried to relax and let the AC and lunch-crowd conversation wash over her. Sipping more slowly, she noticed a bulletin board below the menu, with a sign at the top, *The Grove Groove*. She stood and walked over to read. Among the local real estate agents' business cards were flyers for a lost llama, babysitting services, and a "gently used" Western saddle. She flipped up and read a thank-you card from a local little-league team to the drugstore's owner, for his sponsorship. An index card at the very bottom caught her eye.

Furnished Apartment for Rent.
See Adam Preston for details.

You know you're in a small town when they don't include a phone number. She walked back and sat, just as the girl set down Priss's BLT.

"You want mustard?"

"Sure. But, can you tell me who Adam Preston is, and how I contact him about that apartment?"

The girl walked a few steps and drew a soda from a tall, old-fashioned dispenser. "He's the boss I told you about. The pharmacist." *Snap, snap.*

Priss craned her neck to the pharmacy counter in the back.

"He'll be back after lunch." The girl set the curvy glass in front of Priss and plunked a bottle of mustard next to it. "The apartment is upstairs." She looked at the ceiling. "He's up there now actually."

"Oh, cool." It wouldn't hurt to get some insider

information. "My name is Priss, by the way. I'm moving to Widow's Grove for a while."

The girl's attention sharpened, as if Priss had just moved out of the generic customer category. "I'm Sin, as in S-I-N." *Snap, snap.* "Actually, it's Hyacinth. I shorten it to irritate my mother. That'll teach her for naming me after a stupid flower."

Her smile displayed further rebellion—a huge cubic zirconia was set in her front tooth.

"I can relate. My name came from my mother's massive crush on Elvis."

"That old fat guy?" *Snap. Snap. Snap.* "That blows."

"Tell me about it. What can you tell me about the apartment, or the pharmacist? I really need a place near town."

The girl named a modest rent amount, then considered her next words as she scooped ice cream into a banana-split boat. "Adam is okay. He's kinda hot, for an old guy."

That wasn't the kind of information she was looking for. "I mean—"

"Except he's got a major stick up his butt."

"How so?"

"He's anal. Seriously, terminally, anal. The guy needs to dispense himself a chill pill." She walked to the other end of the counter to deliver the split to a guy in a business suit, leaving Priss to try to reconcile those two facts and how to use them for leverage. If that apartment was presentable, she really needed to rent it.

ADAM TOOK THE last dish from the dishwasher and put it in the cabinet. "Mom, I've got to get back to work." He grabbed a sponge and wiped the sandwich crumbs from the counter. "You've got your phone with you in case you need anything, right?"

"Yes, dear." His mother rose from the kitchen chair, clutched her walker and squeaked her way to her favorite antique wing-back chair in the living room.

When the microwave dinged, he took out the cup of tea and carried it to her. He'd wanted to move her into the apartment that had the view of Hollister, but she insisted on saving the nicer view for a "paying customer."

"Thank you. I'll be fine, don't worry about me." She pulled a soft throw onto her lap. "When I'm off this walker and back on my own pins you won't need to coddle me anymore."

"No worries, Mom. I'm just downstairs." He walked to the door, wondering how many prescriptions had piled up and how Sin was coping with the lunch crowd.

"Adam."

He pulled the door open and turned back to her. "Yeah, Mom?"

"Don't forget, if someone wants to rent the other apartment, I get final say, right?"

"Of course. But I call screening privileges. They'll be living right across the hall and you're too trusting." He closed the door and walked down the stairs that ended in a vestibule; one door led into the store, one led to the alley behind it. He unlocked the door to the store and walked in.

He glanced up front, to the soda fountain. Sin lifted a thumb to let him know all was well then waved him over. Walking up the nearest aisle, he stopped to help old Mrs. Baylor with a suppository recommendation before moving on.

I've got to do something about Sin. She didn't look like a '60s soda jerk—she looked more like Cyndi Lauper at a Halloween party. But how could he approach the situation without hurting her feelings? He'd been through a string of failed hires before Sin, and in spite of her looks he'd come to rely on her. She ran the soda fountain well and he could trust her. The locals were used to her looks. Maybe just a different color uniform would help— one that complemented her hair.

Snap, snap. "Boss, this lady wants to talk to you."

He was going to have to talk to her about chewing that gum. Again. He turned to the lady on the last stool.

Scratch that. A girl.

She had a slim build and wore a knee-length skirt that showed off long, muscled dancer's calves, crossed at the ankle. But it was her face that caught and held him—huge green eyes set in a pretty heart-shaped face. Her brown hair was short and spiked with a widow's peak. She sat looking at him with a small nervous smile.

Time slowed and sound faded.

God, she's enchanting. Even though he was sure he'd never used that word before, it fit. He felt enchanted.

He extended a hand. "Adam Preston."

She gave him a firm, no-nonsense shake. "Priscilla Hart. I'm interested in the apartment you have for rent."

She must have read the skepticism in his expression, because she sighed. "I'm twenty-nine—plenty old enough."

Not for what I was imagining.

"Well, all right. Why don't you follow me? I have an application and background authorization for you to fill out."

There was a line at the prescription counter so he sat her at the consulting window with the forms and got to work.

Fifteen minutes later he'd dealt with the line. The dropped-off scripts could wait. His prospective tenant sat tapping her fingers on the counter. He walked over and picked up the forms. "An interim office manager. Colorado, huh? I don't see a phone number for your previous landlord. I'll need that."

"I need to tell him I'm leaving first." She fussed with the strap of her purse.

She was businesslike and put-together. But after the epic fail of his last tenant, he knew that appearances were deceiving. He frowned.

"You can check. I pay my taxes, am a registered voter and don't have so much as a moving violation."

"But according to this, you don't have a job in Widow's Grove."

"Yet. You'll see from my credit check that I have enough money in the bank to cover a deposit, first and last month's rent."

"But if you can't pay down the road, eviction is a real hassle."

"Look." She stood and slung the oversize purse on her shoulder. "I'm trying to rent an apartment. I am not signing up to guard the president or run the Federal Reserve. Check out my references, then let me know. My cell number is on the fifth form from the bottom." She looked at him as if he were a juicy wad of gum on her shoe. "Do you think you could trust me enough to at least *show* me this apartment? I'll give you time to hide the silver first, if you want."

He had to smile at her, all puffed up and huffy. "Actually, you kind of would be guarding the president. Follow me." He locked the metal door to the drug area then led the way through the door to the stairs. But instead of taking them, he inserted the key to call the elevator.

At the top, he walked to the door to the right and searched his ring for the correct key. "I used to live in the other apartment." He nodded to the door on his left. "But my mother recently broke her hip. Her house is a two-story with a walk-up porch so it wasn't working for her. I was going to move her in here and sell her house but she insisted I move into the house instead."

He found the correct key, opened the door, then stepped back so she could enter. She walked across the oak floor to look through the windows to Hollister. "Great view." Her voice echoed off the high ceilings.

He stayed by the door as she wandered into the kitchen, the bathroom and lastly, the large bedroom, her heels tap-tap-tapping across the wood floor. Generations of Preston-used furniture made the apartment feel cozy.

This apartment was the mirror image of the one across the hall. Growing up, his father had always rented them. It was a good source of additional revenue for the drugstore's start-up, and later the rents had paid Adam's tuition to UCSD.

"I think it's great. I'd like to rent it. Providing, of course, I meet your requirements."

"Okay, well, let me take you across the hall to meet my mother. My requirements take a backseat to hers."

"What does your mother have to do with this?"

"You'd be living right across the hall from her. That means she gets first right of refusal."

He watched her throat move as she swallowed. She squared her shoulders and walked out ahead of him. He crossed the hall and knocked on his mom's door.

"Come in."

He opened the door. "Mom? Do you have a minute to meet a possible tenant?"

"Certainly, bring them in."

"This is Priscilla Hart, an office manager, most recently from Colorado."

The girl—woman—walked past him to where his mother sat, reading a thick book. "Ms. Preston. It's nice to meet you. Your son told me about your recent accident. I'm sorry."

His mom put aside the book. "To hear him talk, I'm a fragile invalid. Nothing could be further from the truth."

"You're reading *Atlas Shrugged!*"

The delight in her voice brought his head up.

"That's one of my favorite books of all time."

His mother's eyes lit up. "Oh? What is it you like about it?"

Priss may not have recognized his mom's "professor voice," but Adam did.

"Her theory of rational self-interest and belief in the power of an individual." At his mother's wave, the girl sank onto the sofa. "I've learned a lot from that book."

His mother had tried for years to get him interested in philosophy, but he'd fallen asleep ten pages into that doorstop of a book. *Sports Illustrated* was more his style. "You read that stuff?"

Priss looked up, yet somehow managed to look down her nose at him. "Are you one of those men who think you have to have a college degree to be intelligent?"

"I never said that. Did I say that?"

With a smug smile, his mother watched him twist on the hook.

"Priscilla, if you have some time, I'd love to discuss this book with you."

Priss nodded.

"Would you mind making us some tea, Priscilla?" His mother gave a small head shake when he started to move.

Priss popped up. His mother explained where to find things in the kitchen.

Once she was in the other room, his mother said, "She's the one."

"I haven't run her background check. She could

be a convicted felon for all I know. She might steal the silver—"

"My silver is all at the house."

"Or murder you in your sleep. You just like her because she likes that Rand woman."

"You're wrong. I like her because she ruffles your oh-so-neat feathers." Her smile held secrets. "And frankly, son, your feathers could use a good ruffling."

PRISS PUSHED THROUGH the door from the stairwell into Hollister Drugs, heading out for another day of job hunting. She loved her new digs. She enjoyed sitting in the overstuffed chair by the window, watching the town wake up, pedestrians shifting from a trickle to a stream as the shops opened. She liked the evenings, too. The lights winked out as the town settled in for sleep. Now if she could only get as lucky in the job market.

At least she could show that do-gooder, Ms. Barnes, that she had a decent place for Nacho to live in. Her credit check and references had come back sterling, so the uptight druggist couldn't find an excuse not to rent to her. But she had no doubt that he'd tried.

She glanced to the prescription counter. Head down, Adam focused on something he was writing while speaking in an undertone to an ancient lady in a Sunday dress and orthopedic shoes. That first day, all Priss had seen was a double-breasted white coat and a wall of upper middle-class attitude. But the past few days she'd caught glimpses of more.

His tanned profile looked chiseled from granite. A sable curl escaped his perfectly gelled hair, falling onto his forehead. Underneath the Mr. Sphincter was a fine-looking man. That weird combination of handsome and uptight increasingly intrigued her. It seemed she kind of liked weird.

"And how is Annie doing, Ms. Talcott?" Adam looked up; his soft brown eyes held concern. "Has she gotten settled in Atlanta?"

The old lady beamed. "Oh, yes. Can you believe? She's expecting again!" The woman set her industrial-strength purse on the counter, unclasped the catch and pulled out her wallet, flipping open a huge accordion photo holder. "Have I showed you my great-grandtwins lately?"

"How old are they now?" Adam's fond smile displayed a killer chin dimple.

Their voices faded as she strode to the front of the store. He really appeared to care about that lady's family. Hell, he even took the time to look at photos.

No doubt about it. Adam Preston was a Nice Guy.

And therefore, suspect.

Four hours later, Priss returned home. She pulled into her space, shut down the engine and waited for Mona to stop wheezing. She'd looked for work at every business in Widow's Grove that her skills could possibly stretch to fit—and a few they wouldn't.

The clock was ticking. Nacho had been in the not-so-caring hands of the county for two weeks now. Every night, a herd of sharp-hooved nightmares thundered through her sleep, all starring Nacho, with the boy being neglected, being bullied—and worse.

She shook her head, shoving her past to the back of her mind for another day.

IT WAS ONLY midmorning on Friday and she was already tired, discouraged and in need of coffee. She'd picked through the meager want ads in the local paper and had been to every business on Hollister. She was beginning to get a whiff of failure on the wind that grew stronger each day.

Today. I'm not quitting until I find a job today.

Throwing her shoulders back, she put on her interview smile, snatched her purse from the floorboard, and stepped out of the convertible. She'd abandoned her heels after that first day. Dressy flats might not show off her legs as well but they hurt less. She strode as fast as her pencil skirt allowed toward the red-and-white-trimmed building. The sign next to the door read The Farmhouse Café.

How hard could waitressing be? After all, her mother had done it for years so it had to be a piece of cake.

A cowbell clanked against the glass door when she stepped onto an oak floor, silvered with use. Empty red vinyl booths marched along the windows to a corner where a potbellied stove squatted. Grizzled men in overalls drank coffee in a booth against the back wall. The place was midmorning-deserted.

A Formica-topped bar faced her. A pale-blonde woman sat sipping coffee on the only occupied stool, a motorcycle helmet and leather jacket on the stool beside her. A big-haired blonde stood on the other side of the bar, in a tightly fitted white pantsuit that advertised Monroe-like curves. She'd borrowed Marilyn's lipstick, too. Her Cupid's-bow mouth was a slash of crimson.

The waitress said something to the girl at the bar, then looked up. "Hey, sweetie. Welcome to the Farmhouse."

Priss walked over and extended a hand to *Marilyn*. "Hello. My name is Priss Hart. I was wondering if you needed any help with your bookkeeping. I'm—"

The blonde patron choked on her coffee. She grabbed a napkin and coughed into it while the waitress patted her back. When the biker chick could speak, she said, "You must not be from around here. Jess is the math whiz of the universe. She does the bookkeeping in her very best dreams."

"Stow it, Sam." Jess shook Priss's hand. "I'm Jesse Jurgen. That sexy hunk in the kitchen is my husband, Carl."

A Nordic giant filled the serving window, waving a spatula in greeting.

Priss nodded to him, then took a breath and pushed the reluctant words past her teeth. "Could you use a waitress, maybe?"

"Sorry, dear, it's just Carl and me."

Hope and relief whooshed out on her breath. She'd have to try Santa Maria, or Solvang. More gas, more commute time. More alone time for Nacho.

Shit.

"You look done in, hon. Have a seat." Jesse turned and lifted a metal carafe from a warming tray. "Want some coffee?"

Priss dropped onto the red vinyl-clad stool next to the biker chick. "I'd love a cup. Thanks."

Jesse poured. "You drink that. It'll buck you up. I'll be right back." She walked from behind the bar to refill the farmers' cups at the back booth.

"I'm Sam Pinelli." The slim woman next to her eyed Priss from over her coffee cup. "You don't know anything about the building trade, do you?"

"I wish."

"My husband has an auto repair and tow shop…"

Priss shook her head.

"I can't help you, then, but you came to the right place. Jess knows everything about everything in Widow's Grove—especially if you're looking for a man."

"That is exactly the last thing I want. I've already got more male in my life than I need." Priss took a sip.

Jesse swished back behind the counter and put the coffeepot on the hot plate.

Sam chuckled, "Well, if you're not looking for love then stay away from Yenta here. And just to be sure, I'd drink only bottled water while you're in Widow's Grove."

Jesse put a hand on her hip. "Samantha Pinelli, you're full of crap. You're so happily married that you're iridescent, for cripes' sakes."

"Now, now, Jess. Climb off your high horse before you split those pants."

"Anyway, we're not talking about you, Pinelli. We're trying to help this sweet thing. What do you do, hon?"

"Temp office management, and bookkeeping. But I'm up for almost anything except cleaning public toilets." She turned her cup in her hands. "And soon, I may have to consider *that*."

Jesse's perfectly plucked eyebrows scrunched. "Well, let's hope it doesn't come to that." She looked Priss up and down from across the counter. "Where are you from, sweetie?"

"Oh, all over." Priss may not have come from a small town, but she knew a local gossip when she saw one. Well, she'd come in for an interview and it seemed she was going to get one, even if it wasn't the type she'd hoped for.

Let the waterboarding begin.

"Are you planning to settle in Widow's Grove?" Jesse pulled up a wooden stool and lowered herself onto it. Her nonchalance didn't quite hide the Grand Inquisitor look in her eye.

Priss didn't like people prying into her life but putting a sob story out on the local telegraph might help her land a job. It's not like she'd be lying; Nacho *was* a sob story.

"My mother died. I've got a ten-year-old half brother who now has no one else but me. And I'm in Widow's Grove until I get him settled somewhere safe." An instinctive shudder ripped through her. She tried to disguise it by straightening her shoulders. "Social Services took him, and they won't release him to me if I don't find a job."

"Jeez, that sucks," Sam said.

Jesse looked as if Revlon had just discontinued her favorite lipstick. "Well. That just will not do." She squinted, tapping crimson nails on the counter. "Let me think a minute."

Sam glanced over at Priss. "You don't know it, but you've just unleashed *The Force, Anakin.*"

"Then I came to the right place after all." Priss leaned toward Sam's stool and said in a stage whisper, "She sure doesn't look like Yoda."

Sam laughed and set her cup down too hard, spilling her coffee.

Jesse grabbed a rag from under the counter and handed it to Sam. "I'm trying to think and you're not helping, Pinelli." Jesse cocked her head and looked Priss over.

Priss felt like she'd just been scanned at the airport.

"I don't suppose you know anything about bartending?"

Well, hell, doesn't that figure? She'd sworn never to have anything to do with her mother's lifestyle, yet here she was, getting sucked into every dirty corner of it. She sighed. "I worked my way through two years of community college bartending."

The crease between Jesse's brows vanished. "Well, then, I've got a job for you." She dusted her hands.

"What job?" Sam asked.

"You remember, Honey from Homestake Realty? She sold you your house, Sam."

"Pompous in pumps. Of course I remember her."

"Well—" Jesse leaned in "—yesterday, she skipped

town with Arnie, the bartender of Bar None. Word is they eloped to the Bahamas. Floyd is *pissed.*"

"You're sending this little pixie to Floyd Henley when he's in a state?"

Priss sat up. "I can handle myself."

Sam shook her head. "If Floyd doesn't eat you for lunch, that crusty bunch of regulars stuck to his bar stools will. You'll be wishing for those public toilets."

Jesse crossed her arms and studied Priss. "Something gives me the feeling this pixie is a scrapper."

"You'd be right." Priss pulled a few dollars from her wallet, slapped them on the counter and stood. "This 'Bar None.' It's downtown?"

"Yep. On Monterrey, off Hollister."

"Thanks for your help." Priss walked to the door. She had to nail that job before someone else did.

"May the Force be with you." Sam's voice drifted through the open door.

"You come back soon and let us know if you get the job!" Jesse called.

Priss waved a hand and kept going.

CHAPTER THREE

THE GOOD NEWS was Bar None was less than a mile from her new apartment, on a side street off Hollister's B & Bs, antique shops and art galleries. Priss stood on the cracked sidewalk under a tree full of gossiping birds, trying to convince her feet to carry her inside.

There *had* to be another way. But if the Yoda of Widow's Grove didn't know of any other jobs, there probably weren't any.

You could try Solvang.

But the cute Danish town was more of a tourist trap than Widow's Grove. She'd be even less likely to find an office job there. Besides, after seeing Nacho's tats and attitude, the closer she worked to Widow's Grove the better. Nacho and unsupervised time probably didn't mix.

Only an open door and one small window framing a neon Schlitz sign marred the redbrick exterior of the bar. She glanced through the branches at the cloudless sky.

I get it, God. But does it have to be this?

A bird-crap missile passed within an inch of her face and plopped at her feet.

"Okay, then. You don't have to be rude about it." Abandoning any hope of reprieve she straightened her skirt and crossed the sidewalk.

Odds are he's not looking for a daytime bartender, anyway. And there's no way I'm leaving Nacho alone nights.

She opened the front door and refrigerated air pebbled her skin, bringing with it the smell of spilled beer, old fryer grease and the ghosts of cigarettes smoked back when it was legal. It stirred memories of more than her bartending days—this scent was her mother's signature perfume. Priss took in the smells again—mostly bitter with very little sweet.

A jukebox she couldn't see through the gloom blared a "welcome home" tune. Booths commandeered the wall to her right; tables filled the floor space. On her left, a long bar took up the rest of the room. A television high in a corner broadcast a baseball game to patrons parked on every stool.

Priss unclenched her fists, her jaw, and her attitude. She put on her friendly bartender face and strode to the bar like she owned it.

The little man who stood behind the long dark wood barrier looked like Tweedledee. Or maybe it was Tweedledum—she always got them confused. His gray hair pulled into a messy ponytail was at serious odds with the bald dome rising above it. He was short and round, but sure didn't look jolly. Jowls and thick features didn't cover the pugnacious thrust of his chin. Even the butt-end unlit stogie in his mouth tilted up—like it was giving everyone the bird.

He swiped a wet rag over the bar. "You're full of crap, Barney. The Giants are gonna wipe the floor with those losers. I got your Tigers hangin'—" His hand headed south to demonstrate but he looked up, saw Priss and froze. "The Antique Emporium is on Hollister, missy."

She put a hand on her hip. "Fernandez has a 2.1 ERA, two saves, two quality starts and it's only April. I'd say the Tigers have it hanging this season."

The lunch crowd's heads swiveled.

The man behind the counter made a growling sound—a predator's warning. "You came in here to talk *baseball?*"

Only one way to handle a bully.

She laid a hand on the bar and leaned on it. "I came here to be your new bartender."

The cigar bounced with his chuckle. "Come back when you're twenty-one, little girl."

She opened her wallet, pulled out her Colorado driver's license and flipped it onto the bar.

He picked it up and squinted at it. "Humph."

A patron spoke up. "Floyd, you should hire her.

A lady would be a welcome change from seeing your ugly mug every day."

Barney, the Tigers fan, pointed at Priss. "Yeah, we want *her!*"

Floyd stared them down. "You don't even know if she can pour a beer."

Priss waited until he turned and glared at her. "So? Try me."

He harrumphed again, leaned against the back counter, and crossed his arms over his considerable chest. "Have at it, missy."

She lifted the opening in the bar at the waitress station and stepped in. Glancing around the setup to get oriented, she smiled at the pale faces bathed in the light above the mirror at her back. They didn't look quite as excited to see her on *this* side of the bar. A few looked like they wanted to play—like a cat plays with a cricket.

She dusted her hands. "Okay, gentlemen. Help me out and tell me your name when you order. That way I'll get to know you faster. Now, what'll it be?"

"A pint of Guinness," a thin man with a slight Scottish burr said. "I'm Ian."

She checked the beer taps—not there. She squeezed past Floyd and found a flat of mixed-brand stout bottles at the other end of the bar. She snagged a bottle, opened it, then upended a clean glass. Tilting it, she poured about half a glass, then set it down so the head wouldn't get out of control.

She grabbed Ian's empty glass and set it in the sink. "Who's next?"

A bald guy with a half-empty beer, said, "I'm Porter. I'll have a martini."

Priss wiped the bar in front of Ian, and laid a new napkin. "Neat or dirty?"

"Always dirty, hon. It's how I roll."

Looking at his wrinkled shirt and fingernails, she had no doubt he spoke the truth.

She poured the rest of the Guinness and placed it in front of Ian, with a perfect thumbs-width head. "Floyd will have to collect from you all—I don't know the prices yet." She glanced around to locate the ingredients. "Vodka or gin, Porter?"

The man reared back on the stool as if she'd slapped him. "What kind of bartender would pollute good vermouth with strained potato offal?"

She raised her hands. "I come in peace." She snatched the shaker from where it sat drying on a towel. "I had to ask. Some groundlings drink it that way." She found the ice, scooped some into the shaker, then gathered the ingredients. Grasping the gin bottle by the neck, she silently counted the measurement and did the same with the vermouth; martini drinkers were notoriously picky. While she shook it, she collected a martini glass and speared two olives on the plastic sword she found next to them. She poured the drink, the last drops filling it to the rim, and set it in front of Porter.

He sipped, then sighed in bliss as his eyes rolled up.

Yes!

"I'm Barney, and I want a mojito." The Tigers fan moved his half-full beer aside.

Another patron hooted from the other end of the bar. "Who you trying to kid? I've never seen you drink anything but Bud."

Barney stuck out a two-day-whiskered chin. "Well, I saw it on a TV show and I want to try it." His rheumy eyes held challenge as he straightened the collar of a shirt that looked dingy, even in dim light. "With two olives."

She hid a smile and turned to Floyd. "Do you have mint leaves?"

"What the hell would I need those for? This ain't the Holiday Inn—this is a workingman's bar."

"Never mind." It was not like Barney would know the difference, anyway. She mixed the lime juice and sugar in a highball glass, stirring until it dissolved. Then she added rum and club soda and split a lime wedge on the rim. She placed it on a clean napkin in front of Barney, leaned over to whisper, "I'll just put the olives on the side, okay?" No way she was putting olives in that supersweet drink.

He nodded, frowning at the glass.

"Well, you gonna drink it or stare at it all day?" Floyd was enjoying this too much. He'd probably sold more high-priced drinks in the last few minutes than he had in a month.

Barney took a sip. His lips twisted and his eyes got big. His Adam's apple quivered—then he swallowed. His lips turned down and his tongue protruded, just a bit. "It's good!" He choked out.

Floyd chuckled. "Glad you think so. That'll be seven bucks."

"Seven bucks!" Barney's eyes bugged. He moved his Bud back, front and center.

A couple wandered in off the street, arm in arm. Summer people, by the looks.

A gray-haired woman in a black rayon waitress uniform with a dowager's hump and wearing orthopedic shoes emerged from a doorway in the back to lead the pair to a table.

"Hey, we don't even know your name." A comparatively younger man halfway down the bar spoke up. Of course "younger" was a relative term. He appeared to be in his forties.

"I'm Priss."

"A bartender named Priss? That's funny!"

Barney had caught his breath from the drink and the price. "Is that like Priscilla?"

She winced. "Yeah, my mom had a crush on Elvis."

"I had a crush on Priscilla!" Porter said.

"She was beautiful, and so sweet," Ian said. "Didn't deserve the crap The King dished out, messing around."

Priss patted her hair spikes. "Well, don't expect me to go all big-hair. Ain't happening."

The patrons laughed, and an argument broke out over which Elvis movie was the best.

Floyd asked, "What's your last name?"

Priss dried her hands on the bar towel she'd tucked into the waist of her skirt. "Hart."

His eyebrows shot up. "No relation to Cora Hart, are you?"

Her hands stilled. "My mother. Why?"

He smiled for the first time since she'd walked through the door. "Because she worked here. Until she couldn't anymore."

Priss shot a glance at the ceiling. *Oh, very funny, God.*

"Your mom was a stand-up gal." He pushed away from the back bar. "You can start tonight."

She swallowed. Winning the clientele over was the easy part. *This* was the hard part. She twisted the towel in her fist. "I can only work the day shift."

"I work the day shift. The job is to cover nights."

"I can't work nights." She was not saving Nacho from the clutches of the county only to put him back into his old life. Or *her* old life.

Nacho, hell, she wasn't putting *herself* back in her mother's old life.

She swallowed her fidgets and foreboding along with her spit and stood awaiting dismissal.

Floyd stared her down. "You came in here for a bartender job and you don't work nights?"

She stared back, hoping he couldn't see her fists shaking in the towel. "That's right."

"What the hell? Why'd you waste my time?"

Barney broke in. "Ah, give her the job, Floyd, you grumpy old fart."

When Floyd shook his head, his jowls flapped. "Why did I become a barkeep? No one wants to listen to *my* problems."

Ian called from the other end of the bar, "You covered nights before, Floyd."

Porter said, "We want *her.*"

He ignored the peanut gallery. "No." His cigar wasn't lit but the fire in his eyes was. "Go home, little girl."

A blast of disappointment blew a hole in her chest. All her air whooshed out.

This job would have been an answer to her problem. Maybe not the *best* answer, but she'd learned long ago that poor girls didn't get the best. She bit the inside of her lip and checked her facial muscles to be sure they didn't telegraph emotion. Another lesson she learned early—predators only took down the weak.

But wait. The only time he'd smiled was when he realized Cora was her mother. For some reason, the misguided dude thought a lot of her mom. A trickle of hope oozed down the edges of the hole in her chest, sealing it so she could breathe again. She wasn't above using guilt, or her innocent looks, to manipulate.

You utilized whatever skills you were given to survive in a jungle.

She'd grown up being tucked in a corner booth of bars, sipping free endless sodas and doing homework. Surely Nacho had, too. She let the corners of her mouth drop and lowered her eyelids in a slow blink—once, then again. "You must have met my half brother, Nacho."

"Yeah." Floyd's cigar tilted higher. He wasn't dumb. She'd have to be careful.

"Well, I'm trying to spring him from Social Services." She let out a sigh, carefully moderated to just short of theatrical. "If I don't have a job, they won't release him to me." She lowered her eyes, tortured the towel in her fists and waited.

And waited. Conversation died. The bar held its breath.

"Oh, what the hell." Floyd grunted in disgust. "I'll take the night shift—for now. You're not gonna last more than a week, anyway."

The old barmaid walked up to the waitress station. "Floyd, I'll get their BLTs. I need a strawberry margarita with sugar, no salt, and a Coors. With a lime." Her eyes flicked toward Priss.

The animosity in the woman's laser stare practically singed the skin off Priss's face. Then she turned and shuffled back through the door she'd emerged from.

What the hell?

Floyd pointed a finger at Priss. "You. We open at ten. Be here at nine tomorrow. I'll show you around. Now, scram. I've got work to do."

She gave a cheery wave to the patrons, and walked out. Happy, yet unsettled at the same time.

Had her mother just helped her get a job?

ADAM LEANED HIS elbows on the outfield chain-link fence, watching the T-ballers. He'd been on his way home but couldn't resist watching the next generation learn America's game.

He pushed his heels into the grass and felt the muscles in his calves tighten. Being in charge of the senior softball league meant he was the first to arrive on game day and the last to leave, but fitting players onto teams, teams into schedules, schedules into play-offs—he loved it.

Pitching with the Widow's Grove Winos wasn't what he'd hoped for in college. Even if he'd made the majors, he'd be retired by now anyway. He rested his chin on his forearms and sighed.

The bantam batter pushed his too-big helmet back and, tongue between his teeth, frowned at the ball on the tee.

The infielders started the chant, "Hey, batter-batter…"

The kid hefted the oversize bat on his shoulder and swung. The whiffle ball sailed off the tee and over the infielders' heads, into the grass of the outfield. The yells of his teammates woke the batter from amazement and he took off, little legs pumping for first.

The entire outfield, plus the shortstop and second baseman, swarmed for the ball, all yelling, "I got it!"

Despite all the waving gloves, the ball landed in the grass.

The coach stood at home plate, face florid, yelling the batter around the bases. The parents in the stands cheered loud enough to raise a flock of mourning doves from the power lines.

The little kid jumped onto home plate with both feet. The dugout emptied and the coach swung him high.

Carley Beauchamp walked up, hands cupped around her mouth, yelling, "Way to go, batter!" She rested her forearms on the fence and gave Adam a shoulder bump. "Better watch it. You're looking at those kids like you want one."

"Not me. Kids are like puppies—adorable, but also unsafe, uncontrollable and messy. When I have the urge, I'll just come borrow yours. I'll get my cute fix, and a solid reminder of why I'm never having any." He leaned over and bumped her shoulder.

He and his best friend Daryl had double-dated back in high school. Adam brought whoever, but the other half had always been Daryl and Carley. Still was.

Her brown eyes held concern, and a few milligrams of pity. "You are a sad case, Preston."

"What are you talking about? Life is good."

"Oh, please. I've known you since second grade so I feel obligated to point out a few things." She lifted her hand, and started ticking points on her fingers. "You live in your mother's house, alone. You dispense corn plasters and Viagra to the over-sixty set during the day, then fill your off-hours running a softball league for potbellied wannabes." She took a breath.

God, he hated when she counted on her fingers. She had so many.

"Your last girlfriend just came out of the closet, and you're down to DatesRUs.com, or recommendations from Jesse, at the Café."

He winced as the darts hit home. They were small but Carley always had dead aim. "Why don't you just fillet me, and have it over with?"

Her fingers encircled his biceps. "Roger's gone, Adam. But you're still here." He'd seen eyes like that behind chain-link fences at the pound. His jaw locked. "We are not discussing that."

"Okay, okay." Her fingers slid off his arm. "Only

because I'm such a good friend, I'm here to save you from a long, lonely future."

"Why am I afraid?"

"A big, strong guy like you, afraid of a date?"

"What date?"

"Well, working in the office at the school does have its advantages. The replacement for your— um—the teacher who left—"

"No." The chain-link twists dug in his forearms when he pushed off and straightened.

"Adam, just listen. Her name is June Sellers, and she's just your type."

"And what, exactly, is my type?"

She rolled her eyes and unholstered those fingers. "Blonde and classy, quiet and ladylike. The type a guy could take home to his mother. You know, a good girl."

The air quotes stung. "Why do you say that like it's bad?"

"It's not. If that's what makes you happy." She dug through her purse a moment and came up with a crumpled Post-it note in hot pink. "I told her about you and she gave me her phone number." She handed it over. "She's expecting your call."

He avoided what looked like peanut butter on the edge and squinted at the smeared writing.

"I just think you deserve more than what you want." She held up a hand to ward off his protest. "I'm only trying to wake your ass up. Life isn't safe, or neat and tidy. I'd think you'd have figured that out after what you lived through." The pity was back in her stare. "When are you going to take off the gloves and live life out loud, Preston?"

"I'm happy as is, thanks, Carley."

THE NEXT DAY, Adam unlocked the glass front door of Hollister Drugs, stepped in, locking it behind him. He followed the scent of freshly brewed coffee to the soda fountain, where Sin stood in her uniform, reading the *Widow's Grove Telegraph,* and sipping coffee from a mug that suggested doing something to oneself that was physically impossible.

With effort, he pulled his eyes from the multi-colored tattoos that twined, full-sleeve, down both her slim arms. "You need to cover those tattoos, and I asked you to take that mug home."

"Well, Happy Monday, Sin." She put down the paper. "We're not open yet. I'll put on the arm warmers when we are, and I don't drink coffee in front of customers, you know that." She set a clean stoneware mug on the counter and poured him a cup. "Aren't you just a ray of sunshine this morning?"

"Good morning, Sin." He reached for the coffee, noticing again how badly her hot pink hair clashed with the uniform. "You sure I can't talk you into a different hair color? Blue? A nice lavender?"

When she smiled, the crystal set in her tooth flashed. "Nah, but thanks, boss."

He saluted her with his cup. "Thanks for the coffee." He noticed his new tenant sat at one of the tables, reading the *Widow's Grove Telegraph*. The paper rustled when she turned a page. He raised an eyebrow at Sin.

She shrugged. "If you trust her enough to live across the hall from your mother, I thought it was safe to invite her in for a cup of coffee before we opened."

He nodded. *I should have thought to do that myself.*

Priss wore a closely fitted pink button-down shirt and dress pants. Her short dark hair had that just-fell-out-of-bed look that had him imagining things he shouldn't.

Her too-big green eyes held a warning that he'd been staring.

He slapped on his "trusted pharmacist" smile to cover his gaffe and carried his coffee to her table. "Morning. Mind if I join you?"

She put down the paper, pulled a phone from her large tapestry purse on the floor and checked the time. "Okay, but I only have a few minutes."

He slid into the fancy wrought-iron chair. "I just wanted to officially welcome you to Widow's

Grove. I realized I hadn't done that yet. Are you finding your way around?"

"So far, so good. I'm enjoying the apartment, but I wondered what passes for fun around here."

"Well, the tourists go on wine tours, and there's shopping—"

She waved a hand. "I mean the locals. What do *you* do for fun?"

"Baseball."

A spark of interest flared in her eyes. "Tell me about that."

"We have little league for the kids and a senior league for adults."

"Women allowed on the teams?"

"They're not banned. But only one team has a woman. It's pretty competitive." He leaned his elbows on the edge of the table. "Do you play?"

She nodded. "High school. And I played first base in a summer league in Boulder."

Enchanting and she played baseball? Too good to be true. "Slow-pitch?"

She made a *pfft* sound of dismissal. "I said I *played*." She leaned an arm over the back of her chair and flashed him a card shark's smile. "Hard ball, baby."

He could talk smack. He just never had, with a woman. He narrowed his eyes. "You any good?"

She held her hand up and blew on her nails. "Point nine two fielding percentage, no errors."

"How many games?"

"Fifteen."

"Nice." A woman on the Winos? Why not? Pete Gilmour sucked at first base. Plus it would give Adam the opportunity to get to know Priss better.

On the other hand... He studied her stand-up hair and the stubborn line of her chin. She was hardly his type. And about as far from safe as it was possible to be.

Still, he'd sure love to see this little dynamo run bases. "You interested in playing?"

"Maybe. Who would I talk to if I was?"

"I run the league, and pitch on one of the teams. I might have a slot. *If* you can hit."

"Two seven five average."

"Not bad for a girl." He didn't let his lips quirk. But he wanted to. She stuck out her chin. "Pretty good for an infielder. Even a guy."

Cute, competitive, and the stats to back it up. *This could be love.*

She folded the paper and slipped it in her purse. "Well, thanks for the tips, and the conversation."

He wanted to keep her here, talking. This lady tugged at his attention and he wanted to understand why. "You never said what brought you to Widow's Grove."

He couldn't say exactly what changed. She didn't move, but she changed, lightning-fast, from a pretty, young woman to a jungle cat—motionless, crouched, wary.

Her fingers tightened on her cup. "Does it matter?"

"It doesn't." He took a slow sip of coffee. "I would guess you're not from a small town."

"Nooo." She said the word as if he'd pulled it from her. When she shrugged, her shoulders lost their firing-squad tension. "I got tired of the big city and decided to slow down for a while."

"Well, you'll find people here friendly. They'll want to get to know you." He raised a hand in a universal gesture of peace. "In a good way. We watch out for our own."

"I've been watching out for myself for years." She stared into her mug long enough to divine the future in the dregs. "I'm from Vegas, originally."

"Not much small town there."

"You'd be surprised. Off the strip, it's a lot like a small town." Her pert nose wrinkled. "People get way up in each other's business. It's part of why I got out of there as soon as I could."

He wanted to keep her talking. "Um, before you go, could give me some advice? You know, as a woman?" He leaned in to whisper.

She backed up.

"What color uniform should I order for Sin?"

Her face went blank a microsecond, then she laughed. It wasn't the delighted tinkle he'd expected from a tiny thing like her. It was an all-in belly laugh, and he glimpsed for the first time, what she'd look like unguarded. Her smile outshone the sun pouring in the window. But what hit harder was her...he fumbled for a word to describe it.

Life force.

A vibrant woman lived inside that wary jungle cat. Her laughter echoed in his bones, making him want to reach out and catch her hand where it lay on the table. He stopped himself in time. What kind of background made a woman that young so wary?

She leaned in, her lips quirking. "A different color is not going to fix that problem."

"I was afraid you would say that."

She chuckled. "I wouldn't worry about it. I like her just the way she is and I'll bet your customers would say the same."

He broke eye contact before it could become another stare. "Yes, but she's just so...out there."

The twinkle in her eye winked out. The jungle cat was back. "Oh, and conformity tops honesty, efficiency and competence in your book?"

"No. But I can dream, can't I?"

A shade of a smile crossed her lips. "Dream on, dude." She lifted her phone, and snapped to attention. "I've got to go."

"Where you off to?"

"I've got to go...to work." She slipped her phone in her purse.

"Great, you found a job. Doing what?"

"Um. Customer service." In one fluid movement, she was on her feet. "Nice talking to you."

He stood. "You have a good day."

She turned and waved to Sin, who came from behind the counter with the keys in her hand. Though he couldn't hear their words, they talked all the way to the door. Sin unlocked it, let out Priss and let in Susie, his checkout girl.

He grabbed his cup to leave but his gaze followed Priss until she passed the edge of the window.

"Ignacio Hart. Report to the office."

The voice on the dorm loudspeaker was soft but Nacho still jumped. He shot a look around to be sure no one saw. Nope. The prisoners were all at breakfast.

They'd told him his half sister would be here to take him today. He'd been shocked, since it was pretty clear that day at the apartment that she didn't give a shit. Besides, she sure didn't look like the motherly type. That was okay by him. He'd already had a mother—didn't need another.

He crammed the last of his T-shirts into his backpack and looked around. The sun hit the floor, crosshatched by the wire in the glass. They said it was there to keep the kids safe.

Yeah, tell me another bedtime story.

Neatly made cots stretched the length of the

high-ceilinged room. His was the only rumpled one. Screw 'em. He was so out of here.

He tossed the backpack over his shoulder, his hands fisted so they wouldn't shake. He couldn't wait to escape this kid warehouse, with their rules, bad food and the wimps sniffling after lights out. The only good thing about this place was that a bus picked him up so he could keep going to the same school. Not that he cared about learning, but all his homies were there.

He walked to the door, wondering if he was heading from a pile of dog crap into an over-his-head shit pile. His mom was dead, his dad was in prison. They were handing him off to a chick he didn't even know, just because half her blood was his mom's. What did that have to do with him?

But the county didn't care. They were happy to have one less body in the warehouse. No one bothered asking the only guy who might care—and he *hated* that.

He used to feel empty inside when his mom went to work at night. Now he felt empty all the time. He wished he had a big family, like his friend Joe. They were loud and yelled a lot but you had to care if you yelled, right?

He took a last quick glance around to be sure he hadn't left anything. The extra weight of the iron cross felt just right in the bottom of the backpack. His teacher talked about how knights in old days had a family coat of arms on their shields when they went into battle. The cross was his. Maybe his mom was full of shit. Maybe all those dead guys back in Spain weren't royalty. But the weight felt right, just the same.

His stomach rumbled, empty, but full of ice. He practiced a badass superhero scowl.

His shoelaces slapped the floor, but he imagined a pair of Avenger's boots, thumping down the stairs. He was tough. His skin was leather. Ice was in his veins, not in his stomach. He was—

His sister stood at the bottom of the stairs, looking up at him. She was little for a grown-up—only a couple inches taller than him. Trying to look cool with her spiked hair and hipster pants, but she was scared. He knew scared when he saw it.

Cool—that made them equal.

He slouched down the last couple of stairs.

"Hi, Nacho. I signed you out of here for good. Have you got all your stuff?"

He glared hard and walked past her. No reason to make it easy.

"Hey, wait." She trotted to catch up, and pushed the door open for him. "It's not really warm enough yet, but I thought you'd like to ride with the top down." She waved her arm at a huge beater Caddy parked at the curb. The paint was sunburnt and it looked like the white leather interior was split in places, but his stomach took a happy dive anyway. He'd look cool pulling up to school in a drop-top.

He followed her, scuffing his feet to act like he didn't want to. The tall brick building loomed at his back, watching to see if he'd get in the car. Whether or not this worked out, there was no way he was going back to that place. He'd run away first.

She patted the door, then swooshed it open like it was a limo. "This is Mona. Mona, this is Nacho."

He snorted and got in. Crazy ran in his family.

She walked to the driver's side and got in but she didn't crank the engine; she just looked at him.

"What?"

"I got us an apartment—a nice one, over Hollister Drugs. You know where that is?"

What, did she think he was an idiot? He nodded.

"I already talked to your school. I've got to work so the bus will drop you off about two blocks from the drugstore. I should be home about the time you get there, but if I'm not…"

When she didn't say more, he had to look at her.

"You're to wait for me outside, on the sidewalk. Got that?"

"Yeah."

"I'll have to take you in and introduce you to the landlord and his mother when I get home from work today. They don't exactly know about you yet, so…" She chewed her lip. "Just wait for me when you get home from school, okay?"

He rolled his eyes. "I'm not retarded."

When she smiled she looked a little like his mom and a little like one of those elf queens in the *Lord of the Rings*. "Noted. Buckle your seat belt." After he did, she handed him a bag from the floorboard then cranked the engine. "I figured you didn't get breakfast."

He opened it. A McMuffin. *Sweet.* "Thanks." He ignored the foil-covered cup of orange juice and dug in.

"What do you think of this town?" She talked loud, over the wind.

"It blows."

"Don't talk with your mouth full."

"Then don't ask me a question after I take a bite."

She looked over at him. "So you're not tied to this place?"

He snorted. "I want to go to a city. Like a real city—like L.A. or something." They had real gangs there. He could take his pick.

She smiled. "Then you're going to like living with me. I move around."

It might be cool, getting to see places. "I can hang with that."

"Great. Then when you get out of school in June, we'll hit the road, okay?"

"Cool." Actually, it *was* cold but he didn't care. The wind whipped by, making it feel like they were going a hundred instead of thirty-five. People in other cars stared. He rested his arm on the door and squinted at them. This part might not be too bad.

Ten minutes later, Priss pulled into the circle in front of his school. Cars ahead and behind them dropped off kids. More kids hopped off the buses parked at the curb. Others milled on the sidewalk, yelling, running. A typical day.

He spotted Diego and almost waved like a butt-wipe second grader. He stopped himself in time. But Diego saw him, and elbowed Joe. Nacho took his time gathering his backpack so they could get a good look at his wheels. It was a beater, but it was a drop-top. With raised shocks and some painted flames—

"We're clear, right, Nacho? You're going to wait for me in front of the store after school?" She looked worried.

"I *got* it." He hopped out and slammed the door, hard, to show her what he thought of her rules.

"Okay, you have a good day, Nacho. See you this afternoon."

He crossed the sidewalk to his *real* family. The one *he* got to choose.

CHAPTER FOUR

PRISS WATCHED NACHO stride to the sidewalk and slap hands with two Hispanic boys. *Well, that went about as well as I could expect.*

When a horn bleated behind her, she moved up ten inches.

A tingle of consequence shivered down her spine and she shifted on the seat. She felt as if today she'd stepped through a door, a demarcation that would separate her life into before and after. She shook it off. Widow's Grove was a way station, a branch to rest on before she flew off to the next adventure.

She wondered how she'd look back on this time. What kind of mother—no, *guardian*—would she be? She inched Mona forward a few feet. Well, she'd be a better one than her mother, that was for sure. Nacho would never have to lie awake, afraid in the dark. She would be what she'd wished her mother had been: attentive, understanding and *present*. She'd also make sure that Nacho felt comfortable talking to her about anything.

In fact, because she wasn't his mother, maybe they could just be friends. Sure, she'd be the one setting down the rules, but somebody had to. He'd understand that.

Good friends. Yeah, that's what I want.

They could take day trips on the weekends, exploring the area. Maybe they'd learn to parasail—or even surf! With happy thoughts she inched her way to the exit, hung a right and headed back to town.

Her shift at the bar didn't start for an hour and a half, and she had one more chore to complete. Ms. Barnes had turned over the papers for Nacho, along with the key to her mother's apartment. Apparently the state had decided Cora Hart's belongings wouldn't help them out of their fiscal crisis. Now Priss had to clear out the rest of the stuff, or pay rent for another week. As much as she was dreading going back there, she didn't have a choice.

And that made her feel trapped. Again.

She rested her arm on Mona's door. The sun winked through the morning cloud cover, then disappeared.

A scene flashed in her mind. One of the last scenes of a long and depressing movie.

Her mom stood at the stove smoking a cigarette, stirring potatoes frying in a cast-iron skillet. "You're going to like him, Priss. He's sweet, employed, and—"

"He's married, Ma."

"Well, he's had a tough go of it. The marriage is not good. He's going to file for a divorce. Soon."

"So, in the meantime, he's going to move in here? Do you realize I go to school with his kids, Ma?"

It was hopeless. All a guy had to do was ask and if Cora Hart wasn't involved with someone else, she was his. She'd done stupid stuff before, like when she hooked up with that sleaze who had cleaned them out two years earlier. But this was a new low. She'd never messed with a married man before. *"Do you know what's going to happen when this gets around school?"*

Her mother tapped the cigarette on the ashtray, put it back in her mouth and turned the greasy potatoes with the spatula. *"You'll like him. We'll make a great family. You'll see."*

Priss pulled Mona to the cracked curb in front of the so-called apartments. The tired paint and robust weeds didn't look any better today. She sat a moment, staring at her memory that had slipped into the present. Something inside her firmed, like clay hardening in the sun.

It's not going to be like that for Nacho. I'm going to listen to him. He's going to know he has a say in what happens. It's going to be him and me first, then everything and everyone else second.

At least for as long as she was here.

She slid the strap of her bag over her shoulder, checked the side mirror for traffic, then stepped out of her car. She strode to the back alley where she'd spied Dumpsters on the way by. Luckily one was empty. She muscled it across the alley and pushed it under the back window of her mother's apartment.

Piece of cake. You can do this.

Today she didn't need the scent of underprivileged that enveloped her when she walked in the door to take her back to those dark days. The ghost of her mother stood in the kitchen, stirring potatoes.

She ignored the vision and stepped into the tiny bedroom where Nacho had slept. Might as well start there. She opened the window, stripped the bed, and tossed the sheets out. She opened a plastic bin that had held his clothes, and filled it with anything that looked personal. There wasn't much: a few Lego pieces, a G.I. Joe figure he'd probably outgrown and a couple of dime-store jigsaw puzzles.

Next, the closet. Her mother's few clothes hung from hangers in limp accusation. She didn't even examine them—straight out the window.

Keeping her head down to avoid ghosts, Priss dragged the trash can from the kitchen into the living room. Everything not belonging to the landlords got dumped in, including ashtrays and the rumpled threadbare sheets on the couch—her mother's last bed. She pulled off the sheets and rolled them into a ball. But before she let them go, she lowered her nose and took a deep lungful of the desperation, hope and sadness that had been her mother.

A barnacled shell, buried so deep in the silt of her psyche that she'd forgotten it, suddenly burst open, spitting out a misshapen pitted, black pearl of guilt.

A strangled sob slipped out before her throat closed.

I should have at least stayed in touch. The pain of learning about her mother's death from a stranger rose in her, fetid and slimy. Had her mother lain in a county hospital bed, breathing like a landed fish, wishing she could see her daughter one last time?

It isn't the child's job to rescue an adult. It's supposed to be the other way around.

Shaking her head at her sentimental foolishness, Priss dropped the sheets in the trash, then walked to the kitchen. The sooner she got out of these backwaters, the better.

A half hour later, the apartment was empty. She took one last quick tour to be sure she hadn't missed anything. She glanced in the bathroom and pulled the door to close it when something brushed her hand. Hanging from a hook on the back of the door was an apron. She remembered it. Her mother's barmaid apron.

The pocket gapped. Priss reached in and pulled out a roll of money, held together with a rubber band. No evening's tips, these—twenties and tens, more than an inch thick. When she slid the band off and unfurled the bills, a piece of paper fell out. She unfolded it to find a list of states, with a line through Nevada, Florida, Michigan and Ohio. What, was she trying for a man in every state? Priss flipped through the bills, counting, stunned by the tally. What had she been saving for? Bail money for Nacho's father before the trial? A deposit on a decent place to live in? Nah. Cora Hart had lived in places like this her entire life, and she'd been way too old a leopard to change her spots.

Priss fingered the rough, dingy white cotton rectangle with its long, dangling ties. Her mother had owned it forever. When it began whispering memories, Priss lifted it off the peg and tossed it over her shoulder to silence it.

Hell, she was back in her mother's world—why not use her old apron? Priss told herself she wasn't being sentimental, just practical; she needed an apron anyway.

The alarm on her phone blatted "Reveille." Time to get to work. She slipped the map and the money into her purse, and took the few steps to the living room.

Snatching up the half-full plastic bin, she walked out, locked the door to the past once more and slipped the key under the door.

ADAM STOOD IN front of his narcotics shelf taking inventory, when a woman's voice screeched in his pocket. Dang it, Sin must've reprogrammed his phone again. He pulled it from his jacket pocket and answered. "Sin, this is not funny. I work with octogenarians and a Lady Gaga ringtone is going to give someone a heart attack."

"That's Eat Your Dead, by the way. Lady Gaga is *pop*." She spit the word like it was spoiled meat. "Special cleanup on aisle four, boss," she whispered, and hung up.

He craned his neck, but couldn't see the aisle from where he stood. He slipped his phone back in his pocket, walked past the cash register, and unlocked the door that kept the drugs secure.

He saw the kid the minute he pulled the door closed behind him. A Hispanic boy with sloppy, too-big clothes stood at the magazine rack with the casual "I'm not doing anything" demeanor of a shoplifter. Sin was an expert at spotting them but this one was more obvious than most. The kid stopped leafing through a muscle-car magazine, shot a glance up the aisle, then slipped the magazine in the waistband of his saggy jeans.

Damn it, these kids never gave up. Where were their parents? He was tired of little delinquents pilfering his stock. It was time to set an example that would deter other kids. The twerp's luck had just run out because Adam was flat *sick* of this. He tipped his chin at Joyce, the cashier—it was the signal to let the kid go.

He followed the boy and once the door closed behind them, Adam grabbed the thief's shirt collar.

"Hey, lemme go!" The punk twisted to see who had a hold of him.

Adam tightened his grip. "Go? The only place you're going is jail." He retrieved his cell from his pocket and scrolled his contacts while the kid struggled.

"I didn't do anything. What're you—a pervert? Lemme go!"

The kid was stronger than Adam would have guessed. He had to twist the boy's T-shirt collar around his fist. "Settle. You'll only make it worse."

"Help!" The kid pulled at his collar, frantic. "Somebody help—he's trying to kidnap me!"

Tourists strolling by slowed, uncertain.

A little old lady in orange Bermuda shorts stopped and glared at him. "What are you doing with that child?"

Oh, hell.

PRISS GUNNED THE engine, running ten miles over the posted twenty-five in the downtown area, checking the rearview mirror for cop strobes. She'd meant to be home a half hour ago, but Floyd had shown up late for work. She couldn't very well walk away from a bar full of patrons.

But damn, it was Nacho's first day with her, and now she'd left him cooling his heels on the sidewalk.

Great way to make a kid feel secure, Hart.

That wasn't the way she'd wanted to start.

Something about the knot of people gathered in front of the drugstore made her heart bang like Mona's engine on a bad day. There was no reason to believe this had anything to do with Nacho, but her shit-meter redlined just the same. Her stomach muscles snapped taut, clicking into defense mode. When she squealed to a stop at the curb, heads swiveled in her direction. She shut off Mona and stood on the seat to see over the small crowd.

"Help me, somebody!" Nacho strained like a dog at the end of a leash, the collar of his T-shirt choking him. Her landlord stood behind him, his fist knotted in cotton, his face redder than Nacho's, fiddling with a phone.

"You let him go!" Priss yelled, vaulting over the passenger-side door.

Bystanders backed away as she charged in like a Pamplona bull.

She grabbed Adam's forearm and squeezed. The muscle, like braided wire, didn't give. "What are you *doing?* Can't you see you're choking him?" When he ignored her, she gave up on the arm, and grabbed Nacho's shoulders instead and looked him in the eyes. "Stop fighting. You're making it worse."

"You'll want to stay out of this." Adam's dark eyes were cool. "He's a shoplifter. I'm calling the cops." He hit a button on the phone and raised it to his ear.

"You. Let. Him. Go." The steely, blood-tipped threat in her voice almost frightened *her*.

Adam let go.

Instinctively, her arms went around the boy's shoulders. "He's my brother."

Nacho struggled in her embrace, then froze. So did Adam.

He hit a button and slowly lowered the phone. "He's *what?*"

She stuck out her chest and tightened her grip on Nacho's shoulders. Righteously indignant was a strong offense. "He's my brother. He wouldn't steal."

God, please, he wouldn't do that, would he?

She had to know. Her eyes traveled down to Nacho. Chin stuck out, lips a tight thin line, eyebrows matching commas of anger over eyes that… were larcenous.

Shit.

There was no doubt in her mind. He'd done it. A flush of heat spread up from her chest. Sweat popped at her hairline, but then freeze-dried in the chill rolling off her landlord.

"Really." He dropped his phone into his pocket, then lifted the hem of Nacho's shirt. He pulled out a magazine with a souped-up hot rod on the cover, garish flames painted on the hood. "You undoubtedly have a receipt for this, then."

Nacho studied his sneakers. Priss squirmed inside as if she were the guilty party.

Apparently—and thankfully—public shaming wasn't entertaining because the crowd broke up, wandering away in ones and twos.

"Look." Priss swallowed, having no idea of what she'd say next. This very morning she'd rescued the kid from Social Services. Now he was facing juvie.

Two government institutions in one day? That has to be some kind of record.

Arguments, pleas and downright supplications whirled through her mind. She tested and discarded each in nanoseconds.

Adam glared at Nacho. Then at her. She could almost see him connecting dots that would lead to the holes in her story.

This was going to take a delicate blend of the truth and every bit of the manipulation she'd learned on the street. She relaxed her face into her "waif" look and raised her rounded eyes. "Could I talk to you for a second? Alone?"

"I'm not taking my eye off him, and no matter what you say, I'm calling the cops."

"I understand." She dug her fingers in the hollows next to Nacho's collarbone. "You. Wait here. If you move—"

He scrunched his shoulders and winced. "I won't. I promise."

Adam's huff made it clear what he thought of a criminal's promises.

"Just over here." She walked five steps, until she stood under the drugstore's green awning.

Adam followed, keeping a wary eye on Nacho.

"I'll pay you for the magazine. And you can keep it."

"That's not the point."

"I know it isn't." She lowered her voice to a whisper, so Adam would have to lean in to hear. "But I just got him out of a group home today. His mom died—*our* mom died—two weeks ago." She set her face in grieving lines, and looked at him from under her lashes. Tears? No, better not push it. "Just this once, could you give him a break? He's only ten, and he's been in that group home since the day we buried our mom. That's bound to have messed him up, you know?"

Adam shook his head. "I'm sorry for your loss. Really. But I've had a rash of petty thefts, and if it weren't for Sin, he'd have gotten away with it. I have to make an example of him."

She touched his forearm. "I'll vouch for him. I'll make him come in through the back door…"

He jerked his arm away as if she'd pinched it. "He is *not* living here."

His distaste sparked tinder—the dried remnants

of every slight that lay scattered in her memory. The behind-the-hand giggles, the "slut spawn" taunts, the smug smile of a blonde girl with a pig nose—they all caught fire in a whoosh.

Her hands fisted. "Oh, yes. He is." It came out as the growled warning of a junkyard dog.

A muscle worked at the side of Adam's jaw. When he leaned in, Priss was suddenly aware of his size. She felt the brush of his fury on her face. "Oh, no. He isn't."

"Read your lease. It bans pets, not kids."

The spasm in his hands told her just when he realized he'd been had. His eyes narrowed to slits. "You *lied* to me!"

"You never asked."

"It never occurred to me to ask a young woman—"

"Well, that's not my fault." When the storm in his eyes worsened, tornado sirens went off in her mind. She'd pushed too far. Her deep, cleansing breath doused the last flickering flames of her anger. "Look. This is not going to be a problem. I'm home from the bar a half hour after he gets home from school, and—"

"The *bar?*"

"My job. I'm a bartender at Bar None."

Fists clenched, he looked up to the inside of the awning. Priss knew it was a prayer on his part, asking for strength.

"You have a problem with how I earn your rent

money, dude?" She tightened the muscles of her chest and core, attempting to smother the anger flare-up that she couldn't afford. The battle wouldn't matter if she lost the war.

He took a step back, eyes narrowed. "Yes, I have many problems actually. You told me you were in customer service."

Ouch. A rare attack of conscience slipped like a shiv between her ribs. "A bartender *is* a customer service job."

He crossed his arms over his chest.

"Look, I promise you that my brother is not going to be a problem." She crooked a finger at Nacho who, in spite of his casual perusal of the street, was listening to every word.

He walked over to Priss immediately.

She pointed a finger at Adam. "You tell this man that you're sorry. And that this is *never* going to happen again."

Maybe the kid did have some survival instinct, because he looked up at the pissed-off pharmacist with tears in his eyes. "I'm really sorry, sir. It won't happen again."

"Damned right it won't. I may not be able to evict you but I'm going to be watching." He studied Nacho as if he were a small, venomous snake. "The only reason I'm not having you arrested is because you just lost your mother." He shot a glance at Priss, and then back. "But you are not allowed in my store. Understood?"

"Yes, sir." Nacho's voice shook.

Is this an act? He was either very good or very sorry. Priss intended to find out which, as soon as she got him upstairs.

"I am *not* happy about this. But it appears I have no choice." Adam turned to look down on her. "For the moment." He turned on his heel, strode to the door, pulled it open, and with one backward glare, walked in.

Priss felt a wasp-sting of regret for having misled him. But she hadn't had a choice; the county had put her back against the wall.

Screw it. He didn't matter. Nacho did.

She took a firm hold of his upper arm and pulled. "You and me, dude. We need to talk." She led him around the building to the back entrance. The entrance she'd been relegated to as a kid. The one she'd worked her ass off to avoid since.

Until today.

CHAPTER FIVE

YOU ARE NOT GOING TO YELL. In spite of the anger singing in her veins, Priss managed to close the apartment door gently.

Nacho crossed to the window that looked down on Hollister. "This is cool."

The setting sun highlighted the soft planes of his face, reminding her that he was still a boy. One who had just lost his old life, such as it was. And she planned to show him that life could be better than he'd known so far—after she killed him. "What the hell were you thinking? Do you know how close you just came to going to juvie?"

He walked past the kitchen, to the bedroom. "Where do I sleep?"

"The big couch in the living room opens to a bed."

"Okay." His voice echoed from the bathroom.

"Get your butt out here. We're not done."

He slouched back in the room, and leaned against the doorjamb, thumbs in his low-rider jeans pockets. She pointed to the table for two between the kitchen and the living area. He walked over, sat and crossed his arms over his chest.

Priss took a deep breath and tamped down the urge to throttle him. "I'm going to ignore the fact that you disregarded my instruction to wait *outside* the pharmacy until I got there." She took a deep breath. *Kinder and gentler.* "But explain to me what possessed you to try to shoplift in this store, of all places? Don't you have any sense of self-preservation?"

He pursed his lips so hard his bottom lip jutted out.

"Why did you do it?" She could play this game. She crossed her arms and waited.

He lasted about thirty seconds. "You're not my mother."

"True thing. Because if I *had* a kid, he'd know better than to pull a bonehead stunt like this. Why did you do it?"

"I don't have to tell you." He moved, just a bit in the seat.

"The court appointed me your guardian. So yeah, you do. But you have choices, you know. I mean, if you went back to county, you could be fostered out. Or maybe adopted."

His head snapped up.

She dropped her hands and held them palm out. She hadn't meant to scare him. "Look, I signed up for this gig. You can count on me to carry it through. But you don't have to stay with me if you don't want to."

"I'm not going back there." His flinty tone told her that it wasn't just an answer to her question—it was a vow.

"That's the smartest thing I've heard you say so far. So that's settled. You stay with me."

He sat up and put his elbows on the table. "So what's for dinner?"

She leaned against the kitchen bar and crossed her arms again. "Tell me why you did it."

"It's no big deal," he huffed, rolling his eyes. "It was our initiation."

"Initiation to what?"

"Me 'n' Joe 'n' Diego. We're starting a gang."

A gang in Disneyland? Good luck with that, kid. She managed not to smile. "Here. In Widow's Grove." He may be from the wrong side of the tracks but she'd be willing to bet the only gang he'd ever seen was on TV.

"Yeah." He made his best "gang" sign, and tried to look badass.

She didn't know whether to kill him or laugh. Taking a deep breath, she paused a moment to get control of both urges. "Okay. Let's get some rules out of the way. First, I'm saying it again. The store is off-limits. Period." She walked over, pulled a key from her pants, and put it on the table in front of Nacho. "This is your key. It opens the alley door and our apartment. Don't lose it."

"Okay." He slipped it into his pocket.

"Second. No law-breaking. We've got enough troubles as it is." She walked to the kitchen. "And last—there's a sweet little old lady across the hall. She's the pharmacist's mother. You're not to bother her, or be loud."

"*He* has a mother?"

"Don't be a brat. You should be happy he didn't call the cops."

"Oh, yeah, I'm just pumped."

"Besides, it was Sin who narked on you."

His eyes got round. "The goddess at the food counter?" He sighed out the words.

"Yep."

"I don't believe it. She's too cool."

"Well, believe it." Priss pulled open the fridge door, happy to have that over with. She thought it had gone pretty well, considering. "So what do you want for dinner? I didn't know what you liked so I got corn dogs, sliders, and frozen pizza."

"Pizza." When he smiled, the change was so startling that she realized it was the first time she'd seen him do it. He transformed from a ten-year-old gangster to a fresh-faced kid in a cereal commercial.

He really is cute. She had to return his smile, longing for the days when pizza could fix everything. Pulling out the frozen pizza, she set it on the counter, then searched the cupboard beneath it for a baking sheet.

One problem handled, her mind turned to the next. *I'm going to have to find a way to smooth it over with the landlord.*

She'd have been glad to leave her street skills behind when she left Vegas. But at the look of distaste on Adam's face when he found out she hadn't told him the whole truth, she'd felt a rare prick of conscience. She refused to be sorry for what she had done. She'd committed to taking care of Nacho and she would use any tool she had in order to do it.

But it was going to cost her.

ADAM SAT IN the crowded auditorium at UC Santa Barbara with June Sellers, the teacher Carley had set him up with, trying not to yawn. June leaned forward in the too-comfy theater seat beside him wearing a silk dress, flowery perfume and a sweet smile.

On the stage, the string quartet played on. And on. He'd heard Bach before, but always in the background, and usually in elevators. The regimented music reminded him of geometry homework in high school—a necessary evil, except in this situation, without the necessary. He locked his jaw as another yawn threatened. Falling asleep on the first date would not bode well for a second date. And he did want a second date. He did.

A couple didn't have to like all the same things to have a successful relationship. After all, she was pretty, classy, feminine, quiet—and he was…bored. He shifted in his seat; even his butt was falling asleep. If someone had asked him to describe his perfect woman three months ago he would have described June, almost down to her flowy dress. But for some reason, his dream, in the flesh, wasn't all he'd imagined.

And that didn't make any sense. Maybe the physical attraction would build like a slow fire as they got to know each other better. Slow fires were good. They were controllable—safe.

The applause of the audience broke his reverie. The quartet members took a bow, and the audience was set free. *Thank God.*

June gathered her light sweater and small purse. "Wasn't that sublime?"

He touched her elbow to guide her to the aisle. "I have to admit, I'm not a huge Bach fan."

"Really? What classical composer do you prefer?"

"Jim Morrison. Or maybe Eric Clapton." He held the door for her. "They're as classic as they come."

He smiled at her scrunched brows as she breezed past him. He waved to Jenny Hastings and her husband, Dave, who was rubbing his eyes as if he'd just woken from a nice nap.

Wanting to impress June, Adam had made reservations for a window table at Demure Damsel,

Widow's Grove's only four-star restaurant, housed in one of the new Victorians lining Hollister.

It was a short drive to the restaurant and once they were inside and seated, Adam studied June's profile as she gazed over the formal English garden in the courtyard of the restaurant. She looked like she'd time-traveled from England with her fine-boned face, big blue eyes and a tiny nose. In the natural light, her skin was pale, almost translucent. Her white-blond hair was twisted up, held with a crystal pin and some kind of magic.

"So, tell me about yourself, June."

She turned to him with a close-lipped smile. "Well, you already know that I'm a schoolteacher. I was raised in Boston." She didn't pronounce it "Baaston." She drew out the *o*'s—a sure sign of class.

"My father is a fine-art importer and he just opened his first gallery in San Francisco. I applied for teaching positions there, but when the opening came up in Widow's Grove I decided to take it for the remainder of the school year. Then we'll see." She looked at her lap. "I'm already missing my parents. This is the furthest I've ever lived from them."

He took a sip of his very nice Napa chardonnay. "What do you like to do? Do you have any hobbies?"

"Oh, yes." Her eyes sparkled and she leaned forward. "I do needlepoint. It's my passion."

"That, and Bach, right?"

"Yes, just so. What do you do in your off-hours?"

"I run the Senior Baseball League in town and I pitch for one of the teams."

"Baseball is your passion, then?" She took a delicate sip of wine.

"I guess you could say that. I was on my college team, then I was recruited by the L.A. Dodgers."

When her eyes widened, staring down, he realized his elbows were on the table. He slid his hands into his lap. "I played with them one season."

Her nostrils flared. "What happened?"

He tasted the sharp tang of bitterness that wasn't due to the wine. "I wasn't good enough."

"Oh. I'm sorry."

The old wound ached like Ms. Clark's rheumatism. He shrugged. "Ancient history."

The black-bow-tied waiter saved him by arriving to take their order. Adam chose a fillet and June ordered salmon in caper sauce.

When the waiter left, she said, "Owning the town pharmacy and caring for the town's residents is a lot of responsibility. It must be a challenging job." She looked at him, her china-blue eyes wide, as if he really was *all* that.

He sat up straighter. It wasn't every day that a pharmacist got to feel like a superhero. And it was in stark contrast to how the last woman he talked to had made him feel.

Priss, that raven-haired little hellcat, had turned on him hissing and spitting, like he'd tried to steal her kitten. He felt a muscle jump in his jaw. "Normally I enjoy the job. Today was a challenge."

"How so?"

He told her the story of the delinquent who turned out to be his tenant. By the time he finished, June's delicately arched brows hovered near her hairline. "That woman lied to you?"

"Yeah."

Her spine was light-pole straight. "I think that's despicable."

He remembered Priss, hand tight around her brother's arm marching him to the alley. Adam wouldn't have wanted to be that kid. By not calling the cops, he may have consigned the boy to a worse fate. "You have to admire her for taking her brother in, though."

"Well, I don't," she sniffed. "She sounds like an alley cat."

The waiter wheeled a cart to their table and began tossing their salads.

More like a mother panther—wild, protective and dangerous.

After the waiter set their salads in front of them, Adam asked, "How do you like Widow's Grove so far?"

As the dinner wore on, the conversation didn't get any more exciting.

It was late when he pulled into June's drive. No generic apartment for June; she'd rented a small cottage behind one of the Victorians that lined the street into town. When he pulled past the big house the headlights illuminated its Mini-Me—a scaled version right down to the baby-blue lattice fretwork on the porch.

He shut down the engine. "You sure were lucky to score this little place."

"It is sweet, isn't it? The owner has an antique store in town. He's one of Daddy's customers."

Adam stepped out of the car and walked around it to open her door. "Well, it fits you." He offered his hand and helped her out.

The night was crisp, starry and quiet. The smell of jasmine came from the bushes at the foot of the porch, mingling with June's perfume, filling his head. He took her hand at the curving stepping-stone walkway. Fine-boned and tiny, it made his look huge by comparison. "Thank you for coming out with me this evening."

"I thoroughly enjoyed it." Together they took the step to the porch. "I'm sorry you didn't."

"On the contrary." He tugged her hand, turning her to him. "I enjoyed being with you." Her smile flashed white in the starlight.

Here we go. He touched her chin, lifting it. He lowered his lips to hers.

Her lips were cool, as if made of the alabaster her skin resembled. It was a composed, chaste contact.

He tilted his head to deepen the kiss, to spark the heat for a slow, warm fire.

Her lips didn't part, and she stepped back. "I'd better get in. It's late." She squeezed his hand, then let go. "Thank you. I hope we can do this again."

Why would you want to? His kiss hadn't even struck a spark in her, much less a fire. But her smile in the dark seemed genuine. "Sure thing. Don't forget to lock up."

After she'd stepped inside and he heard the deadbolt click in place, hands in his pockets, Adam retraced his steps to the car.

No warmth, no tinder. No sparks. He hadn't even managed to drive the chill from her lips.

A vaguely familiar ache hit him like vertigo. Trying to place the feeling, he opened the car door and settled onto the seat. He felt off kilter, as if… The key clicked into the ignition as tumblers clicked in his mind, placing the feeling.

Unfulfilled.

He couldn't say when exactly it had begun, but lately it had been calling to him in quiet moments, whispering. He'd ignored it, staying busy until he ended the day tired enough to fall into a quick coma.

There was a fine shake in his fingers as he started the car and threw it into reverse.

The disquiet was no longer a whisper. It was a voice on the wind.

And the wind was change.

THE NEXT DAY, Priss pulled up behind Bar None and hit the button to raise Mona's top. The dark-bottomed clouds looked like rain. She glanced around the alley while Mona's engine chugged and wheezed and the top lifted.

The iron security gate on the back door of the bar held more rust than paint, and the ripe scent of garbage drifted from the overfilled Dumpster. The backside of Widow's Grove was the flip side of its facade. And here she was, once again on the seamy side.

Pushing her dark thoughts aside, she raised all of Mona's windows, snatched her wallet and apron from the seat, and stepped onto the oil-stained asphalt. At the door, she stopped to tie her mother's apron over her jeans, crossing the ties in the back and tying a bow in the front. An odd feeling flowed over her, as if she were going through the exact motions her mother had countless times before her.

"Not going there today." She may not be able to get away from her mother's life at the moment, but she refused to be pulled into the depression of her surroundings. Maybe she'd find something else soon. And even if that didn't materialize, she knew from experience she could wait out the hard times by keeping her focus on the future.

She pulled out her ring of keys and opened the iron-barred door, then flipped to the key for the metal door. Tonight she'd get Nacho settled—find places for his clothes and the stuff she'd brought from the apartment, then cook him dinner. It might even be fun. Imagining helping Nacho with homework at their small table, she unlocked the door and stepped inside. After turning off the alarm, she flipped on lights and got to work, prepping the bar for the day's business.

Two hours later, the usual suspects perched on stools at the bar. She'd found the patrons were an odd mix of regulars and strolling tourists. She was getting to know the clientele who stopped in for lunch every day. Compared to her past bartending job at a trendy hot spot, this was easy; the most exotic drink she'd been asked to make was a daiquiri.

"Why so down, Barney? The Tigers won last night." Priss polished a glass with the corner of her apron.

The disheveled old guy slumped on his chair watching TV, nursing a Bud which, except for the mojito mistake that first day, was all he ordered. She'd learned he was a retired night guard, living check to Social Security check. She'd seen him count change for his bar tab but he always left her a tip. She'd refused it at first but it had hurt his feelings, so she now just thanked him for his generosity.

He sighed. "My TV died yesterday, right in the middle of 'Sports Beat.'"

Beside him, Porter ate one of his martini olives. "I've gotta run a load to L.A. this week, but when I get back, I'll come over, and we'll see what's what."

"What are you hauling this time?" Ian's Scottish burr always got heavier after his second Guinness.

"Taking washing machines to the city dwellers."

"Don't bother, Porter. The TV's a goner," Barney said.

Priss poured Patrón into the ice-and-mix-filled blender and hit the button. The growl of blades, chewing ice, made her miss some of the conversation. Once the drink was blended, she poured it into a salted margarita glass, added a wedge of lime to the rim, and set it at the waitress station for pickup. "If I'd known earlier, I could have brought you my mom's TV from her apartment. It was rabbit-ears old but I think it still worked."

Gaby, the grumpy old waitress, emerged from the kitchen with a plate of nachos, walked over and snatched the margarita.

Priss slapped on a smile, determined to win over the old hag. "How are you today, Gaby?"

The woman just glared, turned and stalked to the booth.

"What is her problem?"

"Ah, she's okay," Porter said. "She's got a soft side, once you get past the prickly outside."

Priss snorted. "I've seen softer thorns on a cactus." She rinsed the blender pitcher in the sink of soapy water. Her stomach growled. "Anybody need a refill? I'm going to go make myself a sandwich."

Mesmerized by the rowdy game show on the TV, her customers just shook their heads.

She pushed through the swinging door, stepped to the fridge and pulled it open. Trying to choose between ham and turkey, she heard the door open behind her.

The "humph" of disgust announced that Gaby had followed her into the back.

Priss chose the ham, pulled pickles and mustard from the door, and, arms full, kicked the fridge closed behind her.

The old lady stood staring in an old-fashioned black rayon waitress uniform with support-hose sagging. Priss looked back. "What's your problem? What have I ever done to you?"

The woman shook her head and walked to the fridge.

"Most people who dislike me at least give me the courtesy of knowing me first."

The woman pulled two burger patties from a towering stack, closed the fridge and dropped them on the grill where they spit and hissed. "I know you better than I'd like, Miss *Priss*." Her mocking tone made the *Priss* sound like a spoiled-rich bitch.

Priss didn't have a response, so she slathered the bread with mustard, then topped it with the ham and pickles before slapping the sandwich together as fast as she could.

Beating the hag with a ham sandwich would feel good, but it would get her fired. *You need this job. You need this job because of Nacho.*

What the hell had she been thinking, anyway? What was a free bird doing with a kid? What was wrong with her lately?

But she'd made a promise, and now she was in it.

Priss opened the apartment door, juggling an armload of groceries.

Nacho jumped up from the couch. "Why didn't you tell me you went back home?" The plastic container she'd brought from the apartment lay half-emptied at his feet.

"Keep your voice down." She pulled the key out of the door and pushed it shut with her butt. "I had to clean it out or they were going to charge me rent."

"Why didn't you take me with you?"

"You were in school at the time. Give me a hand, will you?" When he didn't move, she schlepped the bags to the counter.

"You had no right to go through our stuff!"

"Yeah, I did. And stop yelling." She set the bags down and dropped her keys with a clatter.

Nacho stood, fists clenched, face red. "How'd you like it if I went through *your* stuff?"

"Well, obviously you already have, because that—" she pointed at the bin "—was in the bottom of my closet."

He plopped on the couch. His bottom lip wobbled and he bit down on it.

She walked over and looked down at the junk on the floor. Hardly personal. A few clothes, outgrown toys and generic jigsaw puzzles.

But the hurt in his eyes seared her. It burned through her adult shell like a laser, leaving a smoking hole right down to the little girl in hated hand-me-downs. That girl knew what it was like to have nothing but junk—junk made precious by its scarcity.

He looked at his hands in his lap. "I didn't get to say goodbye."

"To that trashy apartment?"

"No, to my stuff—my life." His voice wavered, but his teeth were clenched. "It sucked, but it was *mine.*"

She walked over and sat on the couch. "I'm sorry, Nacho, I didn't think." She wanted to touch him, to soothe the pain from his voice, from his fisted hands. From his past. But she knew she didn't have that power, and he wouldn't welcome it even if she did. "You did get to say goodbye to Mom—before she died?"

"Yeah."

"Was she…in pain?" A blade of regret slipped past her armor, stabbing close to her soft parts. Why ask, when she didn't want to know?

"What do you care? You didn't come back, even when she was sick."

"I didn't know—"

"How do I even know you're my sister?" He crossed his arms and tucked his fists under.

Anger was probably easier for him than grief and she was the one in front of him—an easy target. "We have the same last name."

"That doesn't prove anything. I never met you and I'm already ten."

She didn't want to go back there—back to that time. She sat a moment, thinking then said it. "She smoked menthol cigarettes. Lit one right off the other." Turning sideways, she leaned her back against the end of the couch. "She was a bad house-keeper, but could play a mean game of Go Fish, when it was rainy."

Nacho's frown smoothed.

"She was pretty, with her black hair and big eyes. When she went out, she always wore Shalimar perfume and a dress with a belt, to show off her tiny waist."

Bitter and sweet memories swirled in her, blending and hardening into the block of cement that was her past.

Nacho nodded, a small smile at the corner of his lips.

"And she always had to have a man." She pushed away from the back of the couch. "Always."

Nacho said, "Yeah, I guess she was your mom, too."

"Yep, she was." She tamped down the miasma of nostalgia and stood. "Now, what do you want for dinner?"

An hour later, she left Nacho doing science homework at the kitchen table, stepped across the hall and tapped lightly on the door.

"Just a moment!"

Priss heard the squeaky walker approach before the door opened. Apparently she needn't have worried that Olivia would be asleep. She stood in the doorway as perfectly coiffed and dressed as if she had a houseful of company.

"I'm sorry to bother you—"

"Why, hello, Priss. You're not bothering me at all. Come in."

"I can't. I have to keep an eye on..." Priss looked back at her own closed door.

"Your brother?"

Priss whipped her head back. She should have known Adam would be on the phone with his mother right away, warning her of her felonious neighbor. "Yes, Ms. Preston. I just wanted you to know, he won't be a bother to you. I don't know what your son said, but—"

Her smile didn't look afraid. "Don't be silly. I look forward to meeting—Nacho, is it?"

"His given name is Ignacio, although he's offended when people call him that. He's really not a bad boy. He's had a rough time of it lately and…" She shifted to her other foot. "I just don't want you to worry about living across the hall from us."

Olivia laughed. "You'll have to excuse my son. I think this broken hip of mine made him realize that I'm mortal and now he's treating me as if I'm fragile. Nothing could be farther from the truth. I was a college professor for years, but prior to that I taught junior high. It would take a lot more than a ten-year-old to frighten me."

Priss felt a rush of gratitude. At least there was one person in town who wouldn't judge her and Nacho. "Ms. Preston—"

"Olivia, please."

"Olivia, is there anything I can do for you? Pick up some groceries? Run errands?"

"I'm grateful to have many friends, and of course, Adam, who are seeing to my every need, but thank you."

"Oh, well, then…"

Olivia studied her a moment. "You know, I'd love to go out for coffee sometime. You and I could get to know each other a bit better. Would you like that?"

Yes. And no. Priss would love to have a philosophical discussion with Olivia. But watching the woman's bright sparrow eyes, Priss knew Olivia would want to know more about her new neighbors—much more.

Imagining that conversation made Priss want to scuttle across the hall, slam the door and lock it.

But she couldn't afford to offend her landlord's mother. Especially since Olivia seemed inclined to make up her own mind, in spite of God knows what her son had told her about her neighbors. So instead, Priss lifted the corners of her mouth. "Um, sure."

CHAPTER SIX

ADAM BLINKED SWEAT from his eyes and, arms shaking, bench-pressed the bar onto the standards. The clang of weights hitting metal and the grunts of other gym rats blended with the irritating techno beat pulsing from the speakers overhead. He rested a moment then sat up and wiped his face with a towel.

"Are you ready to kick some Santa Maria Marlin butt next weekend, Preston?"

Adam looked up at the gruff voice of the owner of the local gas station, who doubled as the Grove's bookie. "Arm's feeling pretty good, Willie."

"Glad to hear it. Maybe I'll change the odds." He walked away, mumbling to himself.

Adam glanced at the clock. Lunchtime over, he stood and walked toward the locker room. As usual, his feet paused in front of the towering climbing wall. Before he could stop it, his gaze lifted and his stomach plummeted like an elevator with the cables cut, free-falling to the floor of his pelvis.

At the lip near the top of the wall, Roger Maloney, the son of Adam's second baseman, hung suspended by only his hands and a slack safety rope, seemingly contemplating his next move.

Adam's stomach rolled over and whimpered. Fear scrabbled and clawed the inside of his chest. Scrubbing his hands on the back of his shorts, his eyes followed the rope to the pint-size, inadequate balayer on the ground.

Go help. Fresh sweat popped on his forehead. He pushed himself to move but there was a shout from above, flash-freezing him midlean.

"Falling!"

Roger fell, back first, arms and legs relaxed. The belayer was jerked off his feet and pulled into the air. Both Roger and his anchor person laughed like they were on an amusement-park ride.

Insane. Shaking his head and breathing like a buffalo, Adam tottered to the locker room on weak knees. So he had an issue with heights. And closed-in places. And the unexpected. He'd built a life that avoided those risks—well, as much as possible.

So he'd taken the easy way and become a pharmacist because his father had been one. But the career suited him. Prescriptions were black and white. The doctor specified a specific drug, and a fifty-count didn't mean forty-nine, or fifty-one. Black and white were the demarcations of his world and he didn't venture too near the edges.

So what if his life was a bit…boring? It was safe. And there was a lot to be said for safe.

But the memory of his tenant's flashing dark eyes drifted through his mind, tempting him, inviting him to come out and play.

"WHAT CAN I GET YOU?" Jesse stood at the edge of the table, looking from Priss to Olivia, then back again. "I would not have guessed that you two knew each other."

Olivia smiled across at Priss. "Priscilla and her brother are my new neighbors over the drugstore. I'll just have tea, Jesse. Some of that nice lavender I had last time, please."

Priss played with the edges of the menu. "I'll have coffee—the regular stuff, not that sludge you stock for the yuppies."

Jesse just stood there, unmoving, hand on hip. "Well? Did you get the job?"

After Adam's reaction, the last thing Priss wanted was to discuss her new job in front of Olivia. But Jesse wasn't going anywhere until she got an answer. Priss frowned. "I got the job. Thank you for the tip."

Jesse dusted her hands with a smug smile. "Wow, it is not easy to be *this* good." She sashayed to the counter for their drinks.

"Where are you working, dear?" Olivia asked.

Priss had known that going to the café with Olivia was a bad idea. But Nacho was stuck doing detention after school today. She'd taken a chance and knocked on Olivia's door, half hoping she had company and wouldn't be available. No such luck. Her neighbor had been delighted by Priss's invitation.

After ripping apart her closet to find something appropriate to wear, Priss had decided to stay in her dress pants and fitted button-down shirt she'd worn to work.

Olivia was cultured, a college professor no less. Priss was so far out of her league that she was playing ball on a different planet.

She had no illusions. If Olivia didn't approve, Priss and Nacho would be on the street. Adam was looking for an excuse to be rid of them.

But Olivia had taught philosophy and was an avid reader—two of Priss's favorite things. Living across the hall from her was like the siren's call of the sea—and Priss was a sailor.

But there were rogue waves to consider.

And one such wave pulled back revealing a strange lump on the beach of her awareness. *You care what she thinks of you.*

Priss caught herself squirming and tautened to stillness. Hell, Adam had probably already told his mom anyway. Holding her face in studious lines as if it would dress up the truth, Priss said, "I'm the daytime bartender at Bar None." She rushed on. "I've worked it out so I can be home for Nacho in the evenings and the tips will help buy him some extra things. You know, things he probably hasn't had before." *Shut up. Just. Shut. Up.*

"How wonderful that you found a job that enables you to care for your brother." Olivia's smile held no judgments.

The muscles next to Priss's spine unlocked, allowing her to lean against the back cushion. "It's only temporary, until I can find an administrative job."

Jesse returned with their drinks, dropped a wink at Priss, and walked away.

Olivia sipped the tea and sighed. "Lady Grey never disappoints." She set her cup down. "Adam tells me you came to us from Colorado."

"I lived in Boulder. I had a job as an office manager." *Oh, yeah, like you're going to impress a college professor with management experience and your associate's degree.*

"And you gave that up to come here and care for your brother."

"Don't make me out to be a hero." Her face heated. "I didn't come here for him. I came to settle my mother's affairs, such as they are. I didn't know Nacho's father was in prison. I had no intention of taking on a ten-year-old."

Olivia tipped her head, like a bird spying something worth investigating. "Then why did you?"

"I couldn't leave him to Social Services. I tried. I didn't get ten miles out of town." *Shut up, shut up, shut up.* She sipped coffee to keep her lips occupied and considered what to say next.

Olivia gave her a sweet grandmotherly smile.

Priss felt sweat gathering in the dip between her breasts. "I was in foster care for a time when I was young." She glanced up in time to see Jesse walk into the kitchen. No cavalry to save her. Knee bouncing under the table, Priss heard her throat click as she swallowed. "Could we talk about something else?"

"Oh, I'm sorry dear, I didn't mean to pry." Olivia looked as if she'd just trod on someone's blue-ribbon tulip beds.

"No, I'm sorry." Priss watched her hands fidget with her cup. "I can be a bit…abrupt."

"Straightforward talk is a breath of fresh air in this politically correct society. How can we discuss weighty matters if we're afraid to be frank?" Olivia hesitated, as if considering, then set down her cup with a decisive click. "I'd like to invite you to join me and some friends of mine in our book group." When a few drops of coffee splashed from Priss's cup, Olivia raised a hand. "Now, it's nothing formal, or special. We just get together once a month to discuss the book we're reading. We usually choose books with a philosophical bent, which is why I thought you'd be interested."

A shower of glittery sparks went off in Priss's brain. What an opportunity! Then an M-80 exploded in her stomach. *An opportunity to make an ass of yourself.* She shuffled her meager repertoire of polite phrases to convey *no* while still sounding grateful.

Olivia said, "We read *The Handmaid's Tale* last month. This month, we're reading *Lord of the Flies.*"

Regret and temptation warred in her chest. "Ooh, I *loved* that book."

"We've all read it before, of course, but I thought that it would be interesting to read it again and discuss what was new for us."

She couldn't possibly do it. In a roomful of cultured ladies, she'd stand out like a homeless person on a Paris runway.

But *Lord of the Flies* had always been one of her favorite classics. How could she resist? She squinted across the table. Maybe there wouldn't be time to reread it, and that would be that. "When is the meeting?"

"In three weeks."

Priss knew it would seem rude, but she had to know. "Why are you being so nice to me?"

Olivia laughed a tinkling sound of amusement, soothing as wind chimes. "Oh, my dear, I have to admit to being fascinated by you. You're such a dichotomous conundrum."

Priss rolled the pretty words around the palette of her mind, enjoying them. What the hell. She'd already made a poor impression on the male Preston. At worst, in three weeks, his mother would share it.

It was worth taking a chance, even if imagining doing it made her hands shake. Priss smiled across the table. "I'd love to."

Oh, I'm so going down in flames.

"ALL THE TESTS show that Ignacio is a bright child," the principal said. "The subjects he likes, he does well in. Math and science mostly, although Mrs. Devlin tells me he shows artistic talent, as well."

Priss sat in the elementary-school office, trying to get her head around the fact that she was there as a *parent*. When she'd stepped into the one-story redbrick building, her past had overtaken the present. The smell of kids, paper and the wax they polished the floor with opened a portal to the underworld of her past. She shook her head to clear it.

"What subjects isn't he doing well in?"

The careworn brunette glanced at the open folder before her. "Social studies and all language arts—spelling, handwriting and, most especially, reading. I think all these problems stem from his lack of reading skills. Ms. Hart, he's reading more than a grade below his peers." She took off her glasses and laid them on the desk. "Also, this year Ignacio has been acting out quite a bit. He's been disciplined for talking in class, fighting during recess

and throwing food in the cafeteria. This is not un-
usual for a child who has gone through what he has
recently—his mother being sick and then passing."
A shadow of pink rose in her cheeks. "I'm sorry
for your loss, as well."

"Um. Thanks. I'll see that he calms down now
that he's settled with me. We'll work on reading
together, too." She stood. The sooner she got away
from schoolhouse memories the better. "Thank you
for your time."

The principal stood. "Let me know if we can do
anything to help. We have special programs—"

"No, I've got it covered. Thanks." More government help, they didn't need. Priss shook the woman's proffered hand, spun on her heel and scuttled
out.

Closing the door behind her, she checked the
time. School would let out in a few minutes. She
passed a hallway on her way to the front doors.
Under the squeak of chairs and teachers' voices,
she heard in her mind a wisp of laughter. Ugly,
taunting laughter. The ghost of a pig-nosed blonde
girl stalked out of the past and advanced down the
hallway, lips tight and hate in her eyes.

I'll wait outside. Hunching her shoulders and
turning away, Priss headed for the carefree sunshine splashing the world outside the heavy glass
doors.

Minutes later, safely ensconced in Mona, she

heard the bell announcing the end of the school day. Kids poured out of the doors, chattering and laughing. They walked to the chugging buses or to the line of cars pulled up in front of the school.

Priss saw Nacho between the two boys she'd seen that first day. His "gang." Heads together in deep discussion, they walked toward the schoolyard. She stood on Mona's seat to be seen above the trolling cars and yelled over the din, "Hey, Nacho!"

His head jerked up and he looked around. When he saw her waving madly, he spoke to his friends, bumped fists, then walked to the car. "What're you doing here?"

"I had a meeting with your principal."

He opened the door and slouched into the seat, apparently incurious about the results of the meeting.

"Seat belt," she reminded, checking the rearview mirror for a break in the parking-lot traffic. "Where were you going? Home is the opposite way."

"We were just hanging out. No big deal." His face was closed, hard. "Why are you checking up on me all the time? I don't need a babysitter."

She saw a space and gunned the car in Reverse. "Good thing, because I don't do babysitting." The lady in a Lexus SUV blatted her horn. If she'd have been alone, Priss would have flipped the woman the bird. But she was now a role model.

Me, a role model. This kid is in trouble. When they'd inched their way to the exit, she turned left.

"Home is the opposite way," he mocked.

"We're not going home." She sped up as the traffic cleared.

Nacho sat up. "Where are we going?"

"To the library."

He groaned. "Oh, no, not you, too?"

Raising her voice over the wind, she said, "Me, too, what?"

"Mom took me there all the time. Boooring."

Good to know Mom at least made the effort to improve his reading.

"She was always looking up stuff on the computer. We spent hours and hours there."

"Looking up what?"

He rolled his eyes. "Like I noticed."

Mom wasn't a reader. As far as Priss knew, her mother had never stepped foot in a library. *What would she have been looking up?*

"Can I just wait in the car?"

She smiled at her brother's long-suffering look. "You'd better get used to the place, dude. Libraries are one of my favorite places."

His theatrical sigh was so big it almost fogged the windshield.

"How can a brother of mine not like to read?"

"Half brother."

"Oh, then that explains it." Smiling, she took a left into the parking lot.

They walked to the tall front doors of the building, through its columned portico. "We won't be long. I already know the book I want. Then we'll pick out a couple for you."

"Uh-uh. I'm good."

"Not according to the principal, you're not." She opened the door, and held it, inhaling the heady scent of books and freedom. Libraries had been her sanctuary growing up, a safe haven and a portal to worlds that were far more exotic than the poor side of Las Vegas. Programmed from an early age, her nerves settled.

She'd worked her way through the stacks, traveling everywhere: medieval castles, ranches, even other planets. And all for free. She inhaled. "You just haven't found something to catch your interest yet. You will. Some of the best times I've ever had were reading books."

He sighed again. "Just because you have no life, why do you have to take me down with you?"

When he rolled his eyes, she put a hand on the back of his neck and steered him inside. "You don't know what you're missing, but luckily you have me to show you the way."

FIFTEEN MINUTES BEFORE opening, Adam scanned the store's soda fountain. Priss sat at a table, nose in the *Widow's Grove Telegraph*. He'd decided while shaving this morning that if he wanted to mitigate surprises in his life, he was going to have to stay close to Priss. At least that's what he told himself in front of his bathroom mirror.

But standing here, feeling a tugging in his gut like the low-level pull of a magnet, he had to admit that his decision to stay close to Priss, to get to know her, was about more than self-preservation. He may not approve of her brother, her attitude or her rough edges, but he couldn't deny his attraction. And it wasn't just her trim dancer's body, made even sexier by the fact that she seemed totally unaware of it. Lately his mind kept returning to her like an unchecked item on a to-do list. She was absolute chaos to his orderly life. So what was it about Priss that drew him to her?

Now that he finally quit avoiding and just asked the question, his mind spit out the answer. It was her *differentness. Yeah, but you can't get much more "different" than Sin, and the reaction there is not the same at all.*

Instead of carefully considering that revelation, he gave in to the tractor-beam pull. Crossing the floor, he slid into the chair opposite Priss.

The paper rattled when she turned the page. He cleared his throat. "It looks like they haven't caught the guy yet."

She peeked over the top of the paper. "What guy?"

Pointing to the front-page story, he said, "The guy who's been breaking into houses around town the past three months."

She closed the paper and glanced at the article. "Yeah, I read that. It's weird that nothing is damaged or stolen, unless you count the food taken from the fridge."

He crossed his legs and tried to look nonchalant. "I heard you took my mother for coffee."

A wall fell, shuttering her expression. "I drove carefully, had her home in an hour and I didn't corrupt her mind."

She must really think him an ass. "Mom has lots of friends, but they're older so they aren't up to more than stopping by her apartment for a bit. I know she doesn't get out as much as she'd like. Thank you."

"Oh. I didn't do it for you." She flushed. "I mean, I was happy to do it. She's a great lady and I enjoy her company."

She looked like an innocent little girl when she blushed. He knew not to be deceived, but he appreciated it, regardless. "So, how's your brother doing?"

"He hasn't been in the store since that first day and he's not bothering your mother."

He spread his hands and shrugged. "I'm just trying to be nice."

"Yeah, I see that." She raised an eyebrow. "I'm trying to figure out why."

He should have known she'd be suspicious. "Look, I came across a little…militant that day. I was pissed."

"Well, I was a little over the top, too." She shifted in her seat. "I swear I didn't know he had that magazine—never imagined he'd do something like that." Her lips twisted in a wince, as if the words hurt. "But I'm on it now. He won't be a problem."

He searched her intent green eyes. She meant it. "Has he always been a…challenge?"

"I wouldn't know. I met him for the first time at my mother's funeral."

He uncrossed his legs and straightened. "How could you never have met your broth—"

"But we have an understanding, now." She reached for her purse, put the strap over her shoulder, and lifted her chin. "We'll make this work."

"I'm sure you will." He watched her fold the paper. Even her hands were different—long, elegant fingers with blunt-clipped nails. "Well, if he's interested in softball, a new league will be starting up in the summer. I can get you the information, if you want."

She flashed a smile. "Thanks. I'll ask him." She stood and walked away.

Adam sat, watching her go, surprised by his interest and dazzled by her smile.

But there was wild in that smile, too. And he didn't do wild. He slid his chair back, stood, walked to the drug counter and back to his to-do list.

THAT NIGHT PRISS sat on the couch, bare feet tucked under her, reading. She glanced up every so often to the kitchen table, where Nacho was supposed to be reading, but was mostly just sighing and fidgeting. "Dude. Read."

She'd just gotten back to the castaways' island when tap-tap-tapping intruded—Nacho's heel against the rung of the chair. She put the book down. "Maybe it'll help you get into the story if you read it out loud to me."

"No." He ruffled the pages with one hand.

"Yes."

He put his fists to his temples and stared down at the book.

"Nacho—"

He slammed the book shut. "This is so freaking lame. Who gives a crap about some Baggins dude? This guy writes like in another language."

Maybe *The Hobbit* wasn't a good place to start. She'd fallen into the Middle Earth at Nacho's age, but it might be too advanced for his reading level. She stood and walked to the small pile of library books on the counter. "Oh, here's one I know you'll like."

"I don't want to read. I don't *like* to read."

Now he was getting whiny. But if she could find *one* book to spark his interest it could change his whole opinion of reading. She ran her hand along the spine of the hardcover she held and bit back a retort. "Did you ever see *Harry Potter?*"

He glared at her. "How many movies did you go to when you were growing up?"

Of course he hadn't. There was never money for extras in Cora's house. "But it's been on TV."

He sat, a perfect poster child of sullen. "Yeah, like we had cable." He pulled his hand away from his face, palm up. "Helllllooo—rabbit ears?"

"Oh, right." She forced cheeriness in her voice. "That's good, then, you're in for a treat." *God, I sound like a detergent commercial.*

When she tried to put the book in his hands, he sat on them.

She struggled to tamp down the irritation rising up cords in her neck, setting her teeth on edge. Instead of grinding them, she used them to bite her tongue. *You vowed to be understanding and attentive, remember?* All the things her mother hadn't been.

She took a deep breath. Then another. When she was calm enough that her voice wouldn't break glass, she said, "Okay, then I'll read to you."

He sat up. "What, do you think I'm a baby?"

She managed to keep from saying the obvious. Making him madder wouldn't help. "Of course you're not. But I loved being read to. When you don't have to worry about the words, you can make up a story picture in your head. And as you get better at reading on your own, you'll eventually be able to do both at the same time." She stepped to the couch, and patted the arm. "Come, sit. Get comfortable. You're going to love this book. I just know it."

"If I *haveta*." He walked over and plopped down on the couch, leaning his back against the cushioned arm. "But if you *ever* tell my homies you're reading me bedtime stories…"

"Hey, no one will hear it from me." Holding a smile in, she sat on the other end of the couch, pulled down the throw from the back, and spread it over Nacho's feet where they lay next to hers in the middle.

He wasn't as badass as he tried to appear. In fact, he was pretty adorable, with those dark eyes, long lashes and widow's peak. All he needed was some understanding and a little patience. Hopefully this gang-thing was only a phase.

"Okay, be ready to meet a guy who's got it pretty tough. His name is Harry, and he's *way* cool." She opened the book. "Mr. and Mrs. Dursley, of number four, Privet Drive were proud to say that they were perfectly normal, thank you very much…"

NACHO REACHED DOWN to undo the clip on his backpack. "A guy I know stole these from a paint shop."

He upended the pack, spilling colorful spray cans into the weeds.

"Aw, sweet!" Diego said.

"Shut up, fool." Joe scanned the abandoned field behind the warehouse. "You want to get caught?"

When the shoplifting initiation failed, they'd chosen to tag this warehouse. It wasn't far from school, and it sat off by itself at the end of a quiet street. Nacho picked up the orange, yellow and black cans. "You guys do your thing. I'll be around the side."

Joe's eyes widened. "If someone comes down the road or looks from the parking lot, they're gonna see you."

Nacho took a deep breath, happy to see it made his chest pump up. "Yeah, that's not gonna happen. I'm fast. You guys hurry up. I'll see you in a few."

He left his friends fighting over the remaining colors and walked around to the side of the warehouse. They'd decided what each would tag, and even practiced drawing the designs so they'd be faster today. Diego was painting a Beretta, with smoke coming out of the barrel. Joe was printing their gang name, *Widow Makers,* as if the gun was firing it.

This is gonna be legendary. No one could know it was them, of course, but Nacho couldn't wait to hear kids talk about this at school.

He set down the other colors and came up holding only the black can. When Priss's angry death-ray glare floated through his head, something uneasy squirmed in his chest. She'd be flaming pissed if she knew. He rubbed his breastbone with his fist.

"She'll never know." He shook the can, scanning his canvas.

CHAPTER SEVEN

"Yeah, but Garcia has like seventy-five strikeouts, Barney," Priss said as she wiped down the bar while glancing at the game on the TV. The usual suspects lined the other side of the bar. "And he's got a thirty slugging percentage, which is pretty danged good for a pitcher, you gotta admit."

"Ah, the A's suck hind tit." He took a sip of his beer.

She squinted at the grizzled old man. Hair stuck out everywhere—including his ears. "Why are you such a die-hard Tigers fan? Did you used to live in Detroit?"

He puckered his lips and looked into his glass like it held straight lemon juice. "No. I just like them. Is that okay with you?" He slid off the bar stool, hiked his too-big pants, and strode for the bathroom.

Priss watched him go. "What'd I say wrong?"

Porter coughed into his fist. "His grandson is a backup shortstop for the Tigers."

"Wow, that's amazing. He must be so proud. I'm surprised he never mentioned it."

Ian shot a glance over his shoulder, then said in his soft burr, "Barney's ex-wife turned his kids against him. He's never even met his grandson."

Porter said, "But don't bring it up. Barn's real sensitive about it."

"I bet." Priss imagined the old guy sitting in a shabby apartment at night without even the distraction of a TV to keep his regrets at bay. It seemed she and Nacho weren't the only mutts in town, sniffing around the trash cans of polite society.

Her boob vibrated.

She pulled her phone from her bra. She didn't recognize the number, but hit the button anyway. "This is Priss."

"This is Officer Armijo, of the Widow's Grove Police Department. Is this Priscilla Hart?"

"It is." Her heart banged a beat like the drum solo in *Wipeout*. The clock next to the TV read four. Nacho was supposed to be home by now. *Please don't let it be about Nacho—*

"Ignacio Hart gave me your number. He is one of three boys we apprehended for defacing private property."

A depth charge of acid exploded in her stomach. *Shit.* She scrabbled for the pad and pen in the pocket of her apron. "Where is he?" She scribbled the address.

"Ma'am, if you can be here in ten minutes or so, we'll wait, cite him and release him into your custody. Otherwise, you'll have to collect him from the station."

"I'll be there in just a few minutes." She hit End. Her fingers fumbled as she dropped the phone back into her bra.

You can't leave. Floyd's not due here for another half hour.

You can't stay—they'll take Nacho to jail!

"What's wrong?" Barney was back on his stool, his caterpillar eyebrows near his hairline.

"I've got an emergency. I have to go." She scanned the bar. Thank God the lunch rush was over. Only a few tourists sat at tables, sipping margaritas. Floyd lived in Pismo Beach, a half hour away—he may have already left his house, but there was no way he was getting here in the next five minutes.

She couldn't just run out and leave an open cash drawer. But she couldn't shove all the customers out and lock up, either. Panic sizzled across her spine and popped along her nerves. Her mind skittered down dead-end corridors like a rat in a maze.

The door to the kitchen opened and Gaby's bent form shuffled out, her hands full of a basket of chips and a bowl of salsa.

Priss ducked under the waitress station and jogged over to her. "Gaby. I need your help."

The old lady looked at Priss as if she'd broken out of a locked ward. "Really."

"I have an emergency. I have to go—like right now. If you'd just man the bar for a half hour till Floyd—"

"Floyd would be pissed. Sounds like you have a problem." She shuffled by.

Priss grabbed her forearm. "Look, I'm begging you. This is really important. Please?"

The old bat stared lasers at Priss's hand until she let go.

"Seriously. I'll pay you."

Her head jerked up, her greedy little eyes bright. "How much?"

"Twenty-five bucks."

"Don't waste my time." She walked to the table in the corner and set down the chips and salsa.

It was going to take at least five minutes to get to the address the officer had given her. Priss felt the time ticking by in her pounding heartbeat. She blocked Gaby's retreat to the kitchen, "Fifty."

The crone paused. "I can't fix nothing fancy. I can open a beer."

Relief flooded Priss, liquefying her knees. "Thank you, Gaby, I—"

"Pay me now." She put out a hand.

Priss reached into her apron pocket, hoping she had that much on her. "Jesus, do you really think I wouldn't pay up?" *Hurry. Hurry.*

"I wouldn't trust you with a bag of garbage."

Priss pulled out bills and counted them. Forty-five. Gaby's tight lips and crossed arms told her not to even bother asking. She spun to the patrons at the bar. "Can someone lend me a five?" She took the step to the bar. "Please?" She hated that word. Hated the weakness it implied. But she had no choice.

Porter held out his hand to Barney and Ian. "Come on, ante up, men."

Ian handed over a few singles. Barney took an old-fashioned rubber change purse from his pocket and sorted through it with a finger.

Priss felt a pinch in her chest at asking this poor old man for money, even as her head screamed, *hurry!*

Barney contributed two quarters.

Porter added the remainder and handed over the bills and change to her cupped palm.

"You guys are the best. I owe you. Big time." And she hated that, too.

She turned, slapped the bills in Gaby's palm, and poured the change on top. "Even if you are a greedy old bat, I'm grateful." And she was mostly grateful that the old woman didn't stall any longer, counting it.

Priss trotted to the back door. "Tell Floyd I'm sorry. I'll call him."

THE WIDOW MAKERS stood in the parking lot of the Bekins warehouse, waiting for their parents. Two cops stood by their squad car, talking to the warehouse manager.

Nacho glanced at Joe. "Come on, homie, be cool."

"You don't know, man," Joe sniffed once more and took a deep breath. "My uncle is gonna kick my *ass*. For real."

A pale-faced Diego dug stones out of the dirt with the toe of his shoe.

Nacho glanced down the road, not sure he'd be happy to see the beater convertible. He'd be sprung from the cops, but then he'd have to face his pissed-off half sister. He'd stayed chilly when the cops busted them but now his hard-ass act was melting like an Otter Pop in August. He swallowed a thick wad in his throat.

She might send him back to the kid warehouse. *Screw that. I'll just run away.*

But it was one thing to say it; another to do it. He had no money. Nobody would believe he was old enough to work—even if he could escape this shitty burg.

So I'll find somewhere safe to sleep and eat out of Dumpsters behind McDonald's.

He'd come up with lots of possible hideouts, lying awake at night in the group home: the bushes behind the school, the dried-up stream that ran under the freeway overpass. But now that he might really have to use them, they seemed pretty lame. More like dreams he made up so he'd feel better.

Besides, the cops would find him eventually and send him back to the kid warehouse.

God, he couldn't *wait* until he was old enough to be in control of his own life. But he couldn't make time go fast enough. That dream was years off.

In the meantime, Priss had good food, a nice place, and he even kinda liked her reading to him. Plus, that Potter dude was pretty cool; he'd hate to miss what happened next.

The big black Caddy turned into the parking lot. Feeling like he was facing a firing squad, Nacho set his face muscles into the tough-guy look he'd practiced in the mirror a zillion times. He shoved his shaking hands in his armpits.

Priss got out of the car and walked over to talk to the cops. One of them pulled out a pad and started scribbling while she talked. She put her hands out and looked like she was arguing, but not loud. Not pissed, like she'd been with that Adam dude. She tipped her head and smiled up at the cop, but he kept writing.

They're not taking us to jail? He spoke quiet, out of the corner of his mouth. "They're just giving us a ticket!"

His friends didn't look like that made much difference. Hell, the news didn't make him relax much, either. His sister was scarier than the cops.

Priss took the ticket from the cop, said something

to the warehouse manager, and they walked down the side of the building together.

Nacho heard the guy say, "I doubt the owner would agree, but it's pretty good." They stopped by Nacho's creation.

Bekins was in bold black letters that leaned back like the word was going fast. Yellow-tipped orange flames streamed from every letter. He'd just gotten the *B* of the next word done when the law showed up.

"Well, let the owner know that I'm going to pay whatever it costs to clean it off," Priss growled like a pit bull with a toothache. "And I'm taking it out of Nacho's hide."

All the air went out of him. Maybe it would have been better if the cops had taken him to jail.

I am dead meat.

ON THE DRIVE home the only sound was the rumble of Mona's engine and the wind.

Inside Priss's head, it was much noisier.

I am going to kill him. Outrage boiled in her chest, expanding to fill her already filled spaces. *Damned kid.*

But you're not ten years old with a father in prison.

That excuse only works once. He burned that one with the shoplifting stunt.

She wanted to look at him—wanted to know

what his face would tell her. Was he worried? Pissed? But the tendons held her neck lockjaw-tight and staring straight ahead, eyes on the road. Besides, what Nacho felt didn't matter. Not this time.

Pressure built in her skull, then radiated out with a shiver to fill everything inside. When the anger had nowhere else to go, it pushed down into her bones. It made them shake. *I'm giving him what I wanted from a mother. I'm trying to make the kid feel safe and wanted. Then he pulls this shit.*

She opened her mouth to vent some pressure, but then closed it. This wasn't a conversation for driving; she'd wreck the car for sure. Her skin felt taut, bulging with the seething mass of outrage beneath it.

He promised he wasn't going to break any more laws. Little bastard lied to me.

She braked and pulled into the broad alley behind the shops. The smell of hot garbage from the Dumpsters swirled behind the windshield. She halted in one of the oil-stained spaces behind Hollister Drugs. Nacho pulled the door handle before she could throw the car in Park.

"Stop." At her hissed warning, he froze in his seat.

She shut off the engine and slid over until the rigid muscles of her back brushed the door. Nacho wore a "don't give a shit" mask. At least she hoped it was a facade because, if that really was his atti-tude, he was going to be very, very sorry.

"So, this criminal thing with you, it must be ge-netic, huh?" Sarcasm dripped like blood from her razor-wire words.

He glared through the windshield at the brick wall. "Don't you talk about my dad. You don't know shit about me, or him."

"I know you're heading down the road to meet him in prison."

He spun, red fury staining his face. "You don't care!" Saliva flew from his mouth. "You said it the first day I met you!"

The lid blew off the mountain of her temper. "You ungrateful little shit. I dumped a boyfriend and a respectable life in Colorado to come here and bail out your raggedy little ass."

His voice rose full volume, to match hers. "You don't want me! You're just some brown-noser goody-goody who gets off on people thinking you're all holy."

"How can you say that!" Beneath her skin, she was on fire. The flames roared. Any flimsy con-trol she possessed went up in a whoosh. "That is not true! Do-gooders almost took me down when I was a kid. I was trying to save—"

"You never asked if I *wanted* your help! I don't need you. I don't need anybody!" He snatched the door handle and was out of the car faster than she'd have thought possible.

"Don't you *dare* walk away." She got her legs under her, stood on the seat and vaulted over the door.

Nacho stomped around the back of the car, anger rolling off him like the heat off the asphalt.

She stepped in front of him. "We had an agreement! I told you I'd stick by you. And you promised no more law-breaking!"

If looks could slice, she'd be bleeding.

What the hell, she *was* bleeding.

He crossed his arms and spit, "I never said anything! You assumed I agreed." A ray of triumph lit his eyes. "Hey, you did the same with that Adam guy, when you didn't tell him I was moving in. Worked for you."

Her hands spasmed when she realized she'd been had. She fisted them to keep from grabbing him by the shirt and shaking him. Instead, she stabbed a finger at the building. "Get your *ass* upstairs. *Now.*"

He stepped around her, making sure no part of them touched. Once by, he ran for the metal back door. He flung it open and it slammed against the wall with a hollow boom like summer thunder. Then he was gone.

Not caring that the hot metal seared her palms, Priss sagged against the car, suddenly empty to the deepest pit of her guts. Anger was gone. The firestorm had burned through everything inside. Ashes of the anger danced in black spots across her vision. She focused on breathing in. And out.

She'd learned long ago not to trust anyone, figuring if she didn't expect anything of anyone, she couldn't be let down. If this kid could hurt her— and he had hurt her—it was because she'd let him inside her, under her skin.

She moaned and ran a hand through her hair. When had that happened? Why? She'd been soaring through life. Light, free.

Except for the past.

She'd always believed she'd left the past in her rearview mirror. But she'd been wrong. It was still there, stuck like bubble gum to the bottom of her shoe. The past was stretchy and sticky. And not going away.

She stuffed her seared hands in her front pockets.

Long ago she'd learned not to expect the truth from outsiders, but she'd always demanded it of herself. Today it was time for some truth.

She saw herself in Nacho. He may only be half her blood brother but they had the same upbringing. It wasn't much, but seeing her childhood though his eyes, Priss was able to remember that it wasn't *all* bad. That is, until Social Services had "saved" her from her life and thrown her to the wolves.

And leaving Nacho to that fate would have been

like throwing *herself* to the wolves. She may be tough, but she wasn't tough enough to do that.

ADAM STOOD BY the garbage bins out back, trapped. He'd just tossed some empty boxes in when the Caddy roared around the corner. Before he could make himself known, the yelling had commenced. He couldn't very well whistle his way through the alley, pretending to be oblivious. So he stayed where he was while they went at each other like rabid dogs.

The back door slammed against the wall when Nacho barreled through. He caught a glimpse of him tearing up the stairs before the door fell closed again.

Jesus.

He should feel smug, seeing Priss dangle on the other end of a lie of omission. But he didn't. He had a half-baked urge to comfort her.

He sneaked a look around the edge of the Dumpster. She leaned against the car, head hanging—the picture of defeat.

He took a step, then stopped. She'd rip skin off him for having witnessed that. He may not know much about Priss, but he knew pride was a big chunk of what powered that little dynamo.

Like a burrowing animal, empathy opened a hollow space in his chest. She looked so worn down. Clearly she'd taken on too much when she took in that hot mess in tennis shoes. She wasn't obligated to, either—she didn't even know the kid a month ago. No one would have expected it of her.

Then the empty space in his chest filled with something like admiration. That was one brave lady. Even a guy who had none could recognize courage when he saw it. And Priss's combination of courage and vulnerability pulled at him. He wanted to help even though he knew she wouldn't want anyone to see her like this.

Jesus, Preston. You're afraid of heights, flying and just about anything slightly dangerous. Are you afraid of that tiny little bit of a woman, too?

Yep, I am. That *little bit of a woman* stood firmly under the heading *dangerous*.

But still, he couldn't just leave. She may not welcome help, but she needed it.

Oh, man, just don't let me say the wrong thing. Whatever the hell that might be. He took a deep breath, carefully arranged his features to blandness and strode across the alley to her.

When she looked up, he pulled his handkerchief from his back pocket and handed it to her.

"I'm not crying." She took it, sniffed and wiped her eyes.

He shoved his hands deeper into his back pockets to keep from doing something stupid, like putting his arms around her. "Okay."

"I'm not." She blew her nose then straightened.

Her chin went up. "When I get really pissed, this happens. It's like a cough—involuntary."

"I get that."

She started to hand over the dirty handkerchief, but after glancing at it, stuck it in her back pocket. "I suppose it's too much to ask that you didn't hear all that."

"I heard." The tenderness in his voice brought her head up. He fisted his hands in his pockets to keep from touching her arm. He knew Priss wouldn't welcome what she'd only see as pity. "You know he's testing you, right?"

She snorted. "Testing my sanity."

"No. He's afraid. He's testing to see if he can trust you."

Her eyes narrowed. "How would you know? You don't have kids."

"Maybe not, but I was a kid once. I can recognize a frightened boy when I see one."

She studied his face. Adam knew she was deciding if she could trust *him*.

"Look, he's just lost his mom. They took him to a group home, and I can't even begin to imagine what that was like. You came to the rescue, but even though you're blood, you're still a virtual stranger. I've gotta think in his shoes—I'd be pissed, confused and acting out, too."

He shrugged and put his hands out, palm up. "What do you think?"

She cocked her head and watched him. "I think you're a nice guy."

He looked away. "Sometimes it's easier to see things when you're not in the middle of it."

"Is that why you live like you do?"

A lightning-bolt warning zipped through him. "What do you mean?" It was a knee-jerk question, but it was out. He couldn't take it back.

"I don't know you well, and I could be full of crap but—"

"But what?"

"You stand outside of life, looking in—like you're a bystander. You watch people living out their messy lives but you don't get any of the dirt on you." She was still looking up at him, considering. "Why do you do that?"

Her concentration made him squirm. When he realized he was toeing the asphalt like a chastised child, he made himself stop. But he couldn't make himself look at her.

"Hey." Her hand touched his arm. "I just open my mouth and shit falls out. I don't mean anything by it."

Reaching into the car, she grabbed her purse and a square of white apron with long tie strings. "I'd better get upstairs." She tossed the purse strap over her shoulder.

Apparently they'd both learned something today.

He watched her walk away to go deal with Nacho, her small shoulders squared.

He'd taken the easiest path possible in life. Today he'd met someone who'd taken the hardest. If he hadn't failed all those years ago, would it have made all the difference?

PRISS'S HEART SETTLED as she climbed the stairs to the apartment. Talking to Adam had given her an idea—a new direction that could guide her through this dizzying parenting maze.

But the conversation also left her unsettled, as if Adam had jostled something, buried deep. An unnamed emotion stirred, as if awakened. She stepped softly, to lull it back to sleep.

Adam had acted like he really cared. His dark eyes seemed to hold compassion and he'd stood close, as if he wanted to reach out, to touch her.

Taking the last step to the landing, she slung off the soft thought. He'd made it clear from the start that she was—inappropriate. God, she hated that word.

This wasn't her first rodeo. If a guy like that acted all sweet, he probably just wanted one thing from her.

She'd think about that later. She strode the hall to her apartment door. Right now, she had more pressing issues. The Good Cop routine had been an epic fail. It was time for the Bad Cop. She took a deep breath, turned the knob and walked in, kicking the door shut with her heel.

Nacho lay sprawled on the couch, his arm over his eyes.

She tightened the muscles in her chest to shield her heart and prepared to wade into battle for the second time today. "Let's finish this."

He didn't move.

"Oh, you're not talking? Good, because you don't need your mouth in order to listen." She strode to the couch, lifted his feet off it and hung them over the edge.

At her touch, he bolted upright.

"Show a little respect. This is a nice place—no feet on the couch."

A flash of genuine worry shone in his Nacho's eyes before the tough-kid mask fell into place.

She stood over him. "I tried to be the kind of parent that I wish I'd had. But I can see now that was wrong." She lowered herself onto the other end of the couch. "I've got to be the kind of parent you need. And kid, you need discipline."

"I had a parent. I never asked for another one," he muttered under his breath.

"You're grounded. For how long will depend on your behavior. I'm calling here every afternoon at three-thirty and if you're not here to answer the phone, I guarantee you won't like what happens next." She paused to be sure that soaked in. "Homework is to be done by the time I get home. If you need help with anything, we'll work on it after dinner. And from now on, you're reading to *me* every night."

His lips thinned. A storm gathered in her brother's dark eyes.

Oh, God, not again. I can't handle another scream-fest today. But they'd be right back where they started if she didn't get control. Like now. She pushed down the dread and grabbed a fistful of grit.

"I know you'll have plenty of time for all this, because as soon as I can arrange it, we'll no longer have a TV. We're hauling it out of here."

"What?" Nacho's cry of shock and outrage echoed off the high ceilings. "Am I grounded forever? What are we going to do for a TV after that?"

"Welcome to the real world, kid. I have to pay to have your 'artwork' removed. And you will have to repay me." She watched thoughts flicker across his face, knowing he was searching for an angle, a way out. "You have no money. You can't get a job. But if we lose the TV, I don't have to pay for cable anymore. I'm willing to put that toward what you owe me." She shrugged her shoulders. "I'd rather read than watch TV anyway."

She waited. Nacho would consider his options, then choose: running away, Social Services or her. And probably none of those options looked good to him. But she was betting that he'd see her as the least of the evils. At least she was hoping he would.

He opened his mouth, then closed it to a thin line of displeasure.

She released the breath she didn't know she'd been holding, then took another deep one. "Now, spill. Who gave you the paint?"

His eyes cut away. "I bought it."

"You had no money, even if a store would sell spray paint to a kid, which they won't. And don't tell me you stole it. The cop told me the break-in at the paint store was three weeks ago. You were in the group home then."

Silence.

"Who was it?"

He crossed his arms over his chest. "You can't make me tell."

She guessed he wouldn't offer up the thief, but she'd had to try. "Street rules" hadn't changed since she was a kid. If things went down, you took the hit. Ratting may get you out of grown-up trouble but worse awaited you in the hallways. Kids didn't have sentencing limits like grown-ups did. Your debt was never paid in that society.

She, of all people, knew that.

"You don't have to tell me."

His body slackened just a bit.

"But tomorrow you and I are going to the warehouse and you're going to apologize to the owners, then to the paint shop."

He winced. "But I didn't—"

"I know you didn't steal the paint, but you took stolen property. That's part of the price you pay, dude." She walked away, but halfway to the bedroom it hit her—he hadn't agreed. She wasn't having another mess like the last time. She looked back at him. "So we'll head out when I get home, right?"

"Yeah." The word came out battered, defeated. He threw his arm over his eyes.

She walked into her bedroom and closed the door. They both needed time to think. But first, she had a phone call to make. She sat on the edge of the bed and dialed.

"Bar None." Floyd barked.

"It's Priss."

"What the hell's wrong with you? You leave midshift? If I wouldn't be screwing myself, the only view you'd get of this place would be from the other side of the bar."

"I didn't have a choice. I had an emergency. Gaby—"

"Gaby doesn't know which end of a goddamn beer bottle to open, ferchrssake!"

Wincing, she pulled the phone a few inches from her ear. "I didn't leave midshift. I only had a half hour left." She thought about telling him what had happened. Surely he'd understand that she had no choice. But on the way to her mouth, the words hit a wall.

Screw Floyd. What happened in her family was none of his business. Nacho may be behaving like a loser, but Floyd wasn't hearing it from her. "I'm sorry, okay? Is that what you want to hear?" God, she hated groveling. "Now, either fire me, or get your ass back to pouring."

"Let's see if you can manage to work a whole shift tomorrow." His gravel cough was Floyd-speak for a chuckle.

She hung up and fell back onto the bed. *Jesus, what a day.* She'd dodged *that* hand grenade, but Nacho had better be done breaking laws because she was running out of moves.

PRISS LIFTED HER end of the TV, trying to get it over the lip of the elevator on the ground floor. "Come on, Nacho, you're not helping."

On his knees in the elevator, Nacho bent to push. "Making me help with my own punishment is just wrong. Arrrgh!"

The TV shot into the vestibule. Unbalanced, Priss fell on her ass and slid.

The door to the store opened. Adam stood in the doorframe, frowning. "Nacho, what the—what's my TV doing here?"

Priss got to her feet, glaring at her charge. "Right,

sorry—guess I should have run this by you first. Tell the man what's going on, Nacho."

"I'm grounded. Apparently forever because she's getting rid of the TV."

"You're lucky that's all you're losing." She dusted the back of her slacks. "Why don't you wait for me in the car?"

Nacho mumbled something inaudible and slouched out the door to the alley.

She turned back to Adam and tried to catch her breath.

Superman. In his double-breasted lab coat, with his strong-boned face and one brown curl falling onto his forehead, he looked like Clark Kent, right down to the dimple in his chin.

"When you want another TV, let me know. I meant to replace that before you moved in. I'll get a big screen—"

"Nah. We're making like Clapton and going unplugged."

It took him a few seconds to detach his focus from the TV and shift his eyes to her. "You're a Clapton fan?" He said it like a kid would say Disneyland.

"Best guitar player ever. With a nod to Jimi." She bent and grasped the corners of the massive monstrosity of a TV. "Where do you want me to put it?"

His hand settled on her arm, a warm, solid presence. "Just leave it there. I'll have the recyclers pick it up."

When she straightened, his hand slid away, along with the warmth. "You're going to throw it out?"

"That thing has got to be one of the first models adapted to cable."

Barney. A smile unfurled in her chest and found its way to her mouth. "Mind if I give it away?"

"It'd save me a phone call."

"Great, I'll just—" She bent.

Both his hands settled on her arms. "Will you stop? There's no way you can lift that thing."

She knew he had brown eyes. But she'd never noticed they were a rich, dark-chocolate brown. Nor had she noticed the pale lines that radiated from their edges, probably earned on a ball field, squinting into the sun.

He dropped his hands. "Where do you want it?"

"In Mona's trunk?"

"I take it you mean your car. Unless you have an elephant outside." He bent at the knees, and lifted the TV as if it didn't weigh over a hundred pounds. "Open the door for me?"

She hustled to the door and once he was through, Priss trotted to the car where Nacho sat, face forward in the passenger seat. She opened the trunk. "Thanks for doing this." She scanned his biceps, displayed by the pulled-tight lab coat. "It's going to a good cause, I promise. I know a guy who—"

Realizing she was babbling as well as about to betray a confidence, she shut up.

Adam grunted lowering his burden, then walked over and pulled a hank of twine off a wooden pallet beside the large garbage bin to secure the trunk lid. "Even together, the two of you cannot lift that thing out of this car. Don't even try."

"We won't." She took a step toward the car door, but then turned back. "Adam? Thanks. For this." She glanced at Nacho, then lowered her voice. "And for yesterday."

His Superman smile dazzled. "I'll see you at coffee tomorrow morning?"

"I'll be there."

"Good. I want to talk about you playing for our team."

She glanced to the back of Nacho's head. "I don't know. We'll see."

She drove Nacho to school in silence. When she pulled up, he jumped out fast.

"Hey."

He slammed the door. "What?" His eyes scanned the knots of kids on the sidewalk.

She waited until he looked at her. "I'll call you at three-thirty. Get your homework done. I'll be home by four-fifteen or so, and we'll go on the 'apology tour.'"

"Okay."

The resignation in that word gave her hope. "You have a good day."

He turned away with a snort.

It did suck to be him—but he'd earned every bit of it.

A horn blatted. She shot a death-ray stare at the Range Rover soccer mom in the rearview mirror and eased Mona forward two feet in line.

PRISS STOOD LOOKOUT, scanning the alley behind the bar.

Ian lifted one end of the television. "God, this thing weighs a ton!"

"Shhh." Priss said, holding the trunk lid. "He's just on the other side of that door."

Porter lowered the gate of his idling truck, then walked over to help. "Barney's going to be so excited. This is a good thing you're doing, Priss." Together the two guys lifted the TV and carried it to the truck.

"I didn't do anything. My landlord donated it *and* loaded it." She slammed the trunk.

They slid the TV into the truck bed and Porter closed the tailgate. "You got the key to his room?" she asked.

"Right here." Ian tapped the pocket of his slacks. "See you tomorrow, Priss."

She waved as they pulled out. Walking to Mona,

she realized that she'd left her apron inside. Not that it mattered so much, but she'd hate to lose it.

She trotted in, snatched the apron from the end of the bar, then turned to head back out to her car.

Gaby, arms full of fish and chips, pushed out of the swinging kitchen door. She sucked a breath through her teeth that sounded like a snake's warning. "Watch where you're going."

Priss raised her hands.

Gaby squinted at her. "You think you're all high and mighty, giving an old drunk a cast-off from your Big Life. Well, just remember, Miss Priss. I know your true stripes."

Priss didn't have time for a fight. "Yeah, I know. You've got your eye on me."

"That's right. Don't you forget it." The old vulture shuffled off, her gray hair barely visible over her dowager's hump.

Someday I'm going to figure out why she hates me so. But not today—Nacho was waiting.

CHAPTER EIGHT

"LAST APOLOGY COMING UP. I'm sure it'll be easier than this one." Priss hit the gas and Mona fishtailed out of the warehouse's gravel lot and onto the blacktop.

Nacho rested his arm on the car door and his chin on his arm. He looked like one whipped puppy.

She stomped on the niggle of sympathy in her chest before it could grow. He'd earned every bit of the dressing-down he'd gotten from the warehouse owner. But she had to give it to the kid—he had stood tall as he apologized.

Hopefully Nacho had taken the angry man's lecture on morality, free will and good citizenship to heart. Even if it had been applied with a bulldozer.

"I just have one question." She raised her voice to be heard over the wind. "What was the 'B' for?" He'd gotten as far as "Bekins B—" when the cops interrupted.

"Blows."

She bit her lips to keep from smiling. *Bad cops* weren't supposed to be amused by poor behavior, no matter how funny. Checking the directions she'd scrawled on the back of an envelope, she took a left at Foxen Canyon Road.

Wow. She'd never been on this side of town before. The road slipped between rolling hills the color of ripe wheat, with live oaks adding a dusty green accent. The warm sun on her shoulders lifted her spirits. "Isn't this pretty?"

Nacho just grunted, but he did sit up and look around.

A few cotton-ball clouds broke the eye popping blue of the sky, and the smell of hot, growing things swirled in her head.

Less than a mile from the turnoff, the road narrowed as the hills crowded it. Trees closed in, looming overhead. Slowing, she turned into a dirt drive marked by a rusted mailbox on a leaning post and a hand-lettered sign.

The Gaudy Widow
Custom Paint Jobs

Beside the dirt drive, a sagging barbed-wire fence had fallen into the waist-high weeds in places. She shivered in the chill of the deep shade. After a few hundred feet the drive opened into a dooryard.

She braked and let the car idle. "I don't think anyone lives here."

It looked like a strong wind could easily level the dilapidated farmhouse on the right, with its boards sagging and silvered with age. Strategically placed car jacks looked to be the only thing holding up the porch while dark windows seemed to watch the trespassers. A huge barn to the left was in worse shape than the house. She could see through the gaps in the flaked red boards to the blackness within. The big doors stood open.

Nacho pulled the car door handle. "I just want to get this over with." He stepped out, and walked to the barn.

She turned off the engine, left Mona to her death throes and hurried after Nacho. "Wait. That thing could fall on you."

A rusted metal sign on the door read This Property Protected by Smith & Wesson.

Priss peered into the gloom that had swallowed Nacho, her unease ticking like a crazed Geiger counter in her head. When she stepped in, the smell of ancient motor oil and fresh paint assaulted her. Standing in the damp dirt just inside the doors, she waited for her eyes to adjust.

"Oh, wow." Nacho's awestruck voice came from somewhere ahead.

She walked toward it, winding her way through a path lined with damp cardboard boxes and tangled rusted metal as high as her head. The rat maze turned, ending in a huge open area, lit and warmed by large lamps on poles.

In the center, Nacho was on his knees in front

of an old Harley-Davidson. With really tall handlebars and a long, deep seat, it seemed to squat on its broad back tire. The chrome flashed in the lamp's light, but it was the gas tank that drew Priss's eye. Orange-tipped gold flames rose through the black paint, so realistic that when Nacho raised his fingers to touch it, she opened her mouth to warn him.

"Do not touch that!" A Godlike voice boomed from the rafters.

Nacho jerked his hand back as if he *had* been burned.

Priss looked to the hayloft and into the eyes of an enraged yeti.

"Do. Not. Move."

The warning wasn't needed; Priss and Nacho stood, shocked to stillness.

A talking yeti she could *possibly* believe in. But one wearing a faded Grateful Dead T-shirt, jeans and motorcycle boots? The man—for that was the only other option—started backward down the ladder growling unintelligible words, his long frizzy black hair bouncing with every step. His back was broader than the ladder, and the boards under his hairy hands looked like toothpicks in comparison.

At the bottom, he turned and, hands fisted, advanced on Nacho. "Goddamn kids. You come to rip me off too?"

Eyes huge, Nacho just stared.

"Hey!" Priss stepped out of the labyrinth, forced

her cowardly feet forward, and inserted herself between the two. "Back off, dude. He's not hurting anything." Though her brain screamed not to, she turned her back on the huge hunk of attitude with facial hair, and grabbed Nacho's shaking hands. Tightening her lips, she tried to telegraph toughness. Nacho got it. He shook her off and hung his thumbs in the front pockets of his baggy jeans.

"I had a break-in a month ago. I thought—"

She spun. "Bet you get a lot of repeat customers by scaring the crap out of people."

He reached a huge paw into his back pocket and pulled out a purple bandana, folded it lengthwise and tied it around his forehead. It didn't do much to tame his hair, but it made him look marginally more human. "What do you want?"

Priss stepped out from between the two, but not far. "My brother needs to talk to you."

A nanosecond of pure terror crossed Nacho's face.

He needs this. She tightened the muscles in her stomach and made herself still. *He needs this.*

"Um. I didn't steal your paint." His eyes darted, probably scouting the nearest escape route. "But I used it." The rest of his breath huffed out of him. "For tagging."

The man's bushy eyebrows merged when he frowned. "Where?"

"The Bekins warehouse." Nacho's voice shook, but he stood his ground.

Priss kept her fists at her sides, ready to step between them again.

"Oh, yeah, I saw that." He squinted, tugging the beard that covered every bit of skin but his lips. "What's your name?"

"N-nacho."

"Well, N-nacho, not bad work. For a beginner."

Nacho looked like a prisoner whose firing squad had just taken a smoke break.

"But." He pointed a blunt finger. "Defacing private property is a crime, and accepting stolen property can land you in jail." He leaned into Nacho's personal space. "Did you learn anything?"

"Y-yessir."

"What?" It was more a demand than a question.

"Crime costs more than it's worth."

His barely discernible lips quirked. "Good answer."

Priss let out her breath and put a hand on Nacho's shoulder. Under that kind of pressure, what he said would have to be the truth, wouldn't it? "Okay, we can go now." She just wanted out of this creepy place and away from its volatile owner.

Nacho shrugged from under her hand. "Um. Sir?"

"Name's Bear."

Of course it is—no one is named Yeti.

"Mr. Bear—could you tell me how you did this?" Nacho pointed to the flames on the bike's gas tank. "They're epic."

She heard the rumble of Bear's chuckle in his chest first because it was at ear-height.

"It takes years of practice, kid, and the right tools."

Nacho looked up at Bear, hero worship plain on his face. "Would you show me?"

Priss put her hand on the back of Nacho's neck and propelled him ahead of her, straight toward the exit. "Getting late. We gotta go. Sorry to bother you."

They were picking their way through the rusted-wire maze when the Godlike voice echoed through the barn. "You come back sometime. We'll talk."

Nacho had turned and taken a step back, before she snatched his collar and swung him back around. "Don't even think about it."

But before Mona even hit the black top Nacho started in. "Did you see that sweet paint job? Shit, that guy—"

"Don't swear." She glanced to Nacho's happy-kid smile. He smiled so seldom. She tightened her lips to stop her responding smile. *It's not your job to make him happy; it's your job to keep him out of jail. And safe.*

He gave her the puppy-dog eyes. "I could come over after school and hang out with Mr. Bear."

"Doesn't that guy scare the crap out of you? He looks like he eats kids for breakfast." Her fear made the words pour out hot. "Besides, you're grounded, remember?"

Nacho fell back against the seat with a huff.

She kept her eyes on the road as retroactive fear bloomed in her mind. What the heck would she have done if that Bear guy hadn't backed off? Her bluster wouldn't have gone far with a guy twice her size. He looked like a parolee. That lizard Ms. Barnes would lay a little green egg if she knew Nacho was hanging out with a guy like that.

Priss swallowed lead-shot prayer beads of worry. She'd been so busy snatching Nacho from one disaster to the next, she hadn't had time to consider that her brother's safety, his happiness, hell, even his morality—or lack thereof—was on her.

Nacho may try to look tough, but he was just a kid, naive and vulnerable. Brass-knuckled responsibility battered her gut.

Priss thought back to that first day, when she'd only gotten ten miles from here before turning back—where had she thought this road would end?

You didn't think. You reacted.

As she had when she left Las Vegas, all those years ago. She hadn't been looking ahead—she'd been looking over her shoulder, running from where she'd been. And she should know by now that was a good way to end up flying into a closed window.

A BELL SOUNDED when Adam opened the door to The Widow's Adventure Travel Agency. Posters of exotic destinations crowded the walls, vying for attention: Tahiti's white-sand beach seduced, Paris crooked a red-tipped finger, while the cliffs of Dover sang a siren's call.

God, he wanted to go—to all those places.

"Hi, Adam," the owner hailed him. "I got that information you asked about."

"Hey, Nancy." His march from the drugstore ended as he crossed the sun-splashed linoleum. He loved the thought of coming here every month, making plans. "Which one?"

"The Amazon River Cruise." She slid a trifold brochure across the counter. An orange, yellow and black spotted frog on a vivid green leaf stared from the cover.

He breathed out. "Ooooh." A thrill zinged and his stomach plunged on a roller coaster's first dip.

"You'd fly from LAX to either Brazil or Peru, depending on if you want the lower or upper river." She flipped the brochure to a map on the back. "Then you hop on a thirty-passenger ship for your cruise. They also have pontoon-boat excursions into the smaller tributaries. You can do a zip-line canopy tour, a nature..."

He tuned out the rest, imagining himself in a pith helmet, breathing water-laced air, staring through binoculars into the jungle as a diesel engine chugged and water lapped the sides of their small boat....

When he turned the page, his heart tripped into a manic rhythm, pumping an adrenaline surge that weakened his knees. A glossy photo showed a man hanging suspended by a slim rope over a yawning canyon. Mesmerized in vicarious horror, Adam took a few moments to realize Nancy had stopped talking. He glanced up.

Her features were painted with pity. "How many years have we done this?"

A flush of heat surged, boiling up his neck to burn his face. "I can't make up my mind. There are just so many amazing places in the world to see." He slapped the brochure closed and stuck it in his back pocket. "Thanks for this. I've got to get back to the store."

"Wait, Adam—"

The door closed behind him, cutting off the sympathy he didn't want to hear. But he felt it nevertheless in the weight of Nancy's regard until he left the travel agency's plate-glass window behind. As he walked toward Hollister, a coffee-scented breeze from the neighboring bakery's patio cooled his damp face.

I'm not doing that again. Not ever.

But even as he recited the litany, he knew that in a few weeks, his wanting would draw him again to the travel agency like a junkie to a pusher.

Sliding the brochure out of his back pocket, he glanced at the gaudy frog. He imagined himself at an airline terminal, suitcase rolling behind him, the dark maw of the gangway ahead.

At the other end of that black tube stood an airplane, waiting to swallow him. Apprehension crawled over his skin like Amazonian bugs. He shook it off with a shiver.

Feeling a brush at his shoulder, Adam looked up. A boy hurtled past, glancing back, mouth open in a laugh of delight. A shout rang out and another boy ran past, chasing. They looked free, unfettered—familiar.

The kids turned a corner and were gone. Adam stood in the middle of the sidewalk wheezing as a guilt-tipped knife slammed into his gut.

A fluke had slammed both his and Roger's childhoods to a full stop.

But at least I had a chance at adulthood.

The knife sliced again. He lost a lot in the accident. But in the years since, he'd allowed the fear to take everything else—his chosen career, his freedom, and finally, his pride.

And without those, how much of a man was left?

Priss was dead-on right about him. He watched life from the outside, without getting any of it on him. Walking faster, he dodged pedestrians on Hollister. Priss was tiny, but she jumped headfirst into life, swimming through whatever came. What excuse did he have?

Dammit, he was done wasting his life, being afraid. He owed Roger that much.

He didn't know why, but he'd been given a life.

It was time to reclaim it.

AFTER DINNER, PRISS and Nacho assumed their usual positions on opposite ends of the couch. Priss leaned against her end, feet tucked under her, listening.

"Harry himself examined silver unicorn horns at twenty-one Gall—" Frowning in concentration, his mouth moved like a fish taking a breath.

"Sound it out."

"Gall-ee-ons. Galleons?"

"You got it. That's a kind of money. Go on, you're doing good."

"Galleons each and minis—" He did the fish thing again. "Mini-s-cu-l—"

"Miniscule. It means tiny."

"Then why can't they just say that?" He slapped the book closed. "Can't you just read to me? It's a lot more fun."

She stretched her legs out and snuck her toes under the blanket. "There's more to life than fun, dude."

"Not for me. When I grow up, I'm only doing

fun stuff." When her feet bumped his, he pulled his knees up.

"Is eating fun?"

"Yeah."

"Well, how are you going to get money to eat if you don't work?"

"I'll work. But I'm only doing jobs that are fun."

She took a moment, trying to find fault with that logic. "You may be smarter than I thought."

He grinned at her as only a kid who still believed he knew it all could.

"What kind of job would be fun to you?"

He looked over her head, eyes dreamy. "I want to paint cars and stuff. Like Bear does. That bike was *sweet*."

She should have known he'd get back to that. He'd bugged her about it all the way home. Shaking her head, she said, "The sad thing is, Nacho, if things don't change, you're probably not going to get the chance."

"Why not?"

She glanced at the clock in the kitchen. "Let's get your bed made up." She put her feet on the cold floor and stood.

Nacho bounced off the couch. "Why wouldn't I?"

She picked up the throw from the sofa. "I know you're only in elementary school, and you think this stuff you're pulling won't matter when you grow up. But it does." She folded the blanket, smoothing the creases. "You do jail time, you've got a record. Who's gonna hire you then?"

He pulled the cushions off the couch and flung them. "Bear would hire me."

He was probably right. She wouldn't be surprised to hear that guy had a record of his own. "Stack the cushions behind the couch. If you get up in the middle of the night, you're going to trip over them if they're in the middle of the floor."

While he went to retrieve the cushions, Priss bent, grasped the loop, and pulled it to bring out the mattress portion of the sofa. "What I'm trying to tell you is that life isn't as easy for mutts like us." She flipped open the mattress. "Don't get me wrong. Mutts have a lot going for them. They're scrappers—survivors. Some people would rather have a mutt than some foo-foo dog. But we don't come with a pedigree and daddy's bankroll."

Nacho walked to the linen closet in the wall out-side the bathroom and came back with his rolled-up sheets, blanket, and pillow.

"We only have two things going for us that no one can take away."

He dropped the top sheet, shook out the fitted sheet, and together they stretched it over the mat-tress. "What?"

"Our pride and our good reputation."

"Yeah, right." He didn't say "lame," but his eye roll did.

As if his words had twisted a thermostat, the furnace deep inside her roared to life with a blue blaze of heat. "Don't you mock what you don't know." She took a deep breath. "I got accused of something I didn't do when I was a kid." She snatched the top sheet and snapped it so hard it popped like a whip. "Something horrible." Her shudder made the words come out all shaky.

He let go of the sheet and went still. "What happened?"

God, she didn't want to talk about this. But it was up to her to teach him what life was like. She plopped down on the bed. "I'll warn you, this isn't a good bedtime story. But you asked." She patted the mattress. "Sit."

He sat, one foot under him, watching her close.

"I was around your age, when some do-gooder called Social Services on Mom for leaving me alone at night. They took me away and put me in foster care." She fingered the sheet under her hand. "As if the Brenans were better than Mom." She snorted. "They lived in this little house on the outskirts of Vegas and Mr. Brenan worked all the time. They needed the money, but I think he worked two jobs in part to get away from the crazy women in that house. Mrs. Brenan was a social climber. Do you know what that is?"

Nacho nodded. "A mutt that wants to be a show dog."

"Dead-on." She smiled. He really was a smart kid. "I guess by the time I got there, Mrs. Brenan had realized it was never gonna happen for her. But she had Suzie." Priss said it in the same mocking singsong voice she had all those years ago. "She was a year older than me. Mrs. Brenan wanted to get her daughter in commercials to make her famous. And with her blond, curly hair and blue eyes, Suzie was cute. Only one problem." She used her index finger to push up the end of her nose as far as it would go. "She had a pig nose."

Nacho sniggered.

"Mrs. Brenan wanted money for a nose job for her piglet. Mr. Brenan couldn't work any more hours so that's where I came in. Apparently she planned on banking the money the state gave her for me. I didn't care. I just wanted to do my time until Mom landed another job and came to get me."

Nacho leaned forward, rapt as if this were better than a Harry Potter book. "So did they lock you up and starve you?"

"No. It wasn't too bad, at first. I ate what they ate and I got Suzie's hand-me-downs to wear. All brand-name, nice stuff. Nothing was too good for Suzie."

"So, did you get accused of stealing her clothes?"

"No. It was Suzie." Priss winced, remembering, and wrapped her arms around her middle. "She wasn't only spoiled, she was *mean*. Deep down, worm-in-the-apple bad. She didn't want me there from the minute I walked in the door." She shook her head. "Here she had everything, and yet she was jealous of *me*. She did stuff—mean stuff to me behind her mother's back."

The swirling emotions she'd felt back then burst into vivid color in Priss's mind. Indigo, for the sadness. Loneliness was the dark gray of storm clouds. The rage was crimson.

"Priss?"

It was the second time he'd called her name. "Easter was coming. Suzie got it in her head that she wanted a bunny. A real baby bunny." She cleared the wad in her throat. "Mr. Brenan said no. Mrs. Brenan said no. But Suzie kept working on her mom until she got that darned rabbit.

"It was a tiny ball of white-and-brown fluff at first." Priss relaxed her hand, letting go the fistful of sheet. "She named it Sweetness. They put it in a hutch, in the shade in the backyard." She smoothed the wrinkles she'd made in the sheet.

"Everything was okay at first. Suzie loved it when it was little. But it grew into a rabbit. And Suzie didn't think rabbits were as cute as bunnies."

She took a deep breath and looked at the ceiling. Better to say it fast. "I'd sneak out at night when everyone was in bed, to pet him. He really was sweet. And when I saw he didn't have food or water, I took care of him.

"But one night I was cleaning the cage, and I must have made a noise." She glanced at Nacho. He nodded his head to get her to go on. "Mr. Brenan came out. When he figured out that I'd been taking care of Sweetness, he made Suzie get up and clean that cage in her nightgown, yelling at her the whole time about how she wanted the rabbit and she was damned well going to learn some responsibility.

"I knew she'd make me pay." The deep indigo pool of sadness welled in her, a rising flood that carried her back to that day. "But she made Sweetness pay, too.

"I always made an excuse to go out in the backyard in the mornings to check on him. Then one day, about ten days later, he was dead. Lying in the cage like he was sleeping, but his head was wrong, on his neck." The sheet was back in her fists, but she didn't let go. She needed something to hang on to.

"Suzie must have been watching because she came out crying and screaming, saying *I* killed her bunny."

"Oh, man, that's evil," Nacho whispered.

"Mrs. Brenan came out to see what was wrong. Suzie went on and on, hysterical, saying how I was jealous, and I killed Sweetness to get back at her." She took a deep breath.

"She believed Suzie, of course. Or maybe she didn't, but couldn't face what she'd raised. In any case, she stood there ranting at me, telling she was calling Social Services and getting me the hell away from her family.

"And all that time, Suzie stood behind her, smiling."

"Did you kill her?"

"No. But I almost wished I had. Because that day, in the cafeteria, she stood up and told everyone I was a bunny killer."

"Holy sh—" He stopped himself in time.

"Social Services came to the school that day and took me to the group home. I stayed there until Mom got her poop in a pile, found a day job and bailed me out." She let go of the sheet. "But from then on I had a note in my file. Some psycho-babble label, but what it meant was 'bunny killer.'"

The waters of sadness receded, leaving her standing knee high in the stinking mudflat of her childhood. "They say stuff that happens when you're a juvie stays sealed in your records. But school records aren't sealed—and kids never forget."

She laced her fingers, to hide the shake. "So a few years later I'm in high school. And in order to graduate each student had to do so many hours of community service. I wanted to volunteer at the animal shelter—bad. So I went the first day, and had a great time, playing with the puppies, cleaning cages." She tried to say the words without thinking about what they meant. "But there was another girl there from my school, too. She told the people at the shelter about me being a bunny killer. They were nice about it, and even listened to my side of the story." She took a deep breath. "Then they asked me to volunteer elsewhere."

Priss stood. "Stuff is never buried as deep as you hope it will be. I got the heck out of Vegas as soon as I graduated."

Nacho stood, too. "You know what it's like—not to have any say in what happens to you." For the first time since she met him, she heard a sliver of respect in his tone.

"I do know. And I want you to have a say, as you get older. But a record is going to limit your choices." She picked up his pillow and tossed it on the head of the bed. "And we mutts don't get a whole lot of choices to begin with."

ADAM SAT AT his kitchen table after dinner listening to the clock tick, staring at the empty pad in front of him. His mind felt mushy, battered black and blue. He'd spent the past three days in a personal spotlight-style interrogation, breaking down his excuses and motivations, trying to figure out how he'd ended up here.

He'd been so messed up after the accident. Tentative became a way of life—an amniotic sac of insulation from high-impact reality. It had been easier to just go along, to let others decide for him: majoring in pharmacology because his father wanted him to, returning home after college because his mother wanted him to, taking over the family business because everyone had expected him to.

It had taken three days and five pages of pro-and-con lists to dig down to the bedrock of what *Adam Preston* wanted.

He scanned the pile of pages. Luckily, some parts of his current life made it to the "Keeper" list—running the business, living in Widow's Grove and playing softball.

June, though, hadn't made that list. She was a very nice girl, but he now realized why there hadn't been any spark. She was a woman he *thought* he should like.

His mother had never expressed an opinion of the women he dated except to say that she wished he'd settle down with one. So time and again he'd chosen women who he *imagined* his mother would approve of.

You can't get much more pathetic than that.

To take his mind off it, he'd pulled out a blank sheet of paper and written at the top, "My Type." That was an hour ago. It still lay on his kitchen table, as bleak and empty as his future. He didn't know what type of woman would make him feel complete. And how could a guy so unaware ever hope to complete anyone else?

He dropped his chin on his fist. The pen tapped a staccato Morse code on the pad. Maybe it was a message from his brain. Pity he didn't know Morse code.

Priss hadn't been down for coffee the past three mornings. They usually crossed paths a few times a week, but lately he hadn't seen either of his tenants. His mind worried at it like an obsessive compulsive with a lock. Was she all right? Were Nacho and she still fighting? Or was she avoiding him? In the parking lot that day Priss had nailed him in a few words. *Afraid to really live.* She hadn't actually said it, but that's what she'd meant.

And she was right.

Unable to sit any longer staring at his steaming pile of shortcomings, he stood and paced to the living room.

"You're bullshitting yourself, Preston. Just admit it. You're interested in Priss Hart." He strode back to the kitchen. "And that scares you as much as any Amazon cruise." He tucked his hands in the back pockets of his jeans, just so he had something to do with them. "You have determined this to be a fact. The question is, what are you going to do about it?"

He walked another lap.

Thinking about doing something about it, and

actually doing something... Dammit, he'd put *himself* in between these two hard places with all this silly introspection. But he couldn't *unknow* what he now knew, and the knowing tore away what little self-respect he had.

His feet stopped beside the kitchen table covered in lists. "Then you really don't have a choice, do you?" He snatched his car keys from the peg next to the door.

Time to go out there and get some of life on him.

He would run by to say goodnight to his mother, then he'd check in with Priss. Just to be sure she was okay.

And maybe ask her out.

CHAPTER NINE

ADAM STOOD BEFORE Priss's door, his heart unsettled, his fist raised to knock.

I should wait till morning....

Except that by morning he'd have an excuse to wait until evening. He knew this for certain because that's what he'd done the past three days.

You didn't have this much trouble asking June out.

A quieter voice in his head whispered, *Yeah, but June doesn't scare you.*

Rather than exploring why that would be, *or* his budding multiple personalities, he gritted his teeth and let his fist fall into a knock.

The door opened to the limit of the safety chain, revealing Priss's widened eyes and the frown above them. "Is everything all right?"

"Sure. Do you have a minute? I'd like to talk to you."

The door closed and the chain rattled. It opened only enough for a glimpse of Nacho looking up from a jigsaw-puzzle-strewn kitchen table.

Priss stood in the breech, feet planted, holding

the door as if he might try to force his way in. "What is it?" Her words were measured and clipped off at the ends.

If it wouldn't have been seen as cowardly by himself as well as her, he'd have tucked tail and run. "You haven't been down for coffee the past few mornings." He cleared his throat of the forlorn tone. "We were going to discuss you playing baseball with the Winos, remember?"

She shot a glance over her shoulder. "I can't."

"Why not?"

She hissed a whisper. "I don't want to talk about it here."

Nacho bent over the puzzle, but something in his studious disregard told Adam he regarded quite a bit.

Adam took a step back, trying to think of a gracious retreat.

Priss's features remained shuttered, but her eyes spoke the truth. They were dark pools of confusion.

Her unwitting vulnerability puddled his unease like heated candle wax. What would it take to disorient a street-wise warrior who shot first and took no prisoners? He didn't know. But discovering why suddenly mattered to him. He took a step forward. "Come for a walk with me."

"I can't leave Nacho." But her eyes told him she'd like to.

"My mom is right across the hall." He raised his voice. "Mom?"

His mother's door opened so fast that he knew Nacho wasn't the only one listening. "Yes, dear?"

He ignored Priss's frantic head shake. "Would you mind keeping an ear open for Nacho? Priss and I are going for a walk."

"Of course I will."

"Adam, I can't—"

Nacho said, "For chrissake, I'm ten. I think I can handle being alone for a half hour."

"Don't swear." Priss glanced from Nacho to Adam to Olivia, who'd wheeled her walker into the hall. "All right. Hang on." Priss strode back into the apartment, whispered something in Nacho's ear that made him flinch, snatched the jean jacket from the back of the chair, and strode to the door.

It was just after dark as they walked down the street but most of the stores were closed. Downtown Widow's Grove shut down early when it wasn't prime tourist season. A fresh breeze cooled Adam's face and neck. Priss shrugged into her jacket.

"Which way are we going?" she asked.

"Have you been to iCandy?"

She frowned up at him. "I sure hope that's not a stripper bar."

"Guess you're going to have to take that chance." Chuckling, he took her elbow and steered her left. "Now, tell me, why can't you play baseball?"

"I grounded Nacho after his latest debacle." She sighed. "But I'm learning that means I'm grounded too."

"So? Bring him with you." They strolled, hands in pockets, bumping elbows now and again.

"I thought of that, but I'd be so busy keeping my eye on him to be sure he didn't take off, that I'd miss every ball hit my way."

"Then sign him up for Little League. Their games are the same time as ours."

"Yeah, I asked him about that. Zero interest." She shook her head. "And honestly, can you see Nacho playing baseball?"

He imagined the kid in crotch-dragging pin-stripes, baseball cap backwards, flashing gang signs at the other team. "No, probably not." An occasional car passed them. He touched her back to guide her across Hollister at King's Way. The spotlighted flag atop the tall pole in the center of the intersection snapped in the breeze. "Since he enjoys painting, why not sign him up for art classes down at the YMCA?"

Her head snapped up, eyes narrowed. "How do you know about that? We didn't talk about it the day you heard us fighting."

He shrugged, palms out to show he meant no harm. "Widow's Grove is a small town."

Her jacket seemed to deflate, as if her shoulders had shrunk. "I'll look into the YMCA."

At the defeat in her voice, his own shoulders stiffened. In her doorway she'd looked defenseless—his ego had the scratch marks to prove she wasn't. But something like an itch deep in his gut made him want to protect her anyway.

Before he could think better of it, he raised a hand and curled his fingers around her elbow. "Nacho's not stupid. Give him time. If you stay the course, he'll figure it out."

"Yeah, I can hope." But her expression didn't look hopeful.

"So you've lived in Widow's Grove all your life, Nacho?"

The landlord's mother sat at the kitchen table, trying to work on the puzzle. She wasn't very good. She picked up an edge piece, and tried it on the inside.

"No. See that flat part? That means it goes in the frame. On the outside," Nacho said.

"Oh, I see." She picked up another piece.

"I was born in Vegas, but this burg is all that I remember."

"Don't you like it here?"

Should he tell her the truth? A little old lady probably couldn't handle the truth. He just shrugged.

"Priss seems nice. I understand you haven't known each other long."

He focused on the shapes in front of him. "I don't know about nice. She's pretty hard-a—tough."

She looked up, her eyes all twinkly like Mrs. Claus. "Oh, I don't know. I don't think she's half as tough as she acts."

"That's 'cause you haven't made her mad, yet." He turned a piece and tried it again. It was just the right color...

"Do you two look like your mom?" She dug through the pieces in the box.

"Yeah, kinda. We have this thing." He pulled the hair that came down on the center of his forehead to show her. "Our mom was really pretty."

"Looking at you two, I'll bet she was. Was she sick long, Nacho?"

What was with this lady? So full of questions. He didn't want to talk about his mom, but it was a long time to sit, not talking. And besides, Priss would yell if the lady told her he'd been rude. "Yeah. She had umphasema."

He remembered his mom getting out of breath after a short walk. Then the oxygen tanks she wheeled around after her. Then the hospital, when she could hardly talk. She just lay there with a mask over her nose and mouth and looked at him and cried....

"I don't wanna talk about it." The pieces got blurry. His damn nose started running and he wiped it on his sleeve.

"Oh, I'm sorry to make you sad, son." She touched his arm.

He pulled away. "I'm not sad." *And I'm not your son.*

"Nacho."

She didn't say anything else, so he had to look at her.

"Real-life tough guys aren't like in the movies."

"What do you mean?" he asked.

"A famous tough guy once said, 'Courage is being scared to death, and saddling up anyway.'" She smiled. "Do you know who said that?"

He just shook his head.

"John Wayne. You know who he is, don't you?"

"Oh, heck, yeah. The Duke." Even rabbit-ear TVs played his movies.

"Right. Real men cry, Nacho. Then they pull it together and go do what they've got to do." She clicked a puzzle piece into place. "Hey, look at me, I found one!"

She looked so happy, he had to smile. "Maybe there's hope for you yet."

WARM LIGHT SPILLED from the windows a few doors down. Adam steered Priss toward them, enjoying her warmth under his hand. Her short hair grew to a point at the nape of her neck. The pale, vulnerable skin below it begged to be touched.

He pulled his focus away when the door of the shop opened, emitting the cloying smell of sugar and metallic refrigerated air. Two small boys emerged, balancing ice-cream cones with tongue-between-the-teeth focus. Adam reached to catch the door.

"Jeremy, watch that drip." The mother shot Adam a thank-you smile, took the boys' hands, and strolled away.

Priss ducked under his arm.

The wall to the right was essentially made of sugar—filled with jars of brightly colored jujubes, licorice, jelly beans and lemon drops. On the left wall were display cases of handmade brittle, fudge and chocolate. At the case farthest from them, an aproned teen scooped ice cream for the store's only other customer.

Adam breathed in a dizzying miasma of sugar.

"Wow." Priss stood gaping like a girl who'd stumbled into Willy Wonka's factory.

"It does slap your senses, doesn't it?"

"I'd have to pry Nacho off the ceiling of this place from the smell alone."

"What would you like?" He eyed the homemade Almond Rocha.

"I didn't bring any money." She stuffed her hands in the front pockets of her jeans. "I don't want anything, thanks."

"My treat." When he stepped to the chocolate display case, she didn't move. "You want some fudge?"

"I'm good, thank you."

She's embarrassed. She's not rejecting you. He turned to her. "Priss, this is not a big deal."

"Yeah, it is." Her lips pursed, except the center of the bottom one. It jutted in a pooch of cuteness.

"Then you can pay me back." He scanned the jars arrayed on the wall. "What do you think Nacho would like?"

"He doesn't deserve it. He's grounded." She still frowned, but some of the stubbornness relaxed from her lips. She took a step toward the case.

Gotcha.

He pointed to a display atop the case beside them. "How about a sucker?" Rainbow colors swirled, twisting into a nine-inch-diameter week-long sugar rush.

Priss lifted a smaller one, a telephone-cord spiral of yellow, red and green. "I'm paying you back, as soon as we get home."

"Fair enough." He turned to the case and addressed the clerk. "Hi, Gretta. How's your mom doing?"

He continued his small talk with the girl as he picked out a small bag of Rocha for his mother, a small square of fudge for himself, and when Priss closed her eyes in bliss over a peanut-butter cup sample, several of those for her.

By the time they left the candy store, the breeze blowing in their faces had turned cold. Adam shivered in his light shirt.

"You've got to be freezing." She rolled the top of the bag in her fist. "Race you!" She took off.

He stood flat-footed a nanosecond, then ran after her, candy bags rattling with every step.

She must be a great base runner. She was fast. It took him blocks to catch her. Not that he minded watching her fluid grace from behind. Finally, when she slowed in front of the drugstore, he snagged her around the waist from behind and reeled her in. Breathing hard, she laughed up at him as she turned around, an imp's glint in her dark eyes.

His hand tightened across her taut stomach as want boiled from his chest, surging down in a flash point of blazing heat.

Lips open in a pant, she watched him with startled eyes.

They hung suspended in the moment, breathing the rarefied air of between what they were before to whatever they could be, after.

She was so small that he had to bend to reach her lips. Still, he hovered there, waiting. It had to be her choice, too. So close that her breath brushed his lips. She closed the tiny gap with a butterfly kiss, fragile as a sigh.

"I have to go." Her words tumbled out, "I'll get you the money—"

"Don't you ever let someone just *do* something nice for you?"

"Not if I can't pay it back."

His hands came up to cradle her face, to touch the skin he'd known would be satin. It was softer. He brought his head back down to hers and lingered above her lips before tasting the sweetness of chocolate.

Her lips opened, and her tongue touched his in a tentative greeting.

A fizz of desire shot from his chest, making him almost dizzy with the knowing that he hadn't been wrong—she shared the tug he'd felt for weeks. He deepened the kiss, and being Priss, she gave as good as she got. The innocent scent of Ivory soap and chocolate washed over him, combining to create something sexier than exotic perfume.

He wanted to explore her. He wanted to open all her cubbies and drawers to discover clues to the intricate puzzle that was Priss Hart.

By the time she broke the kiss they were both breathing hard. She backed up, fingers over her lips, the look of a startled deer in her eyes.

Then she whirled and was gone, leaving nothing but the slap of her tennis shoes echoing from the alley.

Wow. He stood catching his breath, feeling as

surprised as she'd looked. So much for a cozy, con-
trolled fire.

Sparks, hell. That girl is a firestorm.

PRISS FLEW UP the stairs, trying to leave behind what
had just happened. She stood at the top holding the
railing, catching her breath, her composure, her
equilibrium.

*Damn, that man kisses like Clapton plays the
guitar—natural, easy, pure.*

And she, the one who always kept herself strong
and apart, had simply fallen into him. When had
the uptight, judgmental landlord morphed into a
nice guy who looked like Superman and seemed
to really care?

And when did *that* kind of guy become something she couldn't resist?

She'd always flown with her own kind. If not
out-and-out bad boys, then the dudes on the fringes
of bad—like Ryan. Fun-loving transients, flying
into her life, staying awhile, then flying out. Guys
like that were safe; she understood them, and they
her—nothing deep, nothing lasting. No hooks.

Adam was the polar opposite of transient. And
so not bad. She was the one who chose the truth
first and always; after that kiss, she could no longer deny the attraction. She felt betrayed by her
own curiosity, and her traitorous libido. But why

a good boy all of a sudden? And why hadn't she recognized it sooner?

Trying to leave her thoughts behind, she strode down the hall. Hand on the knob of her apartment door, hearing laughter from inside, she threw it open.

Forearms on the table, Nacho leaned over the puzzle, laughing. "That doesn't belong there! It's not even the right color!"

"Oh, I thought because of the green…" Olivia looked up at Priss and winked.

Nacho said, "Priss, you have to come help. Olivia stinks at this."

"That is rude, and she's Mrs. Preston to you, bud." Amazed by the happy-go-lucky kid in her kitchen, Priss stepped inside and closed the door. He looked as wholesome and normal as a milk-commercial kid. Well, except for the tats.

Olivia smiled. "No, he's right. I'm better with word games." She patted Nacho's hand. "Next time, I'll bring my Scrabble game, and wipe the floor with you, young man."

"Thank you so much for staying, Olivia. You didn't need to."

She managed to make climbing out of a chair and onto a walker look graceful. "I'd much rather be with Nacho than 'hang' by myself." She glanced to him to be sure she got it right.

He gave her two thumbs up.

"Good night, Ignacio."

"'Night, Mrs. Preston."

Priss followed Olivia out and waited until they both were in the hall. "Did you put him under some kind of spell? And when will it wear off?"

Olivia's wheels squeaked to her door. She chuckled. "He's a good boy."

Priss looked back at the open door of their apartment. "He can play that part."

"He's scared to death, you know."

Priss snorted.

"He's testing you to be sure you won't throw him away." Olivia opened her door, then stopped. Priss squirmed inside. Outside, she made sure to hold the woman's stare.

"I didn't think you would." A small, smug smile turned up the corners of Olivia's lips. "You're a good girl. You're going to be good for Adam. Good night." She stepped into her apartment and closed the door, leaving Priss slipping over consonants and vowels that refused to congeal into words.

ADAM HAD EVERY intention of going home. He even made it to his car. But once there, he stood, hand on the door handle. The evening had left him antsy. Unsettled. He could jog home. Maybe that would calm the riot that was raging in his chest. Or—he glanced up and saw the light flip on in his mother's kitchen. Maybe a cup of tea and some innocuous conversation would distract him. Besides, he should tell his mother good-night, and thank her for watching Nacho. It was the least he could do.

At his knock, his mother called, "The door's open, Adam."

She sat in her favorite chair, two steaming cups of tea on the table beside her. "How did you know it was me?"

She patted the chair beside her. "Mother's intuition."

He crossed the room and sat.

"Are you all right?" His mother eyed him like a robin does a particularly juicy worm.

He now knew why worms squirmed. "Yeah, fine, why?" He scooched back in the seat.

"Because you look uncomfortable." She tried to hide a smile behind her teacup.

"I'm not." He should have known this was a bad idea. He set down the teacup and stood. "Okay, so maybe I am." He strode the length of the living room. "I don't know why, but I am."

"Talk to me, Adam."

He stood before the wall of family photos he'd put up at his mother's direction. His parents, on their wedding day. His father, out in front of the store, back when it was still a five-and-dime. He and Roger in Little League uniforms, arms around each other's shoulders.

"Mom, do you think it's possible for a person to change?"

"Of course I do."

"I don't mean small changes. I'm talking a one-eighty." He turned. "My life used to fit me so well. But it's like I woke up one morning and realized it doesn't anymore. It just seems bland and…" He walked back and plopped into the chair. "Boring."

"I'm so glad, son."

"Glad? This is awful. I had it nailed. Life was good. Now I can't count on anything." He stood. "Do you know how unsettling it is to wake up a different person than you thought you were?"

"Change is frightening for everyone, Adam, but even more so for you." She set down her cup. "But it may comfort you to know, you're not becoming a different person. You're becoming Adam again."

"Huh?" He sat down and ran his hand through his hair.

She looked over his head, remembering. "You were such an inquisitive child. Rushing here and there, as if afraid you'd miss some adventure happening while you were in the midst of another." Her hand stole over to touch his knee. "After the accident, you became this Adam—incurious, cautious and quiet." Her hand warmed the cold skin of his knee. "I like that old Adam a lot. Welcome back, son."

"You may remember that Adam, Mom, but he's a stranger to me. It's disconcerting."

"Disconcerting never hurt anyone." Her lips curled to smugness. "I told you Priss was the one."

CHAPTER TEN

THE NEXT MORNING Priss sat at a table in the soda fountain before the pharmacy opened, scanning the paper. "Sin, do you know anything about the YMCA?" She took a sip of coffee.

Behind the soda counter, Sin put her hand on her hip and shot off three gum snaps. "Village People hit in the late seventies."

Priss chuckled, then choked, grabbing a napkin so she wouldn't spray coffee all over the newspaper. When she could talk again, she said, "Oh, God, I needed that. Thanks."

Sin shot her a "humor the crazy lady" look. "Anytime."

Adam walked in.

"Mornin', boss." Sin poured him a cup of coffee.

"Good morning." He glanced at Priss then took the mug from Sin. "Thanks. What's so funny?"

"Got me." *Snap. Snap.* "I gotta restock." She walked to the storeroom at the back of the store.

When Adam crossed the floor and sat, Priss's levity winked out like the New York skyline in a blackout.

"Good morning."

"Hi." Her throat locked in a stranglehold and she coughed to clear it. She couldn't claim to be surprised to see him; after all, she'd come here to talk to him. But now that he sat across from her with the memory of last night in his soft dark eyes, her courage fled as fast as her amusement.

If Nacho can apologize to a pissed-off yeti, you can do this.

"I'm sorry I ran away last night. I owe you—"

He looked away. "For the candy. I know." His jaw in profile was hard.

"—an explanation."

He turned to her, his eyes holding a look of hopeful guardedness.

The truth had seemed simple when she'd been in the shower. When she'd driven Nacho to school. Even when she'd sat down with the paper a few minutes ago. It was still simple—it was just hard to say. She fingered the edges of the newsprint, folding the corners in precise angles. "You scare me."

"I scare *you?*"

"You think that's funny?"

His chuckle looked like it pained him. "I'm not laughing at you. If you knew me better, you'd get the joke." He shrugged. "I'm nothing to be afraid of. What you see is what you get."

"Yeah, and that's what scares me." She folded another corner. This was not going as planned. Planned? Hell, truth was she hadn't thought past spitting out the truth. "Look, what happened last night shouldn't have. You are a 'nice guy.' I don't do nice guys. I'm sure I'm not your normal type, either." She frowned and cocked her head. "It's weird. There's this…"

"Pull."

"Yeah."

"Okay." He drew the word out, as if testing it. "Maybe we should get to know each other better."

A sparkler of excitement fired in her chest, burning hot even as she opened her mouth to say no. *You came down here to finish with him. Do it.*

He rushed on. "Tomorrow's Saturday. I have a game in the morning, but after that why don't we load up Nacho and a picnic lunch and drive up the coast?"

"I—"

"Have you ever seen an elephant seal sunbathing in a bikini?" He waggled his eyebrows.

She smiled. "You say that like I'd want to."

The smile faded in his eyes, replaced by a somehow sexy wistfulness. "Come on, Priss. If you take a chance, I will."

She wanted to say yes. But she needed to say no. She shook her head. "Um. Okay."

THE LUNCHTIME RUSH OVER, Priss wiped down the bar, then checked her stock. The regulars sat engrossed in a game show on TV.

"Three fifty," Ian said.

Barney dismissed him with a wave. "Are you kidding? Dish detergent is expensive. Seven ninety-five."

Numbers flipped and the TV dinged.

Barney took a pull on his beer. "Loser. What would a dude in a chicken suit know about shopping?"

"Everyone okay for now?" After they nodded, Priss grabbed the handle of her bucket. "I'll be right back." She walked to toward the back room, where the industrial ice maker lived.

I should have said no to Adam. She imagined driving up PCH, wind in her hair, Adam beside her. Her heart took a happy skip.

Pushing open the door, she saw Gaby lying on the tile floor, half in, half out of the room-size cooler, her feet on the overturned milk crate they used as a step stool.

Priss's heart broke into a full gallop. She dropped the bucket and ran the few steps to drop on her knees at Gaby's side. She put her fingers to the wrinkly skin at Gaby's neck, feeling for a pulse while she scanned the rayon-clad body for obvious fractures.

Gaby came to with a start, slapping at Priss's hands. "Get away!"

Priss sat back on her heels. "Did you fall? Are you dizzy? Is your—"

"Whatsamatterwithyou?" The old woman struggled to sit up.

Priss reached to help her, but thought better of it just in time.

"Back off." Gaby lowered her feet from the crate. "What do you want? I'm allowed a lunch break."

When Gaby sat up, Priss noticed a yoga mat on the floor under her. "You did this on purpose?"

"Of course I did, you little fool." Joints popping, she crawled to her knees, took a few breaths, then slowly pushed to her feet. She pulled at her bra, straightened her dress, and after shooting Priss a death ray, walked out with all the stiff, awkward dignity of a strutting ostrich.

What the hell?

Priss slid the yoga mat out of the entryway and closed the thick door of the cooler.

Retrieving her bucket, she walked to the ice maker. She scooped, trying to work out what she'd just seen. Gaby had her feet up, in the cold. Did the woman's feet ache? They must. But those old bones, lying on a hard tile floor, even with a mat—that had to hurt, too. Which meant Gaby's feet hurt worse.

It took both hands to drag the ice-filled bucket across the tile. *Why should I feel bad for the old hag?*

She pushed the swinging door open with her butt. Porter saw her and rushed over to carry the bucket.

She followed him behind the bar and slid open the ice bin lid.

The ice rattled, drowning out the TV game show. "Thanks."

"No worries. A little thing like you shouldn't have to do that."

"You do what you have to." She watched Gaby exit the restroom. *I've got it easier than some.* She shook her head to clear out the sympathy. Gaby was as helpless as a cobra, and about as even-tempered.

Priss walked to the end of the bar. "Hey, Barn, you need another beer?" She removed the empty bottle and crumpled the wet napkin beneath it.

"Nope." He pulled out his ancient wallet. "I want to be home in time for the double-header this afternoon." Counting out a few ones he laid them on the bar, then pulled his change purse from the other pocket. He leaned in and whispered, "Did I tell you I got a new TV?"

"You did? I'm so glad." She picked up the bills, a small trickle of satisfaction warming her stomach.

"Yeah. I think my son had it delivered. It's not new, but it's a gem." He pushed the change around the small leather purse, selected two quarters, and laid them on the bar. "Did I ever tell you that my grandson is a backup shortstop for the Tigers?" Pride sparkled in his little blue eyes.

And the trickle in her stomach froze to ice chips. "No, Barn, you never did."

"WHERE ARE WE GOING?" Nacho sat with his head stuck out the window, squinting against the wind like a retriever happy to be out for a ride.

"We're going to check out the Y-M-C-A." She sang the last part.

"What's there?"

"Art classes."

"For you?"

She reached over and ruffled his hair. "No, my cute little brother, for you."

He rolled his eyes. "Why would you think I'd want stupid art classes at the YMCA?"

"Well, Bear said you had talent. This is a way for you to develop it without getting arrested."

"What will *help* is for me to work with Bear, not finger painting with a bunch of losers."

"Nah, they don't do finger painting with kids your age. Anyway, how do you know they're losers if you've never been there?" She turned left into the parking lot of the community center, next to the library.

"Because I've been there." He slouched down in the seat and crossed his arms over his chest. "When I bitch—complained about hanging at the library with Mom, she took me over here." He pointed to the one-story stucco building. "It's just a giant babysitter."

So Mom did try to keep him busy and out of trouble.

While Mona settled, Priss unbuckled her seat belt. Nacho didn't move. "Hey, look at me."

He held still long enough to let her know he didn't want to, but not long enough for her to protest. He turned to her with a bored adolescent look on his face. "What?"

"I'm trying, okay? Do you think you could try a little, too?"

He grunted, undid his seat belt, and got out of the car. But when she rested her hand on his shoulder as they walked to the building, he didn't shrug it off.

They were greeted at the door by the squeak of tennis shoes on waxed wood, shouting and the smell of kid sweat. Walking to the front desk, they passed a picture window to the gym, displaying a basketball game in progress. After getting directions, Priss led the way down a hallway of classrooms to the last one.

The cavernous room was filled with round tables and smelled like tempura paint and library paste. A college-age guy looked up from helping a girl about Nacho's age, who was working with clay.

Nacho heaved the sigh of a prisoner facing a life sentence as the young man came over to greet them.

A half hour later, after renewing *Lord of the Flies,* Priss sat in a comfortable chair at the library, studying. The book club was next week, and though she'd finished her reading, she wanted to make notes so she had at least a shot at not embarrassing herself at the meeting.

But she shifted in her chair, realizing she'd just read the same paragraph twice. She checked her phone. Nacho wouldn't be done for another hour and a half.

Forget about the date with Adam, already— what's wrong with you?

Looking up, she noticed the row of public-use computers. Nacho had said their mom had spent hours at the library, researching something. But what?

She still didn't understand what the wad of money she'd found at her mother's apartment had been earmarked for, or what the cryptic list she'd found meant. Priss closed the book, stood and pulled her wallet from her back pocket. Thumbing through it, she pulled out the scrap of paper that listed all the states with Nevada, Florida, Michigan and Ohio crossed off. Maybe that was a place to start.

It was over an hour later when she gave up. Apparently research on the internet only worked well if you knew what you were looking for. All she knew was that what she wanted wasn't in four states.

What were you doing, Mom?

HAIR STILL WET from the shower, Adam walked out the back door of his house carrying his picnic carton. Balancing the box on his knee, he pulled the door closed and double-checked the lock.

He was a little leery about having left the afternoon's baseball schedule in the hands of Willie the bookie, but the day was pretty, the Winos had won the game and he had a date. Better than a date—no upscale restaurants or elevator music. This was more like a playdate. He bounced down the back stairs and trotted to the one-car garage. Well, if a threesome could be considered a date.

He'd definitely rather leave Nacho home. But he understood that Priss couldn't very well trust the delinquent to stay out of trouble all day. He whistled the opening notes to Clapton's "Layla" while he stashed the carton in the trunk of his car, slid into the seat behind the wheel and backed the Camry out. Even Nacho couldn't ruin this day.

When he pulled up behind the store, Nacho and Priss were waiting beside her land yacht of a car. Nacho wore his usual uniform: crotch-to-knee shorts, untied tennis shoes, and a T-shirt sporting a stylized skull oozing something that didn't bear thinking about.

Priss, on the other hand, looked as fresh and wholesome as the tomboy next door in straight leg jeans, Converse sneakers, and a numbered baseball jersey.

He pulled up beside them. "Hop in. Daylight's burning."

Nacho rolled his eyes.

Priss put her hands out, palms up. "On a beautiful day like this, we're going to drive up Coast Highway in a metal box when we have a convertible we can take? Are you high?"

Adam's heart plunged onto the floorboard with a splat and lay fibrillating as panic mainlined into his blood. Arguments did laps around the inside of his skull. "That thing doesn't even have a roll bar. Aren't you worried about driving Nacho in that?"

The two did an identical head-cock and studied him as if waiting for the punch line.

Shit-shit-shit. If he made a big deal of this he was going to look like a freaked-out wimp. He eyed the monstrosity. "Okay, we'll take your—that." At least when they got in a wreck, they'd have a ton of Detroit steel around them. Of course, that wouldn't matter, because they'd be ejected immediately.

He turned off the engine and raised his car windows.

He should have known that reclaiming his life wouldn't be as easy as it had seemed when he made that vow.

One fear at a time.

If he survived, surely he'd come out on the other side of the drive less afraid, right?

Survive being the key word. He took a deep, steadying breath, squared his shoulders, and opened the car door. "Okay, but I'm driving."

Priss opened her mouth, but after squinting into his eyes for a few seconds, closed it. "Okay."

He unlocked the trunk of his car and lifted out the picnic box.

Nacho bounded for the passenger door as Priss called out, "Dude. Backseat."

The boy huffed, but pulled the front seat forward and plopped into the back.

When she opened the trunk of the Caddy, Adam set the box inside. Priss reached for the towel covering it, but he grabbed her hand. "No peeking. It's a surprise."

She grinned. "Bet it's KFC."

"You'd be very wrong." After making sure her fingers were clear, he slammed the massive trunk lid.

Once they were on the road the wind made it feel like he was going much faster than the posted twenty-five through Widow's Grove. When he turned onto the highway to the coast, he sped up a bit.

"Did we get a hotel room? 'Cuz there's no way we're gonna make it there and back in one day." Nacho whined from the acreage of the backseat.

The seat belt cleaved Priss's chest when she turned. "We talked about this. But it *is* going to be a long day if you start this crap already."

Nacho, who had been strapped into the middle seat, moved to the seat behind Priss.

"Fine, be that way. Buckle in."

The seat belt clicked.

Adam stopped at the intersection with PCH and turned right. When he hit the gas the engine growled and the car surged, spraying gravel. "Whoa. This thing has got some power."

"Hello V-8."

He took it to the speed limit, settling in behind an SUV. Warm wind slid behind the windshield, stirring the hair on his arms, brushing his face. The sun hit the ocean's chop, breaking it into eye-slicing mirror shards.

He pushed his sunglasses up his nose and rested his elbow on the door. Contentment settled over him. This wasn't too bad. Pretty cool, in fact. He glanced at Priss and met her smile.

"Told you."

"Okay, you were right. This time. But under less skilled hands, this would still be a dangerous machine." He ignored her smile. "Where did you get it?"

He let her animated voice flow over him as she told him about the day she found the "unloved gem." God, she was cute. He kept his eyes on the road as much as he was able, nodding in the pauses to keep her talking. How had she not been snatched up by some hip local by now? Maybe she'd scared them all off. He glanced in the rearview mirror. Or her brother had.

"I know there's still work to be done, but Mona is going to be awesome when I get her cherried out."

Nacho leaned in from the backseat. "I'll paint her when I learn how—black with orange flames like Bear had on that bike. Wouldn't that be bad?"

She smiled. "You're right, Nacho, it would. Can you imagine rolling through downtown in a car like that? Man, everybody would drool." She scrubbed a hand over his head, and Nacho ducked out from under. "But that'll have to wait."

"Bear said—" The happy kid dissolved to a cranky toddler.

"Stop." She put up a hand. "Can we have a Bear-free zone, just for this afternoon?"

The kid flopped back against the seat.

The sun still shone warm, but the car went cold. Adam raised an eyebrow at Priss, but she just shook her head. "Bear. Free. Zone."

He turned on the radio, surprised to find it tuned to his favorite station. Jim Morrison wailed at him to keep his eyes on the road and his hands upon the wheel.

Priss leaned back in the seat and turned her face to the sun. "Oh, man, I love the Lizard King."

Then I guess we're not total opposites after all. He tapped his thumbs on the steering wheel to Densmore's backbeat. The road cut inland for a few miles at San Luis Obispo, and when they met the ocean again at Morro Bay, the hills on their right steepened. The coastline tipped into the ocean, exposing its rocky skeleton at the surf. They tooled along in silence.

"Wow, look at that, Nacho." Priss pointed to the vista of grass-covered mountains.

"Seen it."

Priss looked over her shoulder at Nacho. "Mom brought you?"

"Yeah, right. No car, remember? We went to Hearst Castle on a school field trip last year."

"Oh, there's a castle?"

"As close to a castle as money could buy, back in the twenties." Adam pointed to a white spot at the very top of a brushy mount, then put both hands back on the wheel.

Priss clapped her hands. "Oh, I want to see that!"

"It's too late today. They'd be booked up. But I'll bring you back another time, if you'd like."

"Oh, I'd really like." She may have only been referring to the castle, but he read more into her smile.

"Boooorrrringg," Nacho said from the cheap seat.

Adam glanced in the rearview mirror. "Don't worry, Nacho, I promise something really cool is coming up." He slowed and turned left at the sign for the Hearst-San Simeon State Park.

He pulled into a parking space and turned off the key. The breeze carried the smell of dampness, salt and shellfish. Nacho stood on the seat and vaulted out. The car chugged.

Nacho sprinted to where the grass ended and the rocks began.

"Hey, wait up," Priss yelled, opening the car door.

The car continued to cough and sputter. Adam took his hands off the wheel, but hovered, just in case. "What's wrong with this thing?"

Priss stepped out and closed the door. "Oh, she'll quit in a second. Come on, show us the cool stuff."

When he pulled out the key, the car settled with one last wheeze and a fart. He opened the door and stepped out, watching to be sure it was truly done, then followed Priss to the edge of the continent.

The edge dropped four feet onto a floor of black rocks. Small waves pushed in, replenishing the tide pools in the cracks and bowls formed by time and ceaseless pounding.

Nacho said, "Cool starfish."

"This is the second cool thing. The first cool thing is over there." Adam pointed to a sheltered beach, a hundred yards away. "Come on." They walked, grass brushing their legs. He enjoyed watching Priss take in everything at once: the hills, the ocean, the horizon.

A parking lot lay nestled around a white sandy cove that was sheltered by a jutting escarpment.

Nacho squinted. "What's so big about a beach full of rocks?"

"Because those aren't rocks."

Nacho ran up to the rope strung at the edge.

"Don't go any farther." Priss's breath caught. "Oh, gosh, look at that!"

Elephant seals lay sunbathing on the beach. Half-grown pups humped around their seemingly comatose parents, mock-fighting with each other. Their honking bellows sounded like a sugar-fueled, too-loud playdate.

"Way cool," Nacho said.

"The pups will be weaned in a couple of weeks, and then they'll all leave until next year, when they come back to give birth again."

Nacho pointed. "Look at that huge one yelling at her baby."

"See? All kids get yelled at when they screw up," Priss said.

"Yeah, and adults are the same in every species. Look over there, at the one with the spots."

Adam could watch seals any time, but these two humans were much more interesting. He could easily see they were related when they stood side by side with their matching shiny, stand-up hair and widow's peaks. Their faces were small and heart-shaped, but Nacho's eyes were brown, and Priss's were green. Priss's skin was lighter as well—a milky latte to Nacho's coffee tone. Nacho must have inherited his short square body from his father, because Priss had the long, fluid lines of a cat. Or a dancer. Or—

"I'm starving. Can we eat now?" Nacho broke Adam's musings.

"Sure. Then after lunch, we'll explore the tide pools."

The wind played with their clothes on the way back to the car.

Adam opened the trunk and carried the box to a chained-down state-owned picnic table. "Now, for the *pièce de résistance*."

"We're having pizza?" Nacho peered over the side of the box.

"Not hardly." Adam hadn't been able to find his mother's wicker basket, but other than that, the lunch would have made any foodie proud: French cheeses, duck pâté, Greek olive tapenade, salmon-orzo salad, savory ham and butter croissants. He'd have loved to include a bottle of wine, but knew he'd be driving, so he'd settled for sparkling cider. He laid everything out. "Ta da."

"What the h—" Nacho shot a long-suffering look at his sister.

Their faces would have been comic, if this had been funny. Priss's brows scrunched and her lips spread, but her mouth teetered between a smile and a grimace. "Um. Nice."

Their reaction smacked his brain. Standing beside them now it seemed so obvious. *A kid and a street warrior are going to eat* pâté? *You're such an arrogant idiot—thinking only about what you'd be impressed with, instead of considering your audience.* He felt the blood pounding in his face "There may be a KFC in Cambria. I can just—"

"No, no, it's great." She surveyed the dishes. "Do you have any mustard?"

He lifted a small jar of Grey Poupon from the box.

She smiled. "This will work. Here, Nacho, we'll make you a sandwich."

He'd forgotten about Nacho. Well, not forgotten, but when he walked into the Tasteful Widow Italian Market and Deli, he'd gotten carried away, imagining him and Priss on a bluff overlooking the ocean, eating pâté and staring into each other's eyes. *You are pathetic.*

Adam ducked his head, busying himself with the plates and napkins. He should have known that Priss wouldn't like this meal any more than Nacho would.

This was a lunch that June would have liked. Except June would never have agreed to come out and see a bunch of smelly, noisy seals. He'd set out to make a good impression, and ended up making a bad joke.

Priss split two croissants down the middle with a cheese knife, smeared brie on one side, Grey Poupon on the other, and placed thin slices of pro-sciutto ham between.

"Make me one, too, will you?" He sighed. "Nacho, how'd you like to try some salmon?"

"No!" There was no smile in his grimace. "No, thank you."

To her credit, Priss put a dab of everything on her plate.

They ate in inelegant silence.

Priss pointed her fork to a gray blob on her plate. "This is good. What is it?"

"Pâté. Here, it's better this way." He snatched up a cracker, spread some on it with a knife, and held it to her lips.

She bit into it. "Yum. What's it made of?"

"Goose—" He caught the word before it escaped. "Stuff. I'm glad you like it."

Kicking the metal support of the picnic table with a rhythmic, metallic bong, Nacho drained the last of his cider. "Can I get up now?"

Nacho wasn't the only one grateful for a reprieve. Adam stood. "I'll get this cleaned up. Why don't you guys check out the tide pools?"

"You go, Nacho, but stay close to the edge, and don't get wet."

Nacho took off.

Adam crumpled trash in his fist. "I'm sorry. That was stupid of me."

She stepped up close, wrapped her hand around

his bicep and looked up at him with those huge green eyes. "I think you're sweet." She stood tip-toe to kiss his nose. "Thank you for thinking we were worth all this effort."

He put his hand over hers. "Why would you say that? You're worth a lot more than some pâté."

She slid her hand from under his and put the top on the Poupon. "Yeah, maybe. But I'm touched. People don't usually care that much what I think."

An hour later he and Priss sat side by side on the edge of the small cliff, watching Nacho herding small crabs with a stick. His shoes were soaked and his legs were sand-dusted, but it was clear he was enjoying himself.

Once Adam had gotten Priss talking, he'd discovered they had a few things in common besides music and baseball. Priss, too, wanted to see places.

She sat cross-legged, pulling up stems of grass, one at a time. "And so, after school's out, Nacho and I will move on to the next place."

The pâté soured in his stomach. "What? Where?"

"Oh, I don't know. Maybe Boston. Or Boca Raton. Or Seattle. It depends on where I get a job."

Bells went off in his head. "You have a job."

Her eye roll included a head tilt. "Yeah, a great job. Even you thought so."

"Hey, it's a paycheck, right? What about Nacho?"

She shrugged. "Kids are portable. It'd be good for him to see other parts of the country."

He looked out to where the sun neared the horizon. "My legendary luck is running true to form. The most intriguing woman I've met in years walks into my life, and she's on her way to somewhere else."

Priss's small shoulder gave his a gentle bump. "It's only March. Nacho's not out of school till the end of June."

When his pâté sandwich tried to crawl up his throat, he swallowed it again. He'd just made up his mind to grab for the life he wanted.

Three months weren't going to be near long enough.

"We'd better get going, if we want to be back by dark." He stood, and reached a hand down to help Priss up. Her hand fit in his as if it belonged there.

She squeezed his hand. The look in her eyes lit the pilot flame in his chest and the heat cranked up.

CHAPTER ELEVEN

PRISS WOKE MONDAY to an explosive sneeze. Overnight the tickle at the back of her throat had expanded to a full-size feather duster crammed into her sinuses. Glancing at the alarm clock on the nightstand, she threw off the covers, rolled her legs out of bed and sat up. Her head throbbed with every conga drumbeat of her heart. When she blinked, the sandpaper on her lids scoured her eyeballs.

Nacho's head appeared at the doorframe. "You're not up? We're gonna be late." He stepped in. "Wow, you look like crap."

She gently lowered her massive head into her hands. "I tink I'b dying."

He swung his backpack onto his shoulders. "Okay, but can you do it after you take me to school? I've got a spelling test." He leaned his shoulder on the doorjamb as if collecting his cool. "Not that I care."

The oversize T-shirt brushed her knees when she pushed to her feet. "I'll bake you sobe eggs—"

"We don't have time. I ate some Cap'n Crunch."

She sneezed again. "Okay. Hag on. I'm boving." She shuffled for the bathroom.

How do mothers do this?

A half hour later after dropping Nacho off and getting chewed out by Floyd for calling in sick, Priss slid onto a tall stool at the soda fountain and laid her head on the bar.

Sin's gum snapped double-time. "Now that's sanitary."

"Could you snap that gub a little more quietly?" Priss slipped her forearm under her throbbing temple. "Do you dow a good doctor?"

Sin poured her a cup of coffee. "Wouldn't it just be quicker to call the mortuary?"

"Okay. Whateber."

"Anyway, no one would be in their office or clinic yet. But hello—this is a drugstore." She cupped a hand around her mouth and yelled, "Hey, boss, cleanup in the fountain area!"

Priss covered her ears, but it was too late. The echo ricocheted through her skull like a stray bullet.

"Sin, you don't have to bellow." Footsteps and a voice got closer. "I have a cell phone in my pocket."

Sin pointed at Priss. "It will not help business if she's still here when we open." *Snap. Snap.* "I'm just saying."

"Priss?" A hand touched her back. "What's wrong?"

She pushed herself upright. "I hab a cold."

"Let me see." The back of his hand touched her forehead. "No fever. That's good."

His hands bracketed her cheeks. "Do your eyes itch?" His thumbs pulled down her lower lids.

"My eyes, my throat, eben my tongue itches." She dropped her too-big head onto her forearms. "Just leab me here to die."

He chuckled. "You've got hay fever."

She rolled her forehead on her arm. "I don't hab allergies."

He smiled down at her. "I hate to argue with a dying woman, but you do, hon."

Sin's gum interrupted. "I had that once, when I visited my cousins in Pittsburg. I was miserable. I'm never going back there."

His arm came around Priss's waist, helping her to her feet. "Come on, I'll fix you right up." He stopped. "Unless you'd rather see a doctor?"

Widow's Grove trusted Adam as their pharmacist. Surely an entire town couldn't be wrong. But he was a nice guy—and nice guys couldn't be trusted. Right? She looked into his soft brown eyes and saw competence. And concern. And caring. She thought back to what she knew of him: his empathy after her fight with Nacho, how hard he'd tried to make a good impression, on their "date," that smoking kiss on the sidewalk just outside the window. Truth was, for whatever reason, she did trust Adam. She relaxed into him, allowing him to support her. "I'll trust you."

They walked together down the "cold and allergy" aisle. "Do you own a Neti Pot?"

"Whad's dat?"

"Okay, you go upstairs. I'll gather the stuff you need and be up in a few minutes."

"Brig drugs." She missed his warmth as soon as he dropped his arm. "Major drugs."

He smiled. "You're going to feel better in a half hour. Promise."

Within five minutes he was at her door, arms full of relief. He punched two allergy pills out of the foil packet, fetched a glass of cold water, and put both in her hand.

"Those will start working soon, but let's do something for your sinuses in the meantime." He opened a rectangular box.

"Okay, but you deed to know, I'b paying for all dis. What is dat, Aladdin's lamp?"

"Nope. A Neti Pot." He opened a bottle of distilled water and poured it into the "lamp." "You use it to run room temperature salt water through your sinuses…" He opened the cupboard over the stove. "Where's your salt?"

She took it from the table and handed it to him.

"This'll work like a charm." He shook salt in, then mimed how to use it. "Come over to the sink."

She imagined what was going to drain out of her head. "I'b *not* doing dat while you watch."

"Oh, all right. Go in the bathroom, then. Remember to breathe through your mouth."

The treatment was gross and messy, but the salt water shrunk her sinuses almost immediately. The pills must have kicked in too, because she could breathe again.

Glancing in the mirror, she winced. She looked terrible. Why hadn't Adam run screaming? She wet her fingers and spiked the bed-head, brushed her teeth, and tried a quick Visine application to get the red out. She considered lipstick, but decided against. Lipstick was for job interviews and serious dates. This was neither.

Checking to be sure Nacho had flushed the toilet, she mopped the counter with a bath towel. She glanced in the mirror once more, then snatched the lipstick and swiped it across her lips before opening the door.

Adam stood leaning against the counter, his long legs crossed at the ankles, his shoulders blotting out the light from the window over the sink. That one fallen curl on his forehead, the chin dimple. He may be a good boy, but he was a smokin' *hot* good boy. "Better?"

"Yes, thanks to you. I think the drugs are kicking in, too." She stepped out, suddenly aware that they were alone in the apartment.

"Do you want coffee?" He glanced to the cupboard over the counter. Of course he knew where the cups were. This used to be his apartment. She imagined him living here: cooking in her kitchen, showering in her bathroom, lying in her bed. Naked. She swallowed. "No, thanks."

Maybe their thoughts *were* synced, because suddenly his professional look softened, going all smoky. He reached out and the back of his fingers grazed her cheek.

Odd as it was, she really liked this nice guy. He was so cute that day of the picnic, all flustered at having brought pâté. She'd been touched that he had tried so hard. Might as well face facts. Downstairs, she said she trusted him, and in spite of every bit of evidence in her past screaming that she shouldn't— couldn't—she did.

As long as he knew this was temporary, why not give in to the attraction that pulled at her? They could have some fun before she flew off to the next place.

The air seemed warmer, closer all of a sudden. More intimate. Her libido roared to life, imagining his broad hands on her bare skin, his leg, thrown over hers, his...

"Apparently that thing *is* Aladdin's lamp because I feel so much better." She took a step closer. "Can you guess what I wished for?"

His lips twitched. "Too easy. Clear sinuses."

"Well, yeah." Giving in to the tug deep inside, she took the last step that brought her inches from him. The clean smell of his skin filled her head. "But I get three, right?" She ran a finger along his strong jaw and down his neck, to the first button of his shirt. "Want to know my second wish?" She looked up at him, trying for sultry.

She must have achieved some version of it, because his dark chocolate eyes melted to black.

His arm came around her waist to bring her snug against his long length. "I don't know about the second, but I call dibs on the third," he whispered, lowering his head to kiss her.

What was it about his kisses that made them different from anyone else's? It was as if his entire attention gathered to that moment, drawing to a white-hot laser of focus.

And it burned.

With a twist of her fingers, the first shirt button slipped out of its starched prison. She moved to the next.

She was so tired of reasoning with herself, arguing how this wasn't a good idea. Her brain knew it wasn't—she just didn't care.

When he lightened the kiss, she caught his bottom lip with her teeth. He moaned and took her again, making love to her mouth.

She caught fire. The heat fanned out. She felt it in intimate places: the soft hollow of her throat, the tops of her breasts, between her legs. Adam was so buttoned-down. What would happen if she undid all his buttons, and started pushing them, instead?

The thought blew away when he cupped her butt and lifted her slowly over his hard length. Electricity zipped from her core, sending sparks that ignited her lips, her nipples…her need. It was her turn to moan. When he pushed away from the counter, she wrapped her legs around his waist.

"Don't you have to get to work?" She whispered against his lips.

"Oh, hon, I think I might have to be a little late today." Still cupping her bottom and kissing her dizzy, he walked to the bedroom as if he owned it. Which he did.

When they fell onto the rumpled bed the warm smell of her night billowed around them. The thought drifted through her mind that she'd never see this bed the same way again—before *all* thought blew away in the wind that was Adam. He may have been tentative that day on the beach, but he wasn't now.

He lay beside her, reading her face as his hand slipped under her T-shirt. His eyes widened at discovery that she hadn't put on a bra this morning.

She smiled. "Just for fun, right?"

"Oh, yeah, I can get behind that."

She closed her eyes to feel without the distraction of sight. *It's only a brief rest. Enjoy it while you have it.*

And with a flip of a switch, she let go of what she held so tightly.

His lips captured her earlobe and bit lightly. She squirmed. He must have created some magical magnetic pull because when he lifted his hand from her breast, her body followed, arching against the bed.

"Don't move." Adam sat up and shrugged out of his unbuttoned shirt.

She didn't need him to tell her to stay still. The dozens of short white scars marring his chest paralyzed her. When he turned away to toe out of his shoes, the matching scars on his back sucked her breath away. A soft sympathy spread through her chest. These were old scars. Very old. She reached out to smooth one, to ease the pain of it, retroactively.

He flinched, then froze. As if her touch allowed her to read his mind, Priss realized he'd forgotten the scars for just that moment, and was now sorry he had. She lowered her hand. She had no right to know his thoughts.

In one fluid motion, he dropped his pants, stepped out of them, and turned.

She forgot the scars, too. *The buttoned-down pharmacist goes commando?* The long, rigid length of him bounced against his flat belly.

"You're full of surprises, Preston."

A corner of his mouth lifted in a smoky smile full of promise. "Oh, I hope so."

He held out a hand. She took it and he pulled her to her feet. He skimmed his hands over her ribs as if she were an exotic piece of art. Her T-shirt bunched, so she raised her arms and he whisked it off. His gaze warmed her flesh where it lingered.

He lowered his head.

She heard a whimper and realized it was her. He sucked in her hard nipple, then blew a soft breath across it. Tinder caught and flared, the sweet flames roaring under her skin, racing through her, melting all they touched. Her hips bucked against him. It had been a long time.

"So sweet." He said it like a prayer.

Her knees weakened but his hands were there, supporting the backs of her thighs. She had to touch. She grabbed handfuls of his thick hair. His tongue scorched a path across her stomach, trailing nips and kisses. Her eyes closed to better feel. With a rattle of zipper teeth and a brush of air on her belly, she let go of him and watched as he slid her jeans and the damp panties down her legs. No longer supported, she plopped on the bed and her eyelids slid shut.

How had she ever imagined Adam staid and uptight? The man before her was all fluid power, carefully harnessed, but hot. Searing hot.

"Priscilla, watch."

She opened her eyes. Wide.

His dark eyes bored into her, asking, demanding, taking.

When he lowered his head and inhaled, she twitched deep inside. He exhaled, blowing on the fire, teasing it, setting her ablaze. She squirmed beneath him, the watching somehow making this intimate moment more private—even more personal. When his tongue whispered against her sensitive bud, electric heat shot from her sex to her nipples with a flash of pure lust, leaving in its wake an aching hollowness.

Be careful; this man is addictive.

The thought melted before her need. "Adam. Please." She caught his wrists, unable to articulate her yearning.

He looked up and saw it. He must have, because after one last intimate kiss, he fumbled with his jeans on the floor, brought out a condom, opened it with his teeth and unrolled it onto his length.

I wasn't the only one thinking—

Then he was with her, his long body filling the bed, his clean scent filling her head. Lying side by side, he seemed taller—larger. But her need was larger still. She reached for him.

He caught her hands. "Be sure."

"I told you downstairs I trust you." She gave him a flirty smile. "Did you think that only covered dispensing pills?" She twined her fingers with his and curled his hands against her breasts, capturing them both. He kissed her deeply and she threw a leg over his hip and guided him to the edge of her.

He broke off the kiss, settling his head on the other half of her pillow, watching her with heavy-lidded eyes. With a thrust of her hips, he was inside. With a thrust of his, he filled every empty place to overflowing. Her muscles closed around him and squeezed in a grateful spasm.

Still, he watched her with smoky, unfocused eyes, his lips parted in a sigh.

But her need wouldn't wait, not this time. She felt a rumble in the floor of her pelvis and she clung to Adam as it barreled toward them like a locomotive out of a tunnel. He wrapped his arms around her and rolled until he was above her—deep inside her. But then "her" ceased to exist and it was just them—pumping, pulling, straining, as the locomotive caught up and overran them, enveloping them in a cocoon of tympanic sensation. They rode it, rushing fast to the jumping-off place.

With one cry they plunged over the edge, falling together with sparks all around them in a white-hot shower.

When their syncronized breathing slowed, Adam lifted himself on his forearms, his hands cradling her head. He looked down at her. Looked down into her. His tender look seemed to cherish her face. His soft-as-butter smile told her what he saw.

Her stomach muscles jerked tight, slamming the door that had fallen open when she was unaware. Looking away, she squirmed until he rolled off her. But he didn't go far. He lay on his side, one possessive forearm across her chest, his trailing fingers cupping her ribs.

What just happened?

What they had just shared was different from anything she'd experienced before—as if they'd met in the middle, on some other plane. Priss knew they came from different places, with backgrounds and personalities. But in that space, they didn't seem different at all. He wasn't exacting and uptight. He'd been open, and giving, and *there.* She felt as though she'd tasted the essence of Adam Preston. And he was richer than condensed milk.

But sweet stuff could be addictive, especially to a stray more accustomed to scrounging for scraps. She couldn't afford what he offered—not if it left her vulnerable.

She dug deep and found a handful of "don't care." "Wow. That was great." She pulled up the bedsheet and sat up, glancing to the clock on the nightstand. "You have to get to work, huh?" She tossed him a polite stranger's smile.

"What?" He winced like she'd hit him with a whip. "What is this, the after-sex brush-off?"

She flushed, tightened the smile and her resolve, both of which were in danger of slipping. Then where would she be? *Truly naked.* That was so not happening.

Adam raked a hand through his hair. "What just happened was…I don't even have a word for it. You can't tell me that you didn't—"

Get it over with. "Adam, look. You're a nice guy—"

"You've said that before. Several times, in fact." He squinted at her, as if trying to bring reality into focus. "Why do you say it like it's a bad thing?"

"I need you to know, before we go any farther. I keep things temporary—stuff that doesn't matter in places that don't matter. It's the only way this'll work." She felt the muscles in her jaw bunch, and the pressure of her molars grinding. "I've had experiences with 'nice guys.'" She turned away and dropped her legs off the other side of the bed. "No, thank you."

"Look. I don't know what's going on with you right now, but whatever just happened here, that wasn't just me." He grabbed her hand. "And I didn't drag you into this bed. You wanted this as much as I did."

She turned to him, resting one knee on the bed, and took her hand back. "Yeah, I did. It was great. Thank you."

"Thank you?" He bolted upright. "Are you going

to leave me a tip, too? Jesus, Priss. What happened to you? Someone must have hurt you. Bad."

"I don't owe you an explanation." She crossed her arms over her bare chest.

"You're right. You don't." Looking intently into her eyes, he cupped the side of her face. "But I'd like to know."

She would have welcomed his ire; she deserved it. She could have fought his judgments. But his softness stripped her of her only defense—righteous, burning anger. His caring doused the flames like a bucket of water on a campfire, leaving only smoke tendrils and steam.

There was only one piece of armor she had left: the truth.

She sighed. "You don't know me. Our experiences are too different. *We* are too different."

"I may not know much of your life before this, but I know that today, I met the real Priss Hart."

His smug smile stirred the ashes of her anger. "You don't know anything, Preston. But I'll tell you what happened, just so you understand."

He waited.

She grasped herself at the waist to hold her guts in.

"When I left Vegas, I 'lucked out' in Seattle—I got a job as a receptionist with a tech firm. I worked hard, and within a year, I moved up to the HR department. They sent me to classes, and my boss liked me—he was grooming me to move up. I had dreams of someday taking over his job as head of the department." She shook her head. "I was so naive. I thought that if you threw yourself into something, that if you worked really hard, you could make it work. But I didn't know shit." She heard the bitterness pouring out with her words.

"Lots of employees went out to happy hour after work on Fridays. I usually worked late, but one Friday this cute guy stopped me when I was alone in the break room. I knew he was way over my head. He was the Golden Boy of the marketing department, an up-and-comer who had big aspirations and an Ivy League degree to back them up. A real 'nice guy.' Anyway, he talked me into going that night."

Her fingers bit into the skin of her waist. "It was a trendy bar, packed with people who knew what to do. How to act. Then there was me." She took a breath. "So this marketing guy was really nice, buying me drinks, and making me feel like I belonged at his table full of yuppies. When the drinks kept coming, I loosened up. Started to believe I did belong. Oh, yes, I was brilliant." Her mouth twisted. "My head was buzzing and the room was pulsing to the beat of the music when I told him I had to go. He said he'd take me home. Such a nice guy.

"When we got to his car, he was all over me. At first I went with it, but he went too fast. It took me a few minutes, but I realized all he wanted to do was get off. I didn't even factor into the equation." She stared down at the bed he was sure she didn't see— she was back in that car. "I might have been more politically correct, but I'd had too much to drink. I laughed at him. Big mistake. Turns out the worst thing you can do to a nice guy is laugh at him.

"He pushed me out of his car, talking mean and low to me, saying how I was just a piece he'd picked up for the fuck." She pulled in a breath. "But that wasn't the worst. He must've been afraid of what I'd say at the office, so he told everyone he *had* scored in the parking lot. It got back to my department head and I was let go."

"They didn't believe your side of the story?"

"My boss believed me, but it didn't matter. See, in HR, you're held to a higher standard. I signed an agreement when I transferred in that I wouldn't 'date' other employees." She let her hands fall into her lap. Quiet filled the place in her where the story used to be. Speaking it out loud eased something that had been coiled in her for so long that she hadn't noticed it was there.

She also hadn't known talking about it could be so freeing.

Adam broke the silence. "Ah, Priss. Always willing to take all the responsibility. It's one of the deep and wonderful things about you. But it's also your downfall." He held up a hand at her squeak of protest. "Your mistake wasn't in being naive or trusting. It was in thinking that ass was a nice guy."

She shook her head. "You don't get it. It's not about him. All I have control of in this life is myself. That Friday night out at the bar I left myself open to get slammed. That was my fault, so I paid. But I learned."

She looked at him for the first time since she started her story. "That's why I date guys who know the score. I won't leave a hole in anyone's life when I'm gone. And I won't have any holes in mine. More honest that way."

"But you can't think that opening up to someone always ends badly. You're too old to believe—"

"Look, I learned at my mother's knee what happens when you put your happiness in someone else's hands. I'll take care of *me,* thank you very much."

"Do you mean to tell me that you'll never trust someone enough to let them really matter? To let them in close?"

"Oh, really, Adam? And you're just an open book, right?" She raised an eyebrow. Time to redirect the conversation. "Where'd you get the scars?"

HE SHOULD HAVE known she wouldn't bleed without extracting some of his blood in return. He didn't want to say it—didn't want to go back there. But he'd promised to live the life he wanted. Priss was afraid of permanence. He was afraid of—most everything else. Pain was pain, no matter what caused it. And he'd just told her that burdens were lightened when shared. Leave it to Priss to make him prove that he believed in what he preached.

"Roger and I were friends, from the moment we met on the first day of kindergarten. We played on the same Little League team. We were in Cub Scouts together. He lived a couple of blocks from me, and I spent as much time at his house as I spent at my own. I was going to be a major-league pitcher when I grew up, and he was going to be my catcher."

Adam remembered the sandy hair over a freckled nose, and green eyes. He cleared his throat. "And we were both going to be pilots. See, Roger's dad was a pilot for one of the big airlines." He took a breath and let it out. He owed her the whole story. "I was jealous. My dad was only a boring pharmacist."

He lay back against the pillows, determined just to relate the memories, not fall into them.

"We were about Nacho's age when Roger's dad started taking us out to the small airport in Santa Maria, to 'help him' work on his plane. He had part interest in a Cessna 172, and he did the wrenching himself." A thrum started up in his torso, the restless anxiety that had lessened over the years, but still made his voice come out all shaky. "My mom refused to let me fly at first until she saw how *bad* it hurt me to be left on the ground."

Priss touched the Morse code of dashes and divots on his chest. "Tell me what happened."

Her touch was enough to anchor him in the present, allowing him to go on.

"There was nothing different about that day than any other we'd spent flying. The sky was clear, the weather perfect." His eyes drifted closed, but when the old film clip began, he snapped them open. "Ten minutes into the flight, something went wrong. The sound of the engine changed. It coughed and sputtered. Roger and I just sat frozen in the backseat while his dad radioed trouble. He'd turned to go back to the airport right away. But we weren't close enough."

Priss splayed her fingers on his chest, her palm over his heart.

"So he was going to set it down in a farmer's field. He told us to put our heads down and hang on. Roger grabbed my hand. It was so quiet when the engine died. I could hear the wind rushing by the canopy when Roger's dad wasn't calling out a Mayday on the radio.

"They said that he didn't see the high lines because the sun was in his eyes. They said the nose gear clipped it and drove us into the ground. They said—" He took a breath. "It doesn't matter what they said. What happened is I lived. Roger and his dad didn't."

He ran a hand over his face. It came away wet.

Priss's eyes reflected his pain. But she didn't move, just sat waiting for the rest.

"When they finally released me from the hospital, I had to spend a month at home, in bed. And I had a lot of time to think. That's when I decided I was done taking chances. It's why I became a pharmacist, like my dad.

"And it worked, too, right up until I decided I wanted more of a life than just existing in my safe little bubble. That's when I asked you out."

Her eyes widened.

"We're not so different, you and I. We both have scars." He lifted her hand from his chest and put her palm against his, measuring. Her fingers only came to the last joint of his. He knew that he'd spooked her. Knew he was pushing. If he looked at her now, she'd run. Instead he focused on their mismatched hands. "Look, Priss. Maybe we can learn from each other. I can teach you that nice guys are different than you think."

"Okay, but what do I know that I could teach you?" Her voice was small, almost a whisper.

"You can show me what it's like, flying above the radar."

"You already know that the flying part is easy, Preston. It's the landing that's hard."

CHAPTER TWELVE

NACHO SAT ON THE seat next to her, while Priss drove in a new-guy, sex-sated fog. Adam had called in a relief pharmacist to cover for him, and they'd played the day away in bed. After the morning's heavy revelations, they'd kept it light. And hot. When Adam came out of those straight laces... wow. But he hadn't shed his careful, exacting skills with his clothes. His mouth had mapped every inch of her skin. And she'd reveled in discovering his. The wind whipped away the heat in her face and she shifted in her seat, thinking about the intimacies they'd shared. There'd just been enough time to shoo him out the door, hop in the shower and fly to the school to pick up Nacho.

"Hello. Are you listening to me at all?" Nacho waved a hand.

"Oh, sorry. How did you do on the spelling test?"

He huffed a long-suffering sigh. "That wasn't even what I was talking about."

"Hey, I'm on antihistamines. Cut me some slack. Tell me again."

"First, I got a B on my spelling test."

"Hey, that's awesome!" She held up a hand for a high five. "Way to go, Nacho."

"Second, when can I go work with Bear?" He crossed his arms and leaned against the door.

Not a good sign.

"You're still grounded." At the center of town, she turned onto Hollister. "We'll talk about it after that."

"This is bullshit."

"Hey, watch your mouth."

"I *have* been. And I've been watching everything else, too. I'm going to the stupid YMCA art classes. I hate it, but I'm going."

"I know you do. But you just need to stick with it and you'll see—"

"I'm home every time you call after school, aren't I?"

"Yes. And I appreciate it."

"I'm reading every night. I'm doing my homework. I'm doing everything you want. I'm turning into a freakin' nerd, and you don't even notice." His words came out ragged, as if being chewed before he spit them out.

Please don't ruin the day. It's been too perfect. She pushed down her selfish irritation and took a cleansing breath. "I have noticed. I'm very proud of you." At the end of the block, she turned into the alley behind the stores.

He shifted to frown out of the windshield, chin on his chest. "But it doesn't count for shit."

"Hey—"

"I'm never getting off restriction, am I? Just tell me."

"Of course you are. But it isn't like you came home late one day. You damaged property." She parked in her slot and shut down the engine—or tried to. Mona convulsed and sputtered. "Property I had to pay for."

"And you're gonna hold it against me for the rest of my shitty life." He flung off the seat belt and it clanged against the door. "This is prison, and I got a life sentence." He opened the door, stepped out, then slammed it with all the force that ten-year-old muscles possessed.

Mona rocked on her springs. As if startled, her engine quit, midcough.

"I'm not doing this anymore." He walked back the way they'd just come.

"Nacho, where are you going?"

He didn't turn, just waved a hand in dismissal. When he reached the street, he turned right and disappeared around the block wall that separated the alley from the neighborhood behind it.

She grabbed the key and got out to stand, hand on the car, deciding. Follow him, or let him go?

He hadn't thrown a raging tantrum this time. Maybe he was maturing. She'd give him a few minutes to walk off some steam.

But what if he doesn't come back?

Of course he'd come back. He liked their apartment. Their life. Didn't he?

They'd laughed together just last night, eating tacos and working on the jigsaw puzzle, the dropped shredded cheese obscuring the pieces. Yeah, he liked this life.

But it would be dark in an hour. Her fingers tap-danced on the door's ledge.

He's safe. Widow's Grove is Mayberry, for cripe's sakes. Just give him some time to calm down.

Growing up, she hadn't needed a strong hand. But Nacho did. Tough love may seem hard to him. Hell, it was hard on her. But it was working.

Being a good parent means sticking with the hard stuff. Staying the course. He'll thank me someday.

Ignoring the pull in her chest that made her feet want to follow him, she turned and walked for the back door.

He'll be back by the time I put dinner on the table....

But he wasn't.

Priss stood at the stove, stirring the mac 'n' cheese, listening to the seconds tick away in her head. The ticking had gotten louder and louder, the past few minutes. Her heartbeat fell in sync, tripping up and up...

She snapped off the burner on the stove. Where the heck could he be?

Time to go find out.

She trotted to the bedroom to grab a light jacket for herself and one for Nacho. Minutes later, keys in hand, she stepped out of the back door. The red-tinted light falling on the alley told her that dusk was just minutes away—she hurried her steps. She hopped in Mona and cranked the engine. It chugged and chugged, but wouldn't catch. She tried again. And again, until the heady vapor of gas swam in her cleared sinuses.

"Goddamn it, Mona. I do not have time for this." She sat, head leaning on the steering wheel, assessing her options. She could walk, but Nacho had a half-hour head start. Even if she jogged, there was no telling which way he'd gone once he hit the street.

"Please don't make me ask for help." She raised her head, and cranked the engine one more time. Mona chugged, faster and faster. Hope rose, and Priss leaned on the key, as if twisting harder would help. "Come on, you old bitch."

When the chugging slowed, she smacked her palms on the steering wheel. "Fine. That's just fine." Retrieving her purse from the seat, she opened the door and stepped out. She slammed the door then kicked it, to let the car know how she really felt.

Wanting a guy was one thing. But needing one? Neediness was one-sided, and therefore unacceptable. Her mother's life was a map of where *that* road led.

She glanced to the street, the stretching tug in her chest a reminder that Nacho got farther away with every passing minute.

Her muscles tightened, forming the armor she'd need in order to ask a favor.

Get over yourself. It's only a ride. She trudged to the back door of the drugstore.

Ten minutes later Priss sat next to Adam in his sedan, grateful for the heat pouring from the vents. And for him.

He drove to the end of the alley and looked both ways. "Right or left?"

"Right." She snapped her seat belt. "I thought for sure he'd come back." Widow's Grove was a safe town but there were perverts everywhere. She blocked the news stories in her head of kidnapped kids, imprisoned for years. Or the skeletal remains with wild animal teeth marks in them, found in remote areas. A shudder ripped down her spine.

He turned right. "We'll find him. Don't worry." Face forward, he reached his hand across the seat to take hers.

His fingers were a solid anchor. She clung to them and peered into the dusk.

"You're shaking."

"I'm not cold. Could you go faster?"

"I'm at the speed limit now. You just keep watching for him."

Small stuccoed homes perched on postage stamp lawns; the only differences were the details—a wrought-iron fence here, a small rose garden there. "I really appreciate the ride."

"Just keep an eye out." The gentle squeeze of his hand smoothed her sharp-edged nerves. "What set him off?"

She peered down each driveway. If he was hiding, they'd drive right by. Unease prickled her skin from the inside, raising goose bumps. Would he really hide? Not want to come home? Adam braked at a stop sign. "Did he have any money on him? He could have caught a bus."

"Maybe a buck. No more."

Could Nacho have headed to the playground of the school where he hung with his "homies"? His buddies, Joe and Diego. He could have gone to one of their houses! She combed her mind for their surnames. Had he ever told her their last names? What kind of guardian was she, if she didn't even know the last names of Nacho's friends, or where they lived? The fact that it hadn't even occurred to her to ask was her answer.

"Which way?" Adam asked.

The heavy weight of responsibility for another human being hit so hard it seemed to push her

down in the seat. There was a reason she'd traveled light. This was her worst nightmare come true.
She glanced around in the dusk. The houses lining the cross street seemed identical to the ones
ahead. "I don't know." She closed her eyes, imagining Nacho walking to this spot. She imagined
him crossing the street.

What, now you're psychic?

Hell, it made as much sense as the rest of her
life lately. Besides, it was as good a guess as any.
"Straight. I have a hunch that he went to Bear's
place."

Adam flipped on the lights and drove on. "Who
is this Bear guy? Doesn't sound like anyone I
know."

"He owns a custom-paint shop, outside town."
*Surely he wouldn't have tried to walk all the way
out there?*

"What does Nacho want with him?" He scanned
the road, then the houses on the left.

"He wants to learn to paint cars. You know, pin
striping, flames, stuff like that. Slow down." A
group of boys sat on the steps of a porch. Nacho
wasn't among them. "Never mind."

"That could be a good thing for him, don't you
think?"

"You didn't see this guy. He looks exactly like
his name. Only scarier."

"I can check him out if you'd—"

"I'm good, thanks. Nacho's still on restriction anyway."

"But it could be a good outlet for his…talent. Maybe it would keep him busy and out of trouble. You could use it as a reward for good behavior."

Irritation clamped her jaws so tight her teeth hurt. *Just focus on finding Nacho. That's what's important right now.*

They rode in silence for thirty seconds.

Adam broke it. "You know I'm the last one to give Nacho a break. He's a pain in the ass, and he needs to learn some lessons. But if you don't loosen the reins sometimes, how do you know if he's learning those lessons?"

The worry dog snarling in her mind lunged against its chain, snapping it. "And you know this because you have kids, right?"

Adam stared straight ahead, but even in profile she could see his pain in the dash lights.

"Turn right on Foxen Canyon."

There were no streetlights this far out of town. "Do you really think he'd try to walk this far?"

"You don't know how much he's bugged me about coming back to this place. In spite of the fact that Bear is big and scary, Nacho seems to trust him."

"Probably looking for a father figure."

"I never thought about it that way." She squinted

into the darkness. "Slow down, I think it's right around this curve...there."

Before they could turn in at the dirt drive, head-lights bounced toward them. Adam put the car in Park as a huge ancient truck pulled out. "Is that Bear?"

"Yes." There was no mistaking that dark hulk in the cab. No one else was that big.

Adam lowered his window and waved the truck over.

Arm hanging out the window, Bear pulled along-side, peering down into the car. "What do you want now?"

Priss leaned into Adam's lap. "Have you seen my brother?"

"Is he missing?"

When she slumped, Adam's arm came around her waist, supporting her. "AWOL, more like."

"Well, I've been here all afternoon. I haven't seen him. But I'll keep an eye out." He reached into the chest pocket of his plaid lumberjack shirt and pulled out a cell phone. "You'd better give me your number, so I can call if he does show up."

She recited the number and after Bear pulled out, they followed him back toward town.

"Where the hell can he be?" Worry gnawed at her gut like a ravenous dog.

Adam braked to a stop so fast the seat belt locked across Priss's chest. "Do you see him?"

"No. But I have an idea. Your mom's buried in the Widow's Grove Cemetery, right?"

"Oh, good idea." *You should have thought of that.*

He stomped on the gas and the engine roared. Four miles later, the wrought-iron gates came up on their left. The lights flashed on marble headstones when he pulled in. "Where?"

She pointed up the hill, to the newer section. "Up there, on the right."

The skeletal trees looked white and spooky in the headlights. Would he have come here on his own at night? Probably not, but it was the only other place she could think of. "On that little knoll, right there."

Adam turned the car on a diagonal so when he stopped, the lights illuminated the hill.

She could easily see that the area was deserted. Her mother's headstone may not be visible, but Priss knew right where it was. Regret bubbled up from somewhere deep and dark, bathing her brain. *This parenting thing is hard, Mom. You may have been a lousy role model when it came to lots of things, but you tried. I can see that now.* "Maybe some people in our lives are examples to show us what *not* to do."

"Your mom?"

Shit. She'd said that out loud. "Yeah. He's not here. Let's go." Priss felt defeated.

Priss's stomach hurt from holding the muscles

taut and her clenched fingers on the armrest had gone to sleep when the sedan's headlights picked up a flash of white moving along the sidewalk. As they got closer, it coalesced into the band of Nacho's underwear, visible between his sagging jeans, and his dark hoodie.

"There he is!"

Adam braked and Priss was out before the car stopped rocking on its shocks. "Nacho!"

He turned. The stark loneliness etched on his face shot straight into her heart, leaving a smoking hole. When she got close enough, she snatched his hoodie and pulled. Unbalanced, he fell into her, his arms coming around her waist to keep from falling. She hugged him hard. "Holy crap, kid, where have you been?"

"Mph." He mumbled into her chest, taking a step closer to get his feet under him.

"We've been searching forever." Her fingers cupped the back of his head and she held him to her, even after he tried to disentangle himself from her grip.

"Lemme go."

She made herself release him. "Where were you?"

"Just walking."

Not able to let go entirely, she ran her hands down his arms and held on to the bunched fabric of his sleeves.

"I'm fine. Quit hovering already."

"I know. I know." She forced her fingers to relax. "Let's go."

She kept a shaky hand on his neck all the way to the car. "I'm just so glad you're okay. I imagined all kinds of…" She shivered. "If you ever do that again, I'm going to kill you. Seriously."

The dome light came on when Nacho climbed in the back. "Hey, Adam." He slammed the door.

"Hey, Nacho."

Heart still hammering, Priss settled into the front seat. Now that she knew he was okay, she *was* going to kill him. "Thank Adam for driving and helping me find you."

"It's okay—"

"No, it's not."

"I'm sorry, Adam," Nacho mumbled.

She turned and glared over the seat. "You deserve to be grounded for the rest of your life."

"Priss."

Adam's calm look penetrated her anger. Was she overreacting? Apparently. But she'd been too lenient with Nacho at first, and he'd walked all over her, ignoring her rules. Now had she swung too far the other way? Tough love apparently had a shelf life. She sensed Nacho was nearing the end of it. Maybe she did need to loosen up. She rolled her shoulders. "Even though you deserve worse, I'm going to let it slide."

A sigh came from the backseat.

"This time."

She faced front as Adam pulled away from the curb. Easier to cave if she didn't have to look at the kid. "I have noticed that you're trying, Nacho. I appreciate that you didn't throw a fit in the parking lot tonight. It was mature of you to walk away instead. Only next time, don't walk so far, okay?"

"Okay."

In spite of the fact that she wasn't sure it was the right thing, she pushed the words from where they clung. "You keep trying, and I'll look into the car-painting thing."

"Really?"

"I'm not promising anything. If he turns out to be as badass as he looks, the answer is still no. Got it?"

"Yeah, I got it." The little-kid happiness in his voice caught on her rubbed raw places, soothing the sting.

Adam broke in. "I know the police chief. I can ask about Bear, if you'd like."

She smiled across the seat at Adam, grateful for his help tonight. He'd given her much more than just a ride. His solid presence and support had not only helped her keep her head when she would have panicked but it kept her from allowing her anger to make yet another mistake with Nacho. She reached across the seat, took Adam's hand and twined her fingers with his. When he glanced at her, she mouthed, "Thank you."

He winked.

Things were changing. And for this moment anyway, it felt good and right.

ADAM STRODE THE sidewalk. Step one in his plan to take back his life had been a hard one, but it sure was turning out all right. He remembered the afternoon sun falling on the tawny skin of Priss's thigh, and the feel of the firm muscle beneath it. When Priss loosed the tight rein on herself, she undid it all the way. She showed him something about sex that day that he'd never experienced before. Priss didn't *have* sex, she immersed herself, wallowing in it until sated. *Whew.* His body reacted just thinking about it.

Sharing the pain of their pasts had brought them even closer. He now understood better Priss's hard terrain, and knew the volcanic explosions that had formed the woman she'd become. He sensed there'd been even more volcanic eruptions back then, each forming a layer of flinty rock, making her shell harder and harder.

And he wanted to mine them all. To dig down to the soft woman trapped beneath those layers of rock. He hadn't yet glimpsed that woman but knew she existed by her actions. Priss had reached out to befriend his mother. She took on Nacho, and she may work hard not to show it, but last night he'd seen in her fear and in her anger that she loved her half brother.

It's pretty pathetic for a grown man to be jealous of a punk gangster-wannabe.

Step two in his plan was an even steeper one. He pulled open the glass door to the gym and stood in the two-story glass-walled reception area as the bass beat of the music from the kickboxing class reverberated in his chest.

He walked to the towering rock wall; his stomach buzzed like a paper bag full of bees.

Don't look up. You can do this.

Reaching out, Adam grasped a handhold level. A heavy hand fell on his shoulder and he started.

"Not without a harness you don't, Hoss."

He turned to Chris Sagway, the owner of the gym.

"Been watching you eye this for weeks, Adam. Looks like today's the day, huh?" Chris held out a harness made of webbed straps.

"You know I'm not going to get high enough to hurt anything if I fall." Chris had been a year behind Adam in school; he knew about the accident.

"Now, that's not the right attitude for rock climbing. You've got to aim for the top." He pointed up. Way up. "See that bell?"

When Adam raised his eyes, the bottom of his

stomach dropped out from under him. Swaying, he looked down, fast. "Yeah."

"That's what you're shooting for. We'll have you ringing that bell in no time." Chris's confident smile probably reassured most beginners.

Instead, Adam considered how to construct a semigraceful retreat.

"Here, let me help you." Chris showed him how to step in and buckle the harness around his waist, and then tightened the straps around each leg.

It pulled his shorts tight, displaying his package. "Are you sure this is right?"

Chris threaded a nylon rope through the loops at the front of the harness, then winked. "Why do you think the women hang around the rock wall?" He laughed when Adam glanced around. "One of the advantages of the sport, dude."

The nylon rope snaked up high…somewhere Adam chose not to look.

Chris snapped the other end to a clip on a device on his own belt. "It's okay. I've got you." Adam glanced at the sympathy in Chris's eyes, then away.

Dammit, I'm done being the guy that deserves sympathy. Just because I didn't know that when I finally decided to grab on to life that it would turn out to be a nylon rope…

"Belay on. Up you go." Chris tightened the rope. Adam felt a tug at his crotch.

He tightened his stomach muscles, his sphinc-

ter and his resolve. Then reached out for the first
handhold.

Just don't look up. Or down.

Fear echoed from the deepest of dark caverns inside him. He focused on slowing his breathing, then
pulled himself up. His foot found an outcropping.
Blocking the roaring fear in his mind, he reached
for the next handhold, a foot above his head. Sweat
made his fingers slip and he froze for a few heart-
stuttering seconds, trying to decide if he should
take his hand off to wipe it on his shorts.

He decided not to chance it.

Two handholds later, his focus slipped to the
floor, farther away than he'd thought. The room
spun.

The harness jerked and his nose smacked the
wall with an explosion of pain. He snatched the
lifeline in front of his eyes and held on.

"No worries, I've got you." Chris lowered Adam
until his feet touched the thick pad on the floor.

He just barely managed not to sink down to kiss
the blessed surface. His nose throbbed with the
drumbeat of his heart and when he touched it, his
fingers came away bloody.

Chris unhooked himself from the rope and
stepped to the reception desk, grabbed a box of
tissues and handed a few to Adam.

He used them to wipe his face, then leaned
against the wall and tipped his head back, making

sure to keep his eyes closed. He pressed the bridge of his nose to staunch the flow.

"Ten feet isn't bad for the first time." Chris clapped him on the arm.

"Felt like fifty."

"Next time you'll do twenty."

He opened his eyes to look at the wall, upside-down, towering over him. It was intimidating and he'd been terrified. But this hadn't been nearly as scary as scaling the walls of a petite female he knew. And he hadn't run from that.

Maybe there's hope for a coward yet.

"I'M NOT PUTTING down the Tigers, Barn. I'm just pointing out that Cleveland has a deep enough pen to take the pennant," Porter said.

It was a typical day at the bar. The regulars perched on their stools, watching the game like vultures waiting for something to die. The last of the lunch crowd lingered over dessert at a table across the so-called dance floor. Priss poured the last drop of Porter's martini, set the glass in front of him and put the shaker in the sink.

"Excuse me," a lady called from the table. "Could I have another cup of coffee?"

"Sure thing." Priss lifted a pot from the back of the bar and ducked under the waitress station.

Where is Gaby?

"I just don't know why you guys are so down on

the Tigers. Didn't they wipe the floor with Cleveland last weekend?" Barney's voice was becoming shrill. At least he always walked from his dump of an apartment to the bar so she didn't have to worry about him on the road, but still, she wasn't serving him another beer today.

She poured coffee for the ladies with the chic clothes and aging, pampered skin, then walked to the kitchen. Gaby usually mentioned when she was taking a lunch break so her absence was odd.

At the door to the kitchen, Priss paused, and looked through the small window. Gaby sat in the middle of the kitchen on a chair, her worn black orthopedic shoes beside it. Ankle on knee, she cradled her foot.

Oh, God, her feet.

The big toe cocked at an unnatural angle toward the toes, which in turn were pushed over. They looked like dominos, falling. Priss glanced at the other foot which, if possible, looked worse. She winced. How did Gaby walk on those all day? Maybe ice would—

Priss made herself take a step back. Gaby would chew holes in her if she knew Priss had witnessed a moment of weakness.

Suddenly the voices from the bar area made a jump in volume.

"Dammit, Barn, there's no reason to get all riled. I only said—"

"No, I'm not taking any more shit from you two."

Priss walked back to the bar. "Hey. You guys are getting loud."

Barney ignored her, focusing on his buddies. "I come in here every day, and you ride me." He reached into his pocket, fumbled around, and pulled out a few bills and his change purse. "I'm done with you. I'm finding another bar."

His face shone shiny and gray in the dim light over the bar. He swayed on his stool.

Priss was behind him before she was aware of her feet moving. "Hey, Barney. Tell me about the Tigers' infield." She placed a steadying hand on his back. Sweat wicked through his shirt to her palm, but he felt cool. *He does not look good.*

"Nah, screw that." He pushed off the bar and the stool spun. He slid down but when his feet touched the floor he kept sliding, collapsing at her feet.

Priss caught Barney's head on the way down. His eyes rolled back. Though his mouth opened and closed like a fish out of water, nothing but grunted moans came out. "Call 911!" She cradled his head in her lap and lightly slapped his cheeks. "Barney!"

"Ian's calling for help. What can I do?" Porter asked.

She looked up to the circle of familiar faces around her. "Grab me a clean bar towel. Run it under the cold water first, then drag that chair over here. We need to get his feet higher than his head."

When they'd gotten Barney's feet up on the chair, Priss sent Gaby back to the kitchen for some table-cloths to keep him warm.

"The paramedics said they'd be here in five minutes, tops." Ian leaned, hands on knees, breathing as if he'd run a marathon.

"Calm down. We can only handle one patient at a time." She reached into Barney's pocket and withdrew his wallet. "Here." She handed it to Ian. "Find his son's number. Surely he has it in there."

She sat stroking the few hairs on Barney's head, watching his chest rise and fall, willing it…up and down.

A minute or two later, she heard the sweet sound of a siren, getting closer.

She glanced to the blacked-out, pockmarked ceiling. *Thank you, God.*

When the EMTs rushed in, she had to relinquish her charge but she didn't go far. She hovered, explaining what had happened while they loaded Barney on a gurney. They wheeled him out, whispering about a possible heart attack.

When Floyd showed up, Priss told him what had happened and left him calling his insurance broker to be sure he had enough liability insurance, just in case. Leave it to Floyd to focus on the important stuff.

What an ass. She shook her head and walked to the alley, phone in one hand, the wrinkled scrap of paper that Ian had given her from Barney's wallet in the other. She leaned against Mona, who, contrary bitch that she was, had started right up this morning. Priss dialed the number and the phone rang and rang.

"What?" A gruff voice answered.

She squinted at the faded writing. "Is this Michael Conrad?"

"Yeah. Who's this?"

"I'm Priscilla Hart. A friend of your father's. I'm just calling—"

"My father is dead."

So was this man's voice.

Worry stepped out of the way of the blast of anger that barreled up and out of her. "Listen. I don't know or care about your family drama. I'm calling to tell you your dad is ill. He's in the hospital."

"Why would I care?"

"Because he gave you life, asshole. Whatever he did after that, you still owe him." When she heard her voice echoing off the brick of the alley, she made herself take a breath. "So. You drop whatever you're doing. You get your ass to Widow's Grove and take care of your father. Do you hear me? Do not make me hunt you down."

"Who *are* you, lady?"

"Your worst nightmare if you don't show. Soon."

She wanted to throw the phone but settled for stabbing the end button repeatedly.

Why the hell was she so mad? Barney was a sweet old man but it wasn't like she was invested in him. Something ate at the edge of her brain like a ravenous rodent chewing, and chewing. A child, abandoning a parent...

She was the one who wanted truth, above all. Something she'd had to remind herself lately. She had to admit it. The rabid rodent was her own guilt.

Opening the car door, she dropped onto the seat, inserted the key, then sat glaring at the dash. "Do not mess with me today, Mona. I know where the auto graveyard is."

Apparently Mona was smarter than Barney's son. She started right up.

CHAPTER THIRTEEN

TWO DAYS LATER, Adam had a lull in customers and speed-dialed Priss's number.

"Hey, Adam, what's up?"

He heard the tinkle of glasses and running water. "I'm sorry to call you at work, but I just heard back from the police chief about that Bear guy."

"Hang on, let me step out." There was rustling, as if she'd put the phone to her clothes to muffle it. "Guys, I'm taking a break. You okay for a minute?"

He leaned against the alphabetized shelves of pills. He hated that Priss had to work in a bar. She should be working in an office environment where she'd be respected, appreciated, safe.

He heard the squeal of a door opening.

"Okay, spill. Whatcha got?"

"Well, you were right. He goes by Bear, but his real name is Doug Steele. He did five years for manslaughter in Arizona. Killed a guy in a bar fight."

He heard her breath catch. Good.

"What did the chief say about him?"

"That Steele moved here five years ago and that

he keeps to himself. He says the guy just wants to be left alone."

"I sure got that impression when we were out there."

He could almost hear her brain working.

"I need to go out and have a talk with him," Priss said.

Dammit, he'd been afraid of this. He straightened, pushing away from the shelves. "You're not considering—"

"I'm just talking about going out there to find out for myself what this guy's story is."

"Are you considering allowing Nacho, who makes poor decisions already, to hang out with a felon?" When an old lady looked up from the closest aisle, he lowered his voice. "Seriously?"

"I don't know. That's what I need to find out."

"Why?"

"Because shit happens. People can get a bad rep for things that aren't their fault."

"Maybe, but more often people are what they seem."

"Hey, you're the one who brought it up the other night. This is the first thing Nacho has shown interest in. He spends time drawing, every night. His notebook from school is full of flames, doodled in the margins." She sighed. "This flips his switch. And if I can keep that switch flipped—"

"Then I'm going with you."

"No, you are not!"

He knew that challenging Priss head-on was not wise. She was undoubtedly tougher than him. But the memory of that dark hulk in the beat-up truck the other night drifted into his mind. "Yeah, I am. I won't say a word when we get there. But I'll have your back."

"I've got my own back. And Nacho's."

"Dammit, woman. Bravado won't take you very far with a guy like that. He's a mile out of town, and no one would hear, if…" Freeze-frame flashes of several very bad outcomes hit his brain like bullets. "I'm going."

"I don't need you, or your help." *Click.*

He'd hoped that Priss could come to trust him, to let him in and get close. That she would finally let down her guard and allow herself to need someone. He'd thought that because of the week that had just gone by, things had changed. A lot. She'd shared her body with him but also some of her past. And he knew the second was a bigger deal for her.

He also knew he was pushing, hard. But the clock was ticking. School would let out in June and it was already April. Maybe if he really tried hard, he'd find a way to climb all her walls and ring the bell at the top. Did he have enough time?

PRISS SLAMMED OUT the door that evening after dinner to find Adam, legs and arms crossed, leaning against Mona.

God, this is all I need. She stalked over. "I thought I told you—"

He grabbed her arms, pulled her to him and kissed her. A hard, demanding kiss. He wasn't asking this time—he was taking. His hands cradled her head, tipping it, deepening the kiss. Her traitorous body reacted, her heartbeat kicking up as she drank him in like a glass of water. And she was thirsty. Moisture dampened her panties and she heard herself moan.

He ended the kiss. Cool air brushed her neck when his hands slid away.

She stood stunned for the span of a few heartbeats.

"Told you I was going. Give me the keys and get in the car."

The sexual heat morphed to anger, like water on a chemical fire, flaring hot and out of control. "Who the hell do you think you are?"

Adam's dark eyes bored into her. There was no backup in them. "Someone who cares." He held out his hand. "The keys."

Layered emotion swirled in her chest. Outrage, exasperation, and irritation were on top. But beneath it all…was that relief? Screw it. She'd think about that later. Short of kneeing him and leaving him writhing on the pavement, she didn't have a choice anyway. She held the keys over his palm. "Just so we're clear. I handle this. Right?"

"Right." He didn't break eye contact. He meant it. She nodded.

He drove out of town to where the buildings gave way and the golden hills took over. Ten minutes later they turned onto a two-rut track that passed for a driveway and into the false twilight cast by the trees.

"Jeez, this place is spooky." Adam put the car in Park and peered through the windshield at the dilapidated house. "I don't like it."

She unbuckled her belt and opened the door. "You don't have to. I'm doing the talking." Stepping out of the car she closed the door on his grumbling. She wasn't likely to forget that this was *her* responsibility. Not with the weight of it pressing on her shoulders, slowing her feet.

Adam trailed her to the barn. Once inside, surrounded by gloom and stacks of boxes, she yelled, "Hey, Bear! Incoming!"

She needn't have worried that they would surprise him. As soon as they stepped into the glare of the sodium lamps around the perimeter of the middle of the barn, Bear looked up from where he knelt at the side of an old Camaro, a tiny pneumatic sprayer in his big hand.

"What the hell do you want now?" He shoved his safety glasses onto his wild hair. "Did you find the kid?"

"Yes, we did. I left him at home for this visit,

though. I wanted to talk to you." She forced her feet to make the walk to the car.

"So, talk." He seemed to inflate as he stood, taking up a huge chunk of the open space. He towered over Priss like a stuffed namesake she'd seen in a restaurant once.

She heard Adam's throat click when he swallowed.

Grateful for his solid presence at her back, she arranged her face in unintimidated lines. "Nacho has his heart set on learning to paint cars." Going for nonchalant, she reached a hand to lean on the car. "With you."

"Don't touch that!" His voice boomed and she jumped.

"Hey." Adam's voice came from behind her. "No need to yell."

Bear's small eyes looked over her head. "Who're you?"

"That's Adam." She crossed her arms over her chest. "Look, I don't want to offend you, but I heard you'd been in prison."

Bear's forehead wrinkled when his eyebrows shot up. "Well, you got balls, lady. I'll give you that."

She made herself hold his stare, even though her brain screamed to run. "I'm responsible for Nacho. It's my job to ask all the questions."

"You're assuming that I want a kid around the place."

"You told Nacho to come around and you'd show him some stuff. It's all he's talked about since." She stuck out her chin and bluffed tough-like. "Are you the kind of guy who would lie to a kid?"

She heard Adam take a step closer. In spite of her flight reflex's prickle of warning, she stood her ground.

Bear set the paint sprayer gently onto the hood of the car and lumbered away. "Follow me."

She exchanged a quick look with Adam, who gave her a small shake of his head before she turned and followed Bear into the maze on the other side of the barn.

The boxes gave way to a small area at the open back doors of the barn. Trees loomed close to the doorway, filtering light. A stained card table held a coffeemaker, a few chipped truck-stop mugs and two canisters—one of dry coffee creamer and the other of sugar. Several folding chairs sat scattered on the dirt floor.

"Take coffee if you want it." Bear poured himself a cup, then added a liberal dose of sugar. One of the chairs disappeared as he settled onto it.

Though she didn't feel like coffee, Priss got herself a cup. Adam turned one of the chairs and straddled it, though he didn't look in the least relaxed.

Holding the mug of coffee, she perched on the edge of another chair.

"Since you had the guts to show up, I'll tell you

the deal with my time in prison." His eyes darted as if watching their flank for a surprise attack from the trees. "I was pretty wild when I got back from Afghanistan."

"Army?" Adam asked.

She threw him a sharp look. He just looked back at her.

"Delta Force. Sniper." Bear's hand made the cup look like it belonged in a little girl's tea set. "Anyway, back stateside, I was playing pool one night, minding my own business. A guy heard I'd been in the army and started yapping off. You know, all about how our 'Imperial Army' was only over there for an oil grab, yada, yada. Normally I ignore it, but I'd had a few that night and he was more obnoxious than most. Anyway, I punched him. He hit his head against a table on the way down. Broke his neck. The doctors called it a freak accident. If I hadn't been a championship boxer in high school they wouldn't have prosecuted."

His eyes were the deep green of the ocean on a cloud-scudded afternoon. They looked like the windows of a haunted house. "I swore I'd never lose my temper again. And I haven't. I don't."

If what she'd seen the day she and Nacho were here wasn't temper, she'd want to be somewhere far away when that did happen. Like Afghanistan.

"I keep to myself. Don't want trouble with nobody." He buried his nose in his cup and drained it. "But I like kids. Always have. They're honest. If you want to let the boy come out here, I'll try working with him."

Studying what could be seen of his face above the beard, Priss sensed he'd told her the truth. He didn't owe her an explanation. He could have thrown them out but instead he had offered them coffee and shared his story. Plus, the police chief felt he was no danger.

But what if she was wrong? Nacho would be out here for hours at a time, alone with this guy. Who was she to decide?

As close to a mother as he's going to get, that's who.

She looked into Bear's unwavering eyes and went with her gut. "I'll pay you."

Adam stood up. "Priss, I don't think—"

Irritation flared. Adam may have been right the other night but this decision was hers. "The only thing is I don't have much money."

"Let's see if he's really interested first." Bear put the coffee cup on the table and stood. "If he screws around, or is a hassle, he's out. I'm not a babysitter and I can't afford to redo work."

Priss stood and put her untouched coffee on the table. "I'll make sure he understands. Nacho needs something of his own to hang on to. Something he's good at. He really respects your talent." She stuck out a hand.

Her hand disappeared in Bear's but his shake was gentle. Another good sign.

Once they got back to the car, she'd barely closed the door when Adam started in.

"I don't trust that guy."

She'd felt his disapproval boring into her back the whole time they'd been in the barn but had only been able to focus on Bear, and her decision. "Look, I'll admit that it helped having you come out here with me." She took a breath, garnering all the patience and political correctness in her meager store. "But this is my decision."

"Jesus, Priss, he killed a guy. You're going to trust—"

"Yes, I am. I've been taking care of myself many years and I've learned the hard way to be a good judge of people."

"I don't doubt it, but what if—"

"Just because we've had sex, it doesn't give you a say." She faced front, remembering yet another reason she liked to keep things light. She had never let anyone matter enough to tell her what to do— to sway her decisions one way or the other. "Your opinion isn't really relevant, you know?"

"Well, excuse me for caring." He cranked the engine.

"I never asked you to."

His profile was as hard and cold as a marble statue. "That's true. You didn't."

PRISS WALKED OUT of her bathroom, glanced down, then rubbed the toe of her dress shoe on the back of her pants to get the dust off. "Are you sure you'll be okay?"

On the couch, Nacho did his patented eye roll. "You're across the friggin' hall. I think I can handle it."

She remembered back to the nights that she and Nacho had both survived left alone in a drafty bedroom on the wrong side of town. "Yeah, I know you will." She stepped to the door but stopped with her hand on the knob and turned back at him. "I just don't ever want you to have to be afraid again."

"Yeah, yeah."

When he didn't look up from the Harry Potter book, she opened the door and walked out. The click of the door closing sent jitters skittering over her nerves. She pressed her lips together to even the lipstick, brushed invisible specks from her structured jacket, and shot the cuffs.

When Olivia pulled the door open Priss knew she'd messed up. Five women lounged, drinking tea in the living room, dressed in blingy, old-lady sweats and coordinated pastel cotton tops and sneakers.

She slung off her jacket, grateful she'd chosen the fitted white cotton blouse over the satin one.

"Everyone, this is my across-the-hall neighbor, Priss Hart. Priss, this is the Widow's Grove Literary Society, dedicated to bringing good taste to the backwaters of Santa Maria County."

"Oh." Priss swallowed. "As long as there's no pressure…"

"Liv, you're so full of crap." One of the silver-haired ladies stood and walked over to take Priss's hand. "Hon, we're much more likely to drink too much wine and argue the ump's call of the latest Winos' game. I'm Betty."

Olivia's tinkling laugh echoed off the high ceiling and they all came over to introduce themselves.

An hour and a half later, Priss sat in a wing-back chair, bare feet tucked up under her. She'd contributed some to the conversation but mostly listened.

Betty said, "Golding clearly thought that savagery was an unavoidable part of man's makeup. It was bound to come out eventually."

Jane, a former high-school math teacher said, "Haven't we seen that over and over in history? Rome had their circuses, and I'd put reality TV up as an example that we're going the same route in modern times—the lowest common denominator is the standard we're judging by nowadays."

"I don't agree," Priss said.

The heads swiveled to her.

You were right, Mom. I should have listened when you tried to teach me restraint. She bounced her foot to keep it occupied and from carrying her across the room and out the door.

Olivia said, "What do you think, Priss?"

She took a breath. "I think Ralph tried to lead the old way, taking the conch and walking away, assuming everyone would follow."

Bonnie said, "So you think that Jack's kind of primal violence is always going to win out?"

"Not at all. It's just going to take a different kind of leadership today. Democracy only works when the vast majority of people buy into the goals, right?"

Heads nodded.

"Well, when you have a group of people who don't understand, or feel like they can't win in a democratic society, they'll become disenfranchised. Look at the lower class in the U.S. Historically, they bought into the American Dream, thinking if they worked hard their children would achieve a better life."

Olivia glanced over the edge of her teacup. "Yes?"

"Well, the lower classes aren't drinking that Kool-Aid anymore. They don't believe that their children can become president...especially when they look around their neighborhoods and see drug dealers and pimps. We've got to get to the kids. Bring them back into the fold. If they don't believe they have a chance at winning, they're not going to play. Then we all lose, and the *Lord of the Flies* will win." She took a breath.

Not a cup clink or whisper broke the room's silence.

She felt like the ragtag mutt who'd wandered into the Westminster dog show. Her face burned, realizing she'd given away way too much about where she'd come from.

Well, that's that. You gave it your best shot.

Betty cocked her head. "I've never thought about it that way before."

Olivia cleared her throat. "That was a well-thought-out analysis, from a unique perspective." She set down her teacup. "Ladies, I'd say we have a new member. Don't you agree?"

Priss felt like she'd won the blue ribbon.

THE WHOLE THING was pretty easy, actually. He just waited for a day when Priss had to do grocery shopping. That gave him an hour and a half between when he called her until she got home. He always chose a house with kids' stuff in the grass beside the house, and no dog. Most moms worked, so the house would likely be empty. And now that the weather was warmer, he could almost always find one with a window left cracked.

He stood in the dining room, listening to a clock somewhere tick into the silence. Every house had a different smell. Some were stuffy, while others smelled flowery from the stuff they put on the carpet then vacuumed up. But underneath it, they all had one smell in common—a combination of bodies and cooking, damp towels and everyday life. The smell of a home.

His sneakers didn't make a sound as he walked down the carpeted hall. The kitchen door came up on his right and he stepped in, walking to the refrigerator. Crayon-scrawled artwork and photos held on by magnets covered its surface. Photos of a boy younger than him, squatted in the surf, mouth open in a happy squeal. A fat, pretty lady and a tall guy posed for the camera on the front porch, the kid between them. A picture of the same little kid in a cap and gown, graduating from kindergarten. He pulled open the fridge and scanned the contents. "Score." He breathed, lifting the lid on a glass dish of homemade tapioca pudding.

He found a spoon and ate it standing at the counter.

Something touched the back of his legs and he jumped, dropping his spoon.

"Mowrr."

A tabby cat wound around his legs, stepping over his shoes to rub its head on his jeans.

When he bent, his heart tried to beat out of his chest. "You scared me, kitty." The cat arched into his hand, so he picked it up, cradling it like a baby. The cat closed its eyes and purred.

He carried it into the living room and sat on the couch with it. On the wood mantel over the fireplace there were more photos: the mom and dad getting married, two really old people playing golf, and an old-fashioned one of a baby in a long, frilly dress.

Burying his fingers in the cat's soft fur, he sat listening to the echoes of voices that lived here: conversations, shouted play, laughter.

He knew what he was doing was wrong. Even if he didn't hurt anything, he didn't belong here. But he couldn't seem to stop doing it. It was like a magnet that got stronger and stronger, pulling at him until it got where it was hard to breathe around the big empty space in his chest.

Sitting alone and quiet in a family's house, it was like he got filled up again. Like a car at a gas station. It worked, but he knew he was still basically stealing what he needed. It would run out one day and he'd sneak in to another house, even though each time he promised himself he'd never do it again.

Then the other night, walking the sidewalks after dark, he'd looked into normal lives and just watched. Yellow light spilled out of living-room windows. A mom brought a man in a recliner a beer. In the next house, kids sat on the couch; the mom was helping them with homework.

They were like those panoramas he'd seen at a museum once. Dirt and plastic bushes made to look like a desert, a painted sky in the background that looked real because of the backlights. There were Indian statues with buckskin breechcloths and black wigs, meant to show you how those people lived.

And even they were a family. A warrior, a squaw and two little kids.

He knew he was weird. No one else did this. The kids at school all went home at night and didn't even notice everything they had—a house, a pet, a family.

Priss took care of him and their apartment was a lot better place than the kid warehouse, but it wasn't a home. He was trying to do better, to make her want to keep him, but it was hard. It was like there was a war going on inside him all the time.

And he didn't know which side would win.

CHAPTER FOURTEEN

FRIDAY NIGHT, PRISS stirred the pan of gravy on the stove, phone tucked into her shoulder, listening to it ring and ring then go to voice mail. She snatched it and stabbed the end key. No use leaving a message for Barney's son; she'd left seven already. She, Ian and Porter were taking turns visiting Barney in the cardiac care unit where his future was still uncertain. The only sure thing seemed to be that his useless ass son wasn't coming.

"Nacho, come get this puzzle off the table. Adam is going to be here soon and we have nowhere to eat."

He didn't even look up from the book. "But Voldemort is about to steal the stone!"

She couldn't help but smile. Nacho, not wanting to put down a book? He was changing whether he realized it or not.

And here she was, mooning over it.

Crap, is that a lump in the gravy? And that? Shit! She stirred faster. "Dude, if I have to do it, I'm going to just dump the whole thing back in the box."

"No!" He tossed the book down and popped up off the couch. "How can I get it off the table without ruining it?"

"I left a piece of poster board out. Just slide the puzzle on there and carry it into the bedroom."

He walked to the table, picked up some stray pieces and dropped them into the box. "Why can't we just eat around it like we do every other day?"

"Because we're having company. The table has to look nice."

"How can you like that guy? Sin is right. He's got a stick up his butt." Nacho demonstrated, waddling round the table.

"Hey, show some respect." She bent to check the browning pie in the oven. "He's helped us out a bunch. Dinner is the least we can do." *And maybe an apology is in order, too.* Nacho focused on keeping the partially assembled puzzle intact while he slid it onto the thin cardboard.

The tap at the door was soft but she jumped just the same, her eyes flying to the clock on the stove. *He's early!*

"Dude, hurry up."

"I'm going, I'm going." Taking one halting step at a time, Nacho balanced the flimsy puzzle-filled cardboard on his outstretched arms.

Dammit, no time to change. Dusting flour from her jeans, she crossed to the door. "Just lay it on the bed." She said over her shoulder as she opened the door. Strong hands clasped her upper arms and she was jerked into the hall. Off balance, she fell into Adam's arms and his lips found hers, urgent, seeking.

Her hunger fired in a flash-point explosion and she clung, all her focus on the demands of his mouth, her lips issuing her own without consulting her first. Their tongues danced in perfect agreement as her body loosened, opening to him.

Adam ended the kiss and took a long shaky breath. "Hi." He didn't let go.

He smelled heavenly, of night air, soap and pheromones. Her base impulses stood on high alert, a reminder that this man could become an addiction.

"I really like how you say hello." She got her feet under her and took a step back. "Come on in." She held the door as he passed, painfully aware of the fabric of her bra against her stiffened nipples.

HANDS IN HIS pockets to hide what lay between them, Adam stepped into his old apartment, noting subtle changes he hadn't noticed before: the scarlet throw on the back of the old couch, an ornate iron cross hanging on the end of the cabinet in front of him, a framed poster of a mountain landscape on the wall above where the TV used to be. Seeing her things in his old space brought up feelings. Proprietary, possessive feelings. "Sure smells good in here."

"Crap!" Priss ran the few steps to the kitchen,

donned oven mitts and opened the oven, releasing more delicious smells.

Nacho slouched past him.

"Hi, Nacho."

The kid only grunted a reply, continuing on to the table where he swept puzzle pieces into the top of a box.

Priss set a golden crusted pie on the cook top. "Luckily I didn't burn it."

"Wow, is that dessert?" He stepped closer.

"That's dinner." She removed the mitts, then stirred a pan on the stove. "Nacho, we talked about this. Say hello to Adam properly."

Nacho stuck out a tattooed hand.

Adam was so surprised, it took a moment to register that the kid wanted to shake. He extricated his hand from his pocket.

Nacho's grasp was limp. "Hi." He mumbled, his eyes scanning the table, the floor, Priss. He looked anywhere but at Adam.

When he would have withdrawn, Adam held on until the kid's gaze returned to him. "Firm, like you mean it." When Nacho's grip tightened, he nodded and let go. Poor kid, he thought, wondering when the boy's father had exited his life, or even if the guy had ever been in it at all.

"Nacho, will you set the table, please? I'm almost done here." Priss turned off the heat.

"I'll help." Adam reached for the bright red placemats on the counter.

Minutes later he held out Priss's chair, then settled onto his own. "You made chicken potpie from scratch?" He shook the cloth napkin into his lap.

Priss passed the gravy boat across the table to him. "It's no big deal. My mom taught me. She made it on the cold nights in Vegas." She shrugged. "It's not an expensive meal."

"She made it for me, too." Nacho said. His swinging legs had him bouncing in his chair.

The tough-guy exterior sometimes made him forget that Nacho was just a kid. Adam poured the gravy, then passed it to Nacho, on his right. "Tell me about your mom."

"She cooked good." Nacho drowned his plate then passed the gravy to Priss.

"She was uneducated, poor, and had awful taste in men." Priss set the boat on the table and frowning, watched Nacho dig in. "But she was also pretty, hardworking and incredibly optimistic, given her life."

"And she smelled good and she loved us," Nacho said between bites.

"Don't talk with your mouth full." Priss took a small forkful, her expression pensive as she chewed.

"This is really good," Adam said, anxious for a

subject that would erase the sadness from Priss's eyes. "So, have you told him?"

"Nah, I thought I'd save the surprise for tonight."

"Told me what?" Nacho asked.

Priss lifted her glass of iced tea and said in a bored voice, "That I've decided you can work with Bear."

Nacho froze, fork halfway to his open mouth. Delight broke on his face like a happy sunrise. The fork clattered to the plate and his eyebrows rose. "For real?" he breathed.

"Yeah." The tea glass Priss raised to her lips didn't hide her small smile. "We'll give it a shot."

"Holy shit!" Nacho flew out of his chair, threw his arms around her neck and squeezed.

"Whoa, big guy." Priss chuckled, juggling her tea before setting it down and patting Nacho's arm. "No swearing."

Adam hadn't realized the two had identical smiles, having never seen one on the boy. He watched their awkward embrace, tenderness loosening his chest.

No wonder she goes the extra mile. There really is a kid under all the tats and attitude.

As if realizing he'd been uncool, Nacho dropped his arms and backed away. But his smile didn't waver when he sat back down. "Can we go tomorrow?"

Priss's smile looked just as permanent. "Tomorrow's Saturday. Bear's probably not working. But we'll give him a call."

Adam asked, "How're you going to get out there after school, Nacho? The school's on the same side of town, but still, it's probably a good two miles."

Nacho picked up his fork and speared another bite of pie. "I'll walk."

"I don't think so." Priss frowned. "You can stay in after-school care until I get off work, and I'll—"

"But then I won't have any time!"

Adam spoke up. "I have a solution."

Both sets of eyes settled on him.

"I still have my bike from when I was your age, in my garage. You could borrow it."

NACHO AND BEAR'S first meeting had gone well on Saturday, so he allowed Nacho back on Sunday.

Priss had every intention of staying, but after a half hour of listening to Bear explaining technique and equipment to Nacho, she fell asleep. She was awakened by Nacho shaking her shoulder and telling her to leave. She'd already determined that Bear only looked scary and Nacho seemed to be hanging on the man's every word, so she agreed to come pick him up around three.

She dropped Mona's top on the drive back to town, enjoying the scent of warm grass on the breeze. With the passing of the rains, the hills had turned from eye-popping emerald to a dun gold, seemingly overnight. The May sun shone with more intent than it had a few weeks ago, a reminder that time was passing. Too soon, she and Nacho would pack up and fly off on another adventure, somewhere else.

So what was with the nostalgic tug at the thought of leaving? Taking her hand from the wheel, she rubbed her breastbone.

Adam.

When she'd fallen into his arms at the door last night, she'd felt protected. Safe. Happy. It may be an illusion, but it was a soft, pretty one. It seemed even his innocent touch could awaken her body— his guiding hand on the back of her neck crossing a street, the brush of the tender skin at the inside of her elbow, his fingers twined in hers.

Hot sex. That's all it is.

Adam's straight-laced facade disguised an amazingly sensual lover beneath. One she loved to explore. His attention to detail, and his slow, worshipful hands…

It wasn't the sun that heated the crotch of her denim shorts, or sweat that dampened her panties.

You're in lust with him. That's all.

And that was enough. Gravel crunched when she braked and pulled off the deserted road. Pulling her cell phone from her bra, her fingers brushed her pebbled nipple. She hit speed dial.

"Hello?"

His deep voice liquefied her insides.

"Hey, good-lookin', whatcha doin'?"

"I just got back from shopping and I'm cleaning house," Adam said.

She touched herself. "Want some help messing it up again?" The wanting made her voice deep. "Nacho is at Bear's and I'm idling on the side of the road, my fingers in my panties, missing you."

"Jesus, Priss." His breath exploded in her ear. "How quick can you get here?"

He gave her directions and within five minutes she pulled up in front of a tidy brick home surrounded by splashy perennial flower beds. The peaked portico over the round wooden front door made it look like a Hobbit lived there.

She jogged up the concrete steps. Adam, dressed in a T-shirt and sweats, opened the door before she could knock. His gaze raked over her as he took her hand and pulled her inside.

Kicking the door closed, he pressed her against it, forearms bracketing her head, his body centimeters away. "What took you so long?" He buried his face in her neck and pulled a deep breath through his nose. "God, you smell like great sex."

"Do I?" She nipped his shoulder through his T-shirt, grabbed his butt and ground against him. "It's your fault. I was just driving and I started thinking about you, and—"

He groaned and captured her lips. His tongue

darted, doing to her mouth what her southern regions were begging for.

Wanting his skin under her hands, she yanked the T-shirt over his head. She raked her nails up his back and he shivered.

He slid a finger under the cuff of her short shorts, to the wet core of her. He growled deep in his throat. "Jesus, you're hot." He stroked her once and it almost sent her over the edge.

"Hurry." She reached into his sweats and wrapped her hand around his long, rock-hard erection. "I want you." She breathed into his ear and he shivered again. She pulled his sweats down with her other hand.

"Oh, babe, you got me." His hands covered her ass and lifted her.

She wrapped her legs around his waist and her arms around his neck, all the while making love to his mouth.

He guided the head of his cock to the gap in her shorts.

"Hurry—"

When he plunged into her, her back slammed into the door with a thud.

"Yes." She spoke against his mouth, and bit his top lip.

He moaned and his arms came around her, cushioning her from the blow as he slammed into her again.

"Fuck me. Fuck me hard," she panted, grinding her heels into the muscles of his ass.

He slid out the full length of him until only the tip of his cock was inside her. "Hot." He thrust into her. "So hot." He groaned.

She bit the corded muscles along his throat and was rewarded with another thrust. She rode him, both of them straining toward what their bodies so desperately needed. When release came, she screamed. Adam shook as he emptied himself into her.

Their frantic movements slowed, but didn't end. He looked down, his eyes dark and full of nameless emotion as he slid, slowly, in and out. She fell into those eyes and something in her opened—almost as if what he made her feel came from his mind, not his body. A play of emotions flickered across his face but the look in his brown eyes didn't change. They were deep, strong, mysterious.

Her muscles clenched, and as Adam watched, she spiraled into another orgasm that overwhelmed her mind as well as her body. The intensity was too much. Panicked, she slammed her eyes shut to block what she couldn't accept.

She collapsed against his chest, her emotions scrubbed raw and bleeding.

He locked his arms around her waist and carried her to the couch, slipping out of her as he sat. He cradled her in his arms, rocking gently.

She clung, sobbing into the soft spot at the base of his neck.

When the storm of emotions ebbed, she mumbled, "Sorry."

When she would have sat up, his arms tightened. "Shhh."

She had no choice but to relax, head against his chest, absolved from the guilt for continuing to absorb his comfort. They shared the silence a few minutes.

"Needing someone isn't weakness, you know," he whispered.

The words rumbled beneath her ear.

She pushed away, sitting up on the edge of the couch. "Are you kidding? Nothing about what we just did was weak." She pasted on a sexy smile.

His eyes still held a shadow of dark power. "I wasn't talking about the sex."

ADAM WATCHED PRISS'S jerky movements as she finger-combed her hair, knowing she was off balance and ready to run. He didn't want to take a chance—didn't want to push her.

But the month of June was barreling from the future and before he was ready it would roll into the present. Then she'd be gone. He cupped a hand around her thigh, rubbing the satin skin at the inside of her knee in a calming, circular motion. "Tell me about your dad."

Frowning, she cocked her head and looked at him as if he'd asked the distance to the moon. "I never met the man. He was long gone by the time I was born."

"How about Nacho's dad?"

"He's in prison." She scooted farther away. "Why are you always digging around, trying to find out stuff?"

He shot a look at the ceiling. "Maybe you couldn't tell from the past half hour, but I'm interested in you. Very interested in you."

"Sex doesn't require—"

"Jesus, Priss!" The frustration that had fizzed for weeks exploded, propelling the words. "Do you really think that all I want from you is sex?"

She stood, and straightened her sex-rumpled clothes. "I told you that I don't stay. I keep things light."

"Yeah, you did. But why can't we get to know each other in the meantime?"

She glanced around. "Where's the bathroom?"

You've lost her. He pointed to the hall next to the arched doorway to the kitchen. An inky cloud of failure spread through his brain.

The rock walls of Priss's heart had no handholds.

And he wore no safety harness.

Think, dammit.

Priss was all about keeping score. Tit for tat.

Maybe...

He stood and walked to the mantel.

"Well, I've got to get back." Her voice came from behind.

He fingered one of the many trophies his mother kept proudly displayed. "Did I ever tell you that I had the chance to pitch for the Angels?"

Her step was soft. "Really?" She read the base of a trophy three down from where he stood.

"That one's from college. I got a full-ride scholarship." He leaned his elbow on the mantel, trying for a nonchalance that was far from the truth that scurried in panic, wanting to stay buried.

"Did you get hurt?"

Well, kinda. "No, not really."

"Then why don't I know your stats?"

He lifted a photo, pretending to study it. Him, on the mound, throwing a fastball. When the frame creaked, he forced his fingers to loosen a bit. "See, there are home games and away games." He looked up at her. "And for the away games…teams fly to them."

"Oh." Her brows came together and her mouth pursed as if she'd felt a stab of pain.

"I thought I could do it. I never would have taken the job if I hadn't been sure I could do it." He took a breath. "Turns out, I was wrong.

"The past shapes who we are today." He set the picture back on the mantel and turned to Priss. "What made you so independent? So fierce?"

If she'd explain, maybe he could understand—maybe he could learn. Not only about her, but about courage. When she crossed the room, he thought she was leaving. She sat on the couch instead. He let out the breath he held and sat at the other end.

"I was about Nacho's age when Social Services found out that Mom left me home alone nights while she worked. In their infinite wisdom, they decided they could do better." She snorted. "Suffice it to say, they were full of shit. When Mom finally got a day job, she came and bailed me out of the system."

She sat ramrod straight, both feet on the floor, hands in her lap like a manners-school student. She looked like one of those china figurines his mom had all over her house—beautiful, fragile.

"I decided then that I was never going to depend on anyone else again—not even my mom. I took charge. I kept the apartment spotless just in case the social worker showed up to check on us. I took over the checkbook. Made sure the debts were paid." Her index finger picked at the cuticle of her thumb. "But without the tips Mom earned at the bar, there wasn't enough money to pay all the bills. So eventually she had to go back to working nights."

"Did the county find out?"

"I found a lady living in her car. She had some issues but she was nice, just down and out. I made her a deal. She could move in but she had to be there at night." She raised her hands, palm up. "Problem solved."

He shook his head, trying to imagine her at Nacho's age, manipulating the world to find a safe corner for herself. "No wonder you couldn't leave Nacho behind." He whispered, more to himself than to her.

She reached into the collar of her shirt and pulled out her phone and checked the time. "It's getting late. You've got a house to clean and I've got to get to the grocery store before picking up Nacho." She hopped up.

He stood and took her hand. "I'm glad you came."

"Me, too." She ducked her head but not before he caught her blush.

He lifted her chin and gave her a chaste kiss. "Do you and Nacho like barbecue? Because I have a couple of friends coming for dinner tonight. I'd love for you to meet them."

CHAPTER FIFTEEN

HE STEPPED INTO the living room, the old-house smell in his nose, listening to a clock somewhere tick into the silence.

"Adam?" Chip bags crackling, Priss stepped in behind him.

Though he knew it was too late to get out of the dinner at Adam's place, he had to try. "I don't see why I couldn't stay home."

Priss's hand on his back propelled him forward. "You were at Bear's all day. If you want to go after school tomorrow, you're going to be civil tonight. Got it?"

"Yeah, yeah. But I still don't see—"

"Look, I know this isn't your thing. But could you just make the best of it? For me?"

He frowned, glancing around the living room.

"You behave, I'll read you a chapter of Harry Potter tonight. Deal?"

"Yeah, okay."

She ruffled his hair. "Thanks, dude, I appreciate it."

A screen door slapped, he heard steps, then Adam walked through a doorway into the living room.

"Hey, Nacho." But his eyes were on Priss. "Hello, Priss." His voice went all funny. Might as well have hearts coming out of his head, like on little-kid cartoons.

Nacho was already tired of watching them watch each other. "Do you have a TV?"

They looked surprised, like they'd forgotten he was there.

Adam said, "Yeah, sure. You can watch it if it's okay with Priss."

"I'm going to help Adam get ready. You can watch TV until his guests arrive. Then you have to come out and be social. Deal?"

"I guess."

"Carley and Daryl have two kids. You might like them, Nacho. Tanner is just a year older than you, and Penny, the girl, is a bit younger. They'll be here in about an hour. In the meantime, follow me."

They're probably little yuppie clones.

Adam led the way down a narrow hall covered in old photos and turned in at a room with a big desk, bookshelves and a leather couch.

And on the wall next to the door hung a huge flat-screen TV.

"Way cool." He'd seen these in the stores but had never had the chance to watch one.

"You can sit on the couch and watch whatever

you want." Adam handed him a remote. "But don't mess with anything in here. And keep your feet off the couch. Okay?"

"Yeah, sure." He hit the power button. *Like I'm going to steal the furniture?*

When Adam walked out, Nacho jumped, kicking out his feet from under him to land lying on the couch. He crossed one foot over the other on the padded arm of the sofa and started surfing channels. He really missed TV. This night might not be a total waste of time after all.

Ten minutes later, bored with the NASCAR race, he clicked off the TV. He'd forgotten how sucky Sunday-afternoon TV was. Besides, the stuff on the race cars was just decals, not real art.

The hours at Bear's had gone way too fast. He didn't get to actually do anything, but that was okay because he got to watch Bear lay down the base coat for a new design: a cobra on the hood of an old Mustang. Bear explained what he was doing and why, and he even showed him how the sprayers worked.

Nacho glanced at the bookshelves, wondering if maybe Adam had *The Chamber of Secrets*. Even grown-ups read Harry Potter. He stood up and walked closer to read the spines. He should have known—nothing but medical books. What else would a boring pharmacist have? He walked around the desk and sat in the leather rolling chair.

Everything on the desk was laid out just perfect. Even the loose papers were stacked in a neat pile in a leather inbox.

Man, this guy's underwear is too tight.

Adam and Priss were obviously crushing on each other. What did that mean for the kid in the middle? In spite of the bike offer, the jury was still out on this guy. He seemed to be trying but maybe he was just doing it to suck up to Priss.

Nacho lifted a stack of brochures from the desktop, drawn by the bright bird on the top one. He remembered his teacher called it a toucan. He'd forgotten where they were from, but it wasn't the U.S. He undid the rubber band and looked through the pamphlets, one by one. South America, Rome, China. Tahiti looked the best. How fun would it be to play on that beach?

"What are you doing?" Priss stood in the doorway.

He jumped and the brochures fell out of his hand onto the desk. "I was just looking."

She stepped in, hand on hip, looking pissed. "Did Adam say it was okay to go through his stuff?"

"No. But I saw the toucan, and—"

"Where'd you go?" Adam stepped into the doorway. "What the hell?" He hurried over and snatched the brochures from the floor.

All except the toucan one. Priss bent, picked it up and handed it to Adam. "I'm sorry," she mumbled.

"I trusted you in here." Adam looked all embarrassed, like he'd just farted out loud or something.

Nacho looked between Priss and Adam, wondering why they were so mad. Sure, he shouldn't have been snooping but it wasn't like he found a stash of skin mags or something. "I didn't look at anything else—we're studying toucans in school. That's all."

Priss said, "Adam, it's just brochures. No big deal."

His face said otherwise. "The Beauchamps are here." Adam turned and walked out.

Priss grabbed Nacho's wrist. "You promised to behave. You and I are going to talk about this later."

Shit. There goes my time with Bear tomorrow.

He'd never get grown-ups.

PRISS SAT AT a picnic table in Adam's neatly trimmed backyard, a full plate in front of her. The bacon cheeseburger was good but her stomach was too tight to take on much.

God, she could have died when she caught Nacho going through Adam's travel brochures. Would the next eight years be like this, Nacho bumbling from one disaster to another? If so, she didn't think she could take it.

I'm so not cut out for this.

Nacho picked at his food at the kids' table. He sat with the other boy and the little girl but was as separate as a cold moon from shiny stars. Though he and Tanner were only a year apart, they couldn't be more different—Nacho's gangsta-rap style to Tanner's early Justin Bieber. Even four-year-old Penny seemed wary, watching Nacho out of the corner of her eye between bites.

A needle of sympathy pricked the annoyed part of Priss's brain. The kid looked so miserable. And after all, he had no way of knowing that the brochures would be something Adam would want to keep private.

"So what do you do, Priss?" Carley asked, beer in hand.

Here we go. "I'm usually an admin assistant. But it's tough to find office jobs here so I'm bartending at the moment."

Carley swallowed a sip of beer. "I don't know if Adam told you, but I work in the office of the elementary school. I'll keep an eye out for any openings."

Adam's friend seemed nice, in spite of the cashmere sweater tied around her shoulders and the expensive blond tint woven into her shoulder-length hair. "Thanks, but we won't be here much longer."

"Oh. Where are you going?" She shot a look at Adam.

"Nacho and I haven't decided yet but we'll leave after school's out."

Daryl looked up from his baked beans. "Don't you like Widow's Grove?"

Adam's focus was on his plate, but something in the tilt of his head told her he was listening. Hard.

"It's a great town. It's just that I tend to... I mean we, Nacho and I, are going to see more of the United States. Maybe Seattle next."

"You know they have terrible weather," Carley said. "Rains incessantly."

Priss looked down the table to where Adam pushed the potato salad around his plate. *Oh, way to go, Hart. Just blurt out what's in your head. Will I ever learn?*

Carley addressed the kids' table. "Penny, mind your plate. Tanner, help her cut that, will you?"

Apparently that line of conversation was over. Good.

After dinner, Adam and Daryl tossed a football around with the boys. Well, with Tanner, anyway. After ten minutes, Nacho wandered off to hunker down next to Penny, playing in the flower-bed dirt with a toy shovel.

Carley and Priss watched them through the window over the kitchen sink where they washed dishes.

"You'd never met your half brother before you came here?" Carley handed Priss a stainless-steel bowl to dry.

"No. My mother and I were...estranged."

"I can't imagine not having family. My parents had ten siblings between them, and I've got four sisters and a brother. Honestly, I've lost count how many shirttail relatives I've got scattered across the country. We're like rabbits."

Priss placed the bowl on the counter then reached for the glass baking dish Carley held out. "I can't imagine having that much family. Gives me the willies just thinking about it." Remembering her vow to work on being more politically correct, she smiled to soften her words.

"Yeah, Adam told me that you were kind of a loner. Independent to a fault."

Apparently I'm not the only direct person in this town. Priss focused on the dish, but not because it was fragile. "It's the 'fault' part that he stressed, I'm sure."

"On the contrary. He admires the hell out of you. Says you're the—" she looked at the ceiling, searching for the words "—bravest, scrappiest, most steadfast person he's ever met." Her hands stilled in the dishwater. "And though you're as far from his type as humanly possible, I think you're good for him. I've seen changes in Adam lately. It's like he's finally coming to life. And I think you're the cause."

Priss flushed under Carley's studied regard.

"Please don't hurt him."

Priss opened her mouth to explain—to tell Carley she'd been up front from the beginning. Then she closed it. Well-intentioned or not, she didn't owe this woman an explanation.

But for the first time in years, Priss wanted to.

Part of the reason she'd always rested lightly on whatever branch she settled on was to avoid explanations. She didn't need others' judgments and opinions. Especially someone she'd just met. Priss locked her jaw to keep the words in and took the next mixing bowl from Carley's wet hands.

It was good that she and Nacho were leaving. What was it about this town that made her wish to be different from the way she was? The lessons she'd learned at a young age had kept her safe for all these years.

And they would keep her and Nacho safe for years to come, wherever they landed.

A half hour later, they all stood in the living room saying their goodbyes. Adam's arm felt right around her waist, as did his hand resting on her hip. It was almost as if she and Nacho lived here and were saying goodbye to their dinner guests. Then she and Adam would finish cleaning up, see that Nacho had a bath, and they'd walk arm in arm to the master bedroom....

"I'll see you at practice on Wednesday night, Adam. We'll be ready for those Pismo Punks on Saturday." Daryl lifted his car keys from the little antique table next to the door. "Now that's odd."

Carley, who was herding her kids out the door, turned. "What?"

"My Peace Dollar. It's gone."

"Your what?" Priss asked.

He stood staring at his key chain. "My dad was a coin collector. He gave me a 1921 Peace Dollar when I was a kid. I drilled a hole in it, and have carried it on my key chain for years. It's not worth anything except the price of the silver, but it means a lot to me." He looked up. "I know it was there when I came in, because Penny noticed it, driving over here."

Priss scrutinized Nacho's expression.

He glared back. "I didn't do it."

His face was closed and sullen but she glimpsed truth behind the mask. He hadn't done it. This time.

Adam said, "Nacho, if you were looking at it, and—"

"He didn't do it, Adam." She couldn't say what had changed. Maybe she was developing that mother's instinct—but she knew she was right. She put her hand on Nacho's shoulder.

No one moved.

Adam's expression was as careful as his words. "Priss, remember outside the store that day? You said then that Nacho hadn't—"

"I know." A timeworn weariness seeped into the hollow of her bones, weighing her down. "And you were right. Then. But I know Nacho better now, and I'm telling you, he didn't do it."

"You wanna frisk me?" Nacho spit out the words and turned out the pockets of his jeans. He had to grab for the waistband when the pants slipped off his hips.

Carley whispered to Tanner and they started looking, scanning the carpet, checking under the couch.

"Of course not." Adam flushed. "But I didn't take it and Priss didn't. It belonged to the Beauchamps, so…"

Priss didn't have the answer as to what had happened to the coin but she knew that Nacho wasn't it. She sighed. "So, of course you blame the delinquent, right?" She held up a hand to stop Adam's sputtering protest. "I'm not accusing you. Just stating a fact."

Carley shrugged and said, "It's not in the living room. Maybe we can try the kitchen?"

Priss slipped her hand around her brother's shoulders. "Let's go, Nacho. Nice meeting you all. Sorry the evening had to end this way."

The crowd parted for them when they headed for the door.

Nacho didn't shrug out from under her arm until they reached Mona, parked in the driveway with Adam's bike in the backseat. When they got in, he turned to look her in the eye. "I didn't take that guy's dollar."

"I know you didn't." She sent a prayer skyward

then turned the key. Thankfully Mona rumbled to life. She put a hand behind the seat to look over her shoulder and negotiate backing down the two concrete strips that constituted the driveway. "But are you surprised Adam thought you had?" At the bottom, she checked for traffic, pulled out and headed for home.

Head down, Nacho mumbled, "No."

"Remember when we talked about being careful with your reputation? This is what I was trying to tell you. This is where you pay."

"Yeah, I guess so."

They rode in silence, each to their own thoughts. *Adam wouldn't have looked at us if it weren't for the problems at the very beginning.*

Realization hit and she braked at a stop sign hard enough for her back to leave the seat.

Nacho looked over with a frown.

She remembered Adam's shuttered expression. His cool eyes.

He looked at us.

"Here I am, lecturing you…but I'm not clean, either. You've seen me lie, too."

The first time she'd met Adam, she'd lied. She knew he'd assume she'd be living alone in his apartment over the store. A lie of omission was still a lie. Then, that day when Nacho shoplifted that magazine, she'd batted her eyelashes and bullshitted her way out of trouble.

Just like she always did.

She turned left onto tree-lined Hollister.

Sure, she'd needed those skills when she was young. But she still employed them when threatened—and she was an adult now. A role model to her brother.

She thought back to Colorado, and farther back than that, seeing a chain of small deceptions, misrepresentations, manipulations.

Dishonesty.

Shame burned as if vinegar ran through her veins. Those skills were good for a kid who had no power, trying to stay safe in a harzardous world. Using them now was like using a kid's toy wrench to try to fix her car.

Adam *should* have been looking at them both.

It was time to put away the old skills and develop some grown-up ones. But how did one go about doing that when you hadn't a clue as to what those skills were?

She reached over, cupped the back of Nacho's neck. "We both suck, dude." She gave him a shake. "But we're going to try harder, right?"

He pulled away but with a small smile. "Yeah, okay."

Another truth smacked her like an unseen low-lying branch.

You're still doing it.

Deep inside, something shifted. Light fell on the thing she'd been hiding from herself.

A lie of omission....

She had feelings for Adam. Caring, needy feelings that she could hardly admit to herself.

Oh, they were still leaving come the end of June. The day after school released Nacho, they'd be in the wind. But she might as well admit it. This stop would leave a hole in her.

She rolled slowly through town, watching the strolling tourists taking advantage of the stores' later hours.

Well, admitting it to herself was going to have to be good enough for now. New resolution or no, this was one truth she was keeping to herself.

CHAPTER SIXTEEN

PRISS'S HEELS CLICKED on the industrial-tile hallway, the smell of antiseptic, bland food and impending mortality making her want to turn and run. But it was her day to visit Barney so she pulled open the glass door to the cardiac-care unit.

The unit was set up like a big wheel, a nursing station in the middle, bristling with electronics measuring patients' most intimate functions. Nothing in the CCU was private. Death and family drama played out separated from others only by a thin curtain that didn't even reach the floor.

Is this what it was like for Mom? An efficient, generic medical warehouse? A worm of guilt burrowed into her chest. Or was it regret? *Nothing you can do about anything now.* Priss shivered. No one deserved to die like this.

Pasting on a sunny smile, she made herself reach for the curtain around Barney's bed.

He lay sleeping. The unkind afternoon light from the window fell across him, highlighting his grizzled hair, sallow, bloated skin, his awful disease. *Cardiomyopathy.* He'd told her the term, but she'd had to look it up on the library computer. Apparently years of drinking and neglect had hardened his heart to the point of inefficiency. She could see his edema-distended stomach from where she stood.

She walked quietly to sit in the chair beside the bed. As if sensing her, his eyes opened.

"Hey, Barn. How're you feeling?" She took his paper-dry hand.

"Like a lab rat." He cleared his throat. "You shoulda just let me go, that day. This is no way to die."

"Now, that's no way to talk. You're gonna walk out of here." She squeezed his hand. "How could you miss the Tigers win the pennant?"

His jaundiced eyes were sad. "It's okay, Priss. I'm ready to go. I've screwed up this life so bad. Maybe I'll get the chance to come back and try it again."

What worried her more than his condition was his attitude. "It's never too late to start again, Barney."

"Nah, I'm too old and tired." A smile began, faltered, then faded. "The only thing I would like is to see what's left of my family, to say goodbye." He closed his eyes. "To say I'm sorry. But I even screwed that up. They won't come see me."

Sorrow wadded her throat and pooled behind her eyes. She stayed, watching him sleep until the sun's slanting rays reminded her she had to get home to Nacho.

On her way out, she stepped into the empty CCU waiting room to call Barney's son one more time but pulled up short just inside the door. Gaby sat in a chair along the wall, reading a *Hollywood Star* magazine. "Gaby?"

She looked up. Her lips pursed like she'd eaten something sour. "Are you done in there? They only let one in at a time, you know."

Priss hadn't realized the old lady had been visiting Barney. They hadn't even thought to ask if she wanted in on the rotation. "Why didn't you let me know? I would have let you—"

"Oh, don't you try to snow me." She tossed the magazine. It skittered off the table and hit the floor with a plop. "You can act with the others, like you're some good person who really cares." She drilled Priss with a witch's glare. "But I know what you really are."

"And what am I, really, Gaby?" Old lady or not, Priss had taken about all the contempt she could handle. "Are you going to finally tell me what put that bug up your ass about me?"

The old lady stood and pointed a bony finger. "Don't you swear at me. Your mother would be so disappointed."

The truth slammed into her. "You knew my

mother." She'd assumed Gaby had been her mother's replacement.

"I worked beside her for ten years. We were friends. And you know what I never saw, in all those ten years?"

Priss opened her mouth.

"Her daughter." She straightened as much as the widow's hump would allow. "Even when Cora lay in this very hospital, struggling for breath until she couldn't do it anymore, her daughter never came."

"I didn't know." Priss's voice caught on the razor blades in her throat, coming out shredded.

"And whose fault is that?"

An oily black wall of guilt crashed over her. "Mine," she whispered, taking a step back.

"Cora Hart wasn't perfect but she did the best she could raising you. And as soon as you were able, you ran off. You went about your happy life and threw her on the trash heap."

"Did she say that?" The words came out all skinny, as if not wanting to know the answer had squeezed them flat.

"Pah," Gaby spit out. "She didn't see you clear. She was proud that you went to 'make something better of yourself.'"

Priss took a grateful breath.

"She tried to find you, you know."

The air left Priss's lungs like a too-full balloon. She took another step back.

"Yes, she did." Gaby nodded, seeming gratified by something on Priss's face. "She saved every free penny she could to hire a private detective. She spent hours at the library, trying to find some trace of you on the internet." Gaby shuffled to the door on worn, misshapen slippers.

"But you were having a great time, so I guess that's okay."

Priss fell into the chair that was, luckily, at the back of her knees.

WHEN HIS PHONE blatted "Blood-Soaked," Adam snatched it from the counter and answered it. "Dang it, Sin. Will you stop changing my ring—"

"Love target at ten o'clock," she whispered, and hung up.

He scanned the empty soda fountain, glimpsing only the ends of Priss's brown spiky hair over the Scholl's display. His heart double-clutched from first gear to third.

Get ready to eat crow. You earned it.

Before he could chicken out, he stepped out of the drug room, locked the door, put the "Back in Ten Minutes" sign on the counter and strode to the front of the store.

She sat hunched, elbows on the table, chin in one hand, the spoon in the other dripping melted ice cream as she stared out the window.

"You're going to ruin your dinner."

When she looked up, his heart ignored the clutch, ramming straight to top gear. Her green eyes, usually so full of life, were soulless. Haunted.

"What is it?" He dropped into the chair beside her. "Is Nacho okay?"

"He's fine. At least he was last I saw him. Bear has to come to town later so he's bringing him home." She took her elbows off the table and looked down, as if surprised to see the melting hot-fudge sundae. "Want to share? I was just drowning my sorrows in ice cream."

"Does it work?" He reached for a spoon from a place setting on the next table. "It looks better than the crow I was going to order."

"What's that mean?" She dipped her spoon into the puff of whipped cream that perched like a drunken clown's hat on the vanilla puddle.

He pushed the words out. "It means that I owe you and Nacho an apology. A big one."

"You found out Nacho didn't take that dollar."

"Yeah. Daryl called me this morning. Penny had it. She was going to speak up but when I got upset she was afraid she'd be in trouble, so she didn't." There, he'd said it but he still wasn't brave enough to hold her gaze. "I'm sorry, Priss. I should have—"

She squared her shoulders and looked down at the ice cream. "It's okay."

"No, it's not. I didn't believe you. I falsely accused Nacho. He has enough problems without that." Adam shoveled a heaping spoonful of hot fudge onto his spoon, hoping ice-cream therapy really did work. "I need to find a way to make it up to both of you."

Her smile was a sad one but he was glad to see it just the same.

"This really smart guy I know told me that it doesn't work that way. Relationships don't always have to be an even exchange."

"And did he convince you?"

"I'm working on it." She took a spoonful.

"So what's wrong, Priss?"

She stared out the window long enough that he started to worry it could be about him. Did she want to break up with him? Wait—were they even together? Maybe—

"You know, I thought I had it all together before I hit Widow's Grove." She sighed. "Today I found out I've been flying blind for ten years."

"How so?"

"You're not the only one who misjudges people. Suffice it to say I'm learning that people deserve second chances. And third chances. And if they're family, maybe even more than that." She shook her head. "But I can't do anything about that now. It's the problem I *can* do something about that has me stumped."

He'd rather hear about the family part, but he

knew her. That subject was clearly closed. "What's the problem?" He took another bite of ice cream.

"Well, I have this customer at work. A friend. He's in intensive care and he's giving up." She laid her spoon on the table.

"I'm sorry."

"It's so sad. He's such a nice guy. I'm sure he's made mistakes in his life but who hasn't?" Her words sped up. "I mean, who is his son to judge? It's real easy to sit back and look at all the bad things your parents did. But you know, they did the best—"

"Wait, slow down. What did his son do?"

"Nothing. That's the problem."

He shook his head. "You've lost me."

"His son won't come see his dad. All Barney wants before he dies is to talk to him, and the idiot refuses to come."

"You've called him?"

She had been hanging around Nacho long enough that she now had the eye roll down. "Only twenty times. He won't even pick up the phone anymore."

Worry niggled at his brain. Worry that she was harassing a total stranger. Worry that she wouldn't appreciate him pointing out that fact. "Priss, do you really think what you're doing is a good idea? I mean, you don't know this guy, right?"

"No. And I don't want to know him. I just want

him to visit his damned father." She dropped her cheek on her fist. "Loser."

"Okay, so forget about him. What about other family members? Does he have any female—"

"Shit!" She bolted upright, lethargy gone. "I'm an idiot, and you're brilliant!" She hopped up, leaned over, took his face in her hands and gave him a loud, smacking kiss. "Why didn't I think of that?"

Sin gave them a flat stare and Adam flushed. "Not that I mind being brilliant, but what—"

"Barney's grandson is a Tiger!" She spread her arms as if he'd just given her the secret to the universe.

"That would make him even more dangerous than his son. Aren't there any nice old ladies in the family?"

"What kind of baseball fan are you, Adam?" She put a hand on her hip. "He plays shortstop for the Detroit Tigers."

"That's great. I'm sure Barney's proud. But how does that—"

"For such a brilliant guy, you can be slow sometimes." She snapped her fingers. "Hey, Sin, could I have Sunday's *LA Times*?" She strode to the counter. "Come on, cough it up. I know you do the crossword every friggin' day."

Sin does the LA Times *Crossword?* He took another spoonful of ice cream to cool off his brain. "The world's gone mad." But he didn't say it loud enough for either of the women to hear. He had some sense of self-preservation.

Sin took out a section and handed the rest over to Priss.

"What are you doing?" he asked, fairly sure he didn't want to know.

Priss ruffled through, took one section and strode back to the table. "Barney's son is not talking to me. Even if he picked up my call, he wouldn't give me his son's number. And I hardly think he'd be listed in the phone book even if I knew where he lived, which I don't." She scanned page after page. "But I do know where he'll be every Saturday for the next month." She dropped the paper on the table and stabbed a finger at a column. "The Tigers' schedule."

Alarm skittered up his spine. "Priss, you're not thinking about going to see him."

She looked at him like he was an odd bug. "Well, I hardly think if I call the home office for his cell number, that they'll give it to me."

She had a point. But there had to be another way. Her aloof look and tightened jaw told him how far he'd get poking holes in her plan. "What's his name?"

She frowned. "Um…"

"You mean you're going to see a guy, and you don't even know his name?"

"Hang on, hang on. It'll come to me." She put

her fingers to her temples, as if she could pull the name out of her head. "It was something about an animal...not a tiger. A...Otter! That's it!"

"His grandson's name is Otter?"

"Sandy Otto. Porter told me Barney's son had his name legally changed to his mother's maiden name."

"Before you go off on some crazy chase, let me make some calls. I've stayed in touch with some baseball people. Maybe I can get you a number."

The rumble of glass-pack mufflers rattled the sundae dishes stacked behind the counter. A midnight-black Chevy truck from the sixties pulled to the curb in front of the store. Violet ghost flames ran its length and flattened chrome tailpipes almost dragged the pavement. The passenger door opened and Nacho hopped out. Bear climbed out the other side, walked to the bed and lifted out Adam's old bike.

Priss put an arm around Adam's neck. "Gotta go start dinner." She pulled him down and laid one on him. Not a smack this time, but a searing, grown-woman kiss.

"'Scuse me, boss," Sin said. "But Ms. Feeney is at the prescription counter with a hemorrhoid ring."

Priss let go of the back of his neck, but he saw in her eyes she hadn't wanted to. "Thanks, Adam. I mean it."

"No reason to thank me, yet." He glanced out

the window. Nacho stood waving goodbye to the truck that was pulling away from the curb. "Nacho may be a few minutes coming upstairs. I need to talk to him."

"He won't bite."

He whipped his head around. Was he that obvious?

Priss's smile was tender. "Under all that attitude is a lost kid, Adam. Talk to that kid, not the one you see, and you'll do fine." Then she was gone, jogging down the aisle toward the back door.

"No running in the store!" he yelled after her. Ignoring Sin's raised pierced eyebrow and Ms. Feeney's hemorrhoid ring, he walked to the front door.

NACHO LIFTED THE bike onto the sidewalk and headed for the alley, hoping Priss would make good on her promise of pizza for dinner.

"Hey, Nacho." Adam's voice came from behind.

His stomach clenched, cutting off a growl. He turned. "Yeah?" *What now?*

Adam walked up. "How'd the bike do today?"

Wary, he frowned. "Okay."

Adam put his hands in his back pockets but didn't say anything.

"Oh, and thanks for letting me use it."

"No problem. It was just sitting in the garage." He ran his fingers across the seat. "It was a good bike—still is, I guess."

Why is he just standing there? If I'm in trouble, he should just yell and get it over with.

But Adam didn't seem mad. He seemed all nervous, like he had in the office yesterday, with his brochures.

"I owe you an apology. My friend found the dollar. Penny had it."

It took Nacho a few seconds to overcome the shock of hearing an adult apologize. "That's okay." He rolled the bike toward the alley. When Adam touched his shoulder, he stopped.

Adam walked around, to look him in the face. "No, it's not. It had to hurt to get called out in front of people you didn't know for something you didn't do." He held out a hand. "A man apologizes when he knows he's wrong."

Even more surprised by this offer, Nacho shook the outstretched adult hand.

Adam blew out a breath. "Whew. Glad that's over."

He was nervous to talk to me? This day was getting weirder by the minute.

"C'mon, I'll walk you back. How did it go at Bear's today?"

Nacho wheeled the bike through the alley. "Oh man, you shoulda seen. He's got this shortie faring from a guy's Harley that wraps around above the headlight. He's airbrushing a skull chewing barbed wire on it. It's gonna be legendary."

"Sounds amazing."

"It is. Then Bear's got these rims he's gotta powder-coat. He says maybe he'll let me help."

"You're lucky to get to work with him." Adam smiled. "You're going to do fine."

Why is he being so nice all of a sudden? He doesn't really care.

Does he?

CHAPTER SEVENTEEN

PRISS STOPPED, MIDPOUR. "What are— What's wrong?"

The bright light from the open door seared her bar-adjusted eyes but she'd recognize that broad-shouldered silhouette anywhere. She put down the martini shaker as Adam strode to the bar.

"Everything's fine." He leaned his forearms on the bar. "Oh, hi, Gaby. How are you feeling?"

"Fair to middlin'. Those shoe inserts you gave me helped." Gaby lifted her drink tray and walked away.

Priss closed her mouth. It made sense that Adam would know most everyone in here; he was the town's pharmacist. But for some reason, she'd never thought about that before.

She finished pouring. Wiping her hands on her apron, she shot a look around, seeing her workspace through a stranger's eyes. Well, hardly a stranger's. She snatched a crumpled napkin from the bar and swiped a wet spot with a towel. "What are you doing here?"

"Hey, Adam." Porter raised his glass in salute.

Adam waved, but his eyes remained on her. "Can you take a quick break?"

She checked her customers' drink levels. "Can you guys live without me for ten minutes?"

Attention locked on the game show, they murmured assent.

She tipped her chin toward the back door and untied her apron.

Blinded by the bright noon sunshine of the alley, she grasped his upper arm and he led her to where Mona sat like an elephant seal basking in the sun. "Did you get a number for Sandy Otto?" She leaned against the car door, hope rising in her chest. "You did, didn't you?"

"No. That's what I came to tell you. My source couldn't get access." He leaned on the door beside her. "But you'll be there for your friend, and I know that will be—"

She pounded a fist on Mona's side. "Shit."

"He's only a backup shortstop but the teams take great pains to protect their players. There are lots of crazies out there."

"Dammit. I'll have to go to him." The cogs in her brain whirred, considering the logistics.

"Why is this your problem?" He turned and took her sore hand, running his thumb over the back. "Look, I know you have a soft spot for the old guy and you're a loyal friend. I admire you for it, really,

I do. But, Priss, you've known this guy for, what, two months?"

His frown burrowed, digging into a place she didn't want to go. She looked at her feet. "He's a sad old man. Can't you imagine lying in a bed all alone, waiting to die?"

"You're right. It's incredibly sad." Adam's regard illuminated her deep dark corners like an interrogator's spotlight. "But you're not normally the warm and fuzzy type so this makes even less sense to me." He held out his hands. "I'm just trying to understand you."

Suddenly the liquefied sludge of guilt, pain and regret that had heated in her gut the past few days pushed up through the crust she'd built over the years.

"So, what are you saying? I'm too tough?" The superheated words burned coming out. "I can't be human? Care about other people? Oh, no, not Priss Hart. She's a hard-ass." She crossed her arms to cover truth. "She doesn't have feelings like the 'other people.' You know, the ones who have money and class, and…what the hell are you looking at?"

"What is this really about, Priss?"

His dark eyes captured her and like the sun through a magnifying glass, the focus made her squirm.

"Why does this hurt you so?"

"Because I let my mother die, all alone!" Her

shout echoed off the brick building, coming back to slap her in the face. "I left and never looked back. Oh, I made excuses. I ran her faults through my head over and over, until I brainwashed myself into believing that she didn't deserve better...."

She hauled in a breath and tried to hold back the words, but what could stop lava?

"She didn't deserve that. She was just a lost little girl in a woman's body, trying to fill a hole in herself with the next man, and the next man. All she wanted was someone to accept her, to love her. I'm her *daughter,* and I walked away. I blamed her for everything shitty in my life. Don't you see what a colossally horrific thing that was to do?" She wiped her sleeve across her nose. "The last few days, every time I close my eyes I see her lying in that hospital bed trying to pull in air like a fish flopping on a bank. And where was I? Off, flying blind, thinking I was a success. Thinking I was—"

He pulled her to his chest and wrapped his arms around her.

She'd have been okay if he'd just let her get mad. But nice was her undoing—always had been. Her eyes leaked onto his shirt.

After some time, he whispered into her hair, "Priss, you've got it all wrong." His voice rumbled through his chest, against her cheek. "I'm sure your mother didn't want you crippled and chained to her."

His hand rubbed her back in soothing circles, and too destroyed to argue, she just listened, accepting the comfort that poured into the hole in her chest like cool water.

"Think about it, hon. If that were you, would you want Nacho hovering, suffering with you? Or would you want him out in the world, living a full life?"

The truth in his words trickled into her parched soul. She stayed in the caring circle of his arms only a few seconds more, afraid if she stayed any longer she'd never leave. She sniffed and backed up, wiping her cheeks. "How did you get so damned smart, Preston?"

"I'm not smart at all. You were just too close to see the truth." He pulled an ironed handkerchief from his back pocket and handed it to her.

Grateful to have found the only man under seventy who still carried a linen handkerchief, Priss took it, mopping her face and his shirt with it. It gave her something to do to avoid looking at him. "You may be right, Adam, but I can't see that part right now. Just let me hurt, okay?"

ADAM LEANED AGAINST the car, his brain considering and discarding excuses like a veteran postal employee sorted mail. Priss had given him another glimpse of the vulnerable woman behind all the tough. And he didn't want to slam that door. But babysitting Nacho for two days was about as crazy an idea he'd ever heard. "I do understand why you feel the need to go, Priss, I do." Head down, he walked away a few steps, then back. "But this guy could be a psycho for all you know."

"Everybody knows the Cubs snatch up all the psychos." She gave him a wan smile.

"How about if I go with you?" He stopped in front of her and took her hand.

"Thanks, Adam. But this is something I have to do. For me. Besides, you're my babysitter."

"What?" He backed up a step.

"I can't ask your mother to take Nacho on. She's off the walker now and she's a love, but he's too much for her."

"How about…" His brain couldn't fill in the blank. She sure as hell wouldn't allow Nacho to stay with Bear. And after last weekend, Adam wasn't going to suggest the Beauchamps.

She spread her hands. "See?" She pushed away from the car. "I've got to get back to work. I know I'm asking a lot. Just think about it, will you?"

She took the step that separated them, twining her fingers in his. When she looked up his heart kicked his ribs. Swimming in the depth of her sea-green eyes was that passionate, sensitive woman he'd chased. But now he saw more. He saw that she felt those same things for *him*.

Startled, he glanced at her expression. Still open

and hopeful but what he'd seen in her eyes wasn't there anymore. Could he have seen more than she'd allowed herself to?

Or was he putting his wishes into her eyes?

She stood on tiptoe and kissed him, a soft, quick kiss. "No matter what you decide, thank you, Adam. For everything." She turned and walked to the door, opened it and flashed him a Mona Lisa smile.

A WEEK LATER, Priss threaded her arms through the straps of her duffel bag and shrugged it onto her back. "Now, Nacho, you're going to take good care of Adam, right?" She lifted her fanny pack from the kitchen table and clipped it around her waist. "Remember, he's a rookie."

"Oh, yeah, don't worry." Nacho rubbed his hands together.

"Not funny, Nacho. I mean it."

Luckily, Adam was smiling, even if it looked artificial. "We'll be fine. Do you have my car keys? I gassed it up last night."

He'd threatened not to keep an eye on Nacho if she tried to drive Mona to LAX, so she'd agreed to take his "reliable" car. She patted her pocket. "Right here."

"I still wish you'd wait three weeks, when the Tigers come to San Fran. The three of us could make a weekend of it."

"I'm not sure Barney will be around that long." *And by then, Nacho and I will be packing to move.* "I'd better get going." She walked over to where Nacho sat doing homework at the kitchen table, looking innocent. "Nacho, you've got my phone, right?" She'd insisted on leaving her phone with him, just in case he needed to call Adam.

He pulled the phone from his pocket and held it up.

"You behave, kid. I mean it. If I'm lucky, I'll be back Monday night. But latest, Tuesday." She gave him a quick, fierce hug.

He shrugged her off. "Yeah, yeah. I got it, already."

Adam followed her out of the apartment, closing the door behind him. When she turned to say goodbye, he thrust a wad of neatly folded bills into her hand.

"I have enough money."

"I know. But keep it, just in case. You can give it back when you come home."

"Adam, I've got it. Promise." She handed the bills back. "But thank you."

"It's just that Tropicana Field is in a crappy part of St. Petersburg." His lips pursed.

"I've got reservations at the Holiday Inn, and I'll take a taxi to the game. Will you stop worrying?" She stood on tiptoe to kiss him goodbye and hopefully distract him from his questions.

His lips distracted her instead. He enfolded her in the familiar comfort of his arms and whispered in her ear. "I'll hold you in my heart until you're back."

She squeezed her eyes closed and absorbed his words. They sank down deep, spreading like a warm blanket over her worries. She pulled in his comforting scent, and was flooded with reasons not to leave.

"Ah, excuse me, but shouldn't you be getting on the road?" Olivia stood in the hall, watching them with a little cat's smile.

They hadn't even heard her door open. Adam's arms loosened. "She's right. You need to go. And I need to get Nacho to school."

Nacho had the bike now but she still drove him to school; it made her feel "parently." Besides, Nacho liked being seen in Mona. "I put your name on the school list so they won't hassle you. You have the permission slip for treatment, in case—"

"I've got it. Will you stop worrying? Try to enjoy your time off."

She'd been shocked when Floyd gave her the day off to help Barney, even if he'd made it clear it would be unpaid. "Okay, I'm outta here." She ran her hand down Adam's arm and squeezed his fingers once, hard, then forced herself to let go. "Olivia, you'll make sure these two don't blow up the building while I'm gone, right?"

"You know I won't let my two best guys get into trouble." She hugged Priss. "You just see that you don't find any in Florida."

"No worries." She hiked her duffel higher, waved to Adam, then descended the stairs.

IT WAS FULL dark by the time Priss stepped out of the terminal and into Tampa's damp blanket to flag down a taxi.

When she opened the taxicab's door, the smell of cheap incense overwhelmed her, but she got in anyway.

"Where you to?" The driver nodded his head in rhythm to the sitar and drum music pounding from the radio.

She cracked the window. "Are there any cheap hotels within walking distance of Tropicana Field?"

His eyes lit up. "Oh, yes, mum. I know the perfect one." He accelerated away from the curb before she'd even closed the door.

The next twenty miles, Priss alternated between worrying about her driver's erratic lane changes and how fast the meter was racking up her fare. She'd dipped into her savings as much as she dared; if she used any more she and Nacho wouldn't have enough to leave Widow's Grove come June. She should have enough for the cab fare back—*if* she ate one very cheap meal a day.

Adam's offer was sweet but she couldn't take

his money. Even if her debt wasn't monetary, she owed him way too much already. The only other large amount of money she had was the wad she'd found in her mother's apron...and she was saving that for Nacho. If he didn't want to go to college, it would get him into a trade school. Or set him up with equipment, if this car-painting thing turned out to be what he wanted to do.

She sighed in relief when the cabbie slowed and took an off-ramp—but then she got a look at the neighborhood. Streetlights illuminated black-and-gray vignettes of cracked concrete and trash, neon and decay. Storefronts squatted behind metal accordion gates. The only sign of life was the men who slunk wolflike along the sidewalks and stood sentinel on street corners.

The taxi pulled into the drive of a long, low cinder-block building with yellow fluorescent lights under the eaves. The blinking neon sign out front announced it to be "The agoon Tr vel Lodg" over a hand-painted sign of a palm tree and blue water.

"Here you are, mum."

She counted out money, handed it over the seat and stepped out. Angry men's voices came on the damp air. Shouts rang out. She knew this place. The taxi pulled around and squealed out of the lot, leaving her in her past. Watching the shadowy corners of the parking lot out of the corner of her eye, Priss crossed the crumbly asphalt to the office, which turned out to be a four-by-four vestibule. On the other side of bulletproof glass sat a grizzled old man watching TV.

"How much for a room?"

He pulled the toothpick from the gap in his front teeth. "By the night or by the hour?"

"The night."

"Thirty bucks."

"Get out." She put a hand on her hip and glared. "Do I look like a rich tourist to you?" Some things never changed.

He eyed her faded T-shirt and backward baseball cap. "Okay. A double."

She grumbled and slapped a twenty into the teller's slot under the glass.

He slid back a ring with a key and an orange plastic palm tree with a flaking number four on it.

The room was about what she expected: bare ceiling bulb, scarred wood desk and threadbare carpet. The rattling air conditioner under the window wheezed out the ghosts of ancient cigarettes that had died here. After checking the lock and hooking the safety chain, she crossed to the bathroom. Pitted fixtures and a black-flecked mirror were at least marginally clean. If you didn't inspect the corners too close.

Dropping her backpack on the only chair, she pulled the extra blanket from the closet to spread over the bed. It should be halfway clean since most people wouldn't want to use it, given the weather and the substandard AC.

Flipping off the light, she crossed the room guided by the sodium lamp through the crack in the plastic blackout curtains.

She dropped onto the bed, unlaced her tennis shoes and swung her socked feet onto the bed without touching the yucky carpet. The bed sagged in the middle but wasn't too awful. She lay back and rested her head on her arm.

She should sleep like a baby. The traffic sounds and shuffled noises through the paper-thin walls were the familiar sounds of her childhood. But instead, fear came on like a predator's feet. It crept in the steps walking past her door and in the murmured voices around her. Like she had as a child, she lay frozen on the bed, making a deal with God—if she didn't move, she'd be kept safe.

You're not that scared little girl any more. You're a grown-up and you can take care of yourself.

Had she checked the locks?

She jumped at a knock behind her head. When it became a rhythmic bumping, she sighed, trying to block the picture in her head of what was going on next door.

I wonder what Nacho and Adam are doing?

God, she wished she had her phone to call them. Just to hear their voices…. Nacho would probably be working on his jigsaw puzzle before bed. Or

maybe Olivia had come over and they were all playing Scrabble. Homesickness engulfed her in a wave
so strong she ached. How she'd love to have Adam's
arms around her right now. She rolled into a ball.

Maybe he'll go with us. A small voice whispered
from deep in her mind.

*Oh, yeah, that's going to happen. His business
is in Widow's Grove. His family is there. His roots
are there.*

And Adam's roots went deep. He was like a big
oak, while she and Nacho were just sparrows, staying to rest for a while…but how nice would it be to
stay in those sheltering branches?

You don't stay.

Well, it wasn't like she'd be breaking some universal law if she did.

*You know how it works. If something matters,
you start to count on it. When it's taken away it
leaves a hole and you have to start all over, sealing it up.*

And this time, it wouldn't only be her that would
be hurt. She had Nacho to think about.

Sure was a pretty dream though.

When the banging finally stopped next door, she
lay sweating, listening to the traffic.

ADAM CARRIED THE empty pizza carton to the trash,
glad that his offering had scored points. "So what
happens now?" He'd helped Nacho with a couple

of math-story problems before dinner but now the evening stretched ahead like a field planted with land mines.

Nacho just shrugged and picked at the red place-mat in front of him.

You didn't really dream he'd make it easy, did you?

Adam grabbed the sponge from the sink and wiped down the clean counter. "What do you want to be when you grow up?"

The boy heaved a long-suffering sigh. "Do all grown-ups go to class to learn what questions to ask kids? They must, because you all ask the same thing."

"Work with me here. I'm just trying to get to know you."

"I wanna be in a gang." His expression was tough but the words sounded tentative, as if he were test-ing them out for the first time.

Jesus. What the heck do you say to that?

Priss was braver than he'd known, taking this on. But she'd told him to look deeper. He paused mid-swipe and studied Nacho, slouched in the chair, kicking the legs, and shooting looks at Adam out of the corner of his eye.

He's nervous, too.

And you're the adult.

"Well, that's one option." He tossed the sponge in the sink and made himself walk around the counter, pull out a chair and sit. "It reminds me of the old Who song."

"Who?"

"Yeah, they're an old band. Pete Townshend is a legend. In one of his lyrics, he said, 'Here's the new boss, same as the old boss.'"

"What's that supposed to mean?" The kid's chin went up.

Just like Priss's, before she set her feet and got stubborn.

"You don't like people telling you what to do, right?"

He crossed his skinny arms. "Damn straight."

"Well, don't you think the leader of the gang is going to tell you what to do? What people to hit, what corner to sell drugs on?"

Nacho snorted. "Dude, you been watching too many Denzel Washington movies."

"Yeah, well, maybe. But my point is, why not be your own boss? Look at me. I've got my own business."

"Oh, yeah, stand around all day and talk to old ladies about their feet. Sign me up."

"One of the coolest things about being an adult is that *you* get to choose. You could go to college—"

"Can you really see a universe where that happens?" Nacho squinted at him.

He smiled, hearing Priss's words coming out of Nacho's mouth. Maybe she was rubbing off on the

kid. "Sure I can. You're smart. You can do anything you want to."

Nacho's cheeks reddened and he looked away.
"Well, I don't want to do that."

"Okay, maybe trade school. Or after high school
you could start a custom-painting business, like
Bear's."

"Oh, man, that would be cool."

There *was* a kid in there. Adam saw it in the
disbelieving hope in Nacho's eyes, heard it in the
boy's reverent tone.

"Think about it, that's all I'm saying." Adam
smiled. "Well, I have some ordering to do for the
store."

"I'll go get the puzzle out of the bedroom."
Nacho stood. "Priss had a cleaning fit before you
came and made me put it away *again*."

"Hang on. I have another idea." Adam walked to
the living room and pulled his secret weapon out
of his backpack. "How'd you like to read instead?"
He held up the book.

Nacho walked over, took *Harry Potter and the
Chamber of Secrets* from Adam's hand and stared
down at the cover. "This is awesome!" He looked
up, unsure. "Is this for me?"

Adam chuckled. "It's all yours."

"Wow. Thanks." Nacho walked to the couch and
jumped, landing on his back.

"Feet off the couch." Adam stood there, feeling like a superhero for the simple act of making a child happy. A warm heat rose in his chest, bringing with it a gratified smile.

No wonder she does it.

PRISS EASED THROUGH two Detroit fans to the front of the crowd at the door to the visiting team's locker room. It was the only place she could be sure to catch Sandy Otto.

The game had been great, even though the base runners looked like ants from her cheap seat. Hoping to bank some good karma, she'd cheered on the Tigers to the win. Her stomach growled a grinding protest. Her seat had been cheap but ballpark food was ungodly expensive. She'd pick up something to eat on the walk back to the hotel.

The sun burned through her shirt, adding to the sweaty sheen on her skin. Damn, this trip had convinced her that this bird wouldn't be flying south anytime soon. She was not a fan of humidity.

The door opened and the baseball fans pressed her on either side as a phalanx of players exited.

Priss's heart sped up. If she missed him here, she'd only have one other chance, on Sunday. She scanned the faces that passed.

There!

A young redhead carrying a gym bag stopped, blocked by a player signing a kid's autograph.

"Sandy! Sandy Otto!"

He looked up with a TV host's fake smile. "Hi."

"I'm Priss Hart. I know your dad. Can I talk to you for a minute?"

He stepped out of the flow of traffic. "How do you know my dad?"

She'd thought he'd be more likely to stop if she'd said that. "Well, actually I've only talked to your dad. Your grandfather is a good friend of mine."

His smile blinked out. "My grandfather is dead."

"He's not. But he's gravely ill. I thought—"

"Well, he's had ten years more than my grandma. Worry over his drinking killed her." He looked over her head. "Now, if you'll excuse me."

"Barney's very proud of you." She touched Sandy's forearm to stop him. "Surely you wouldn't deny an old man a chance to see you before he dies?"

He stared down at her hand until she removed it.

"Like I said, my grandfather's dead." He walked away.

CHAPTER EIGHTEEN

PRISS PACED OUTSIDE the same door, in the middle o
the same Detroit fans after the game the next day
She had to try once more—for Barney. For her mom

For herself.

Lying in her ratty bed last night, she'd run argu
ments through her mind, trying to come up with
the perfect words to convince Barney's grandson
to visit his grandfather.

That, and imagining what was happening a
home.

Funny, but after the distraction of the game yes
terday, she'd felt a tug in her chest as if a rubbe
band connecting her to California had pulled tight
She justified it because Nacho was there. Might a
well admit it; she loved that little shit.

But it wasn't Nacho that had her tossing and
turning late into the night. She missed Adam, too
At first she'd blamed the missing on her greedy
body. But when she was still awake after midnight
she had to admit it was more than that.

Adam had made it clear that he hadn't wantec
her to make this trip.

And yet...

He'd accepted that she had to go. He'd held her while the guilt she could no longer hold in poured out.

And in spite of understanding Nacho as much as a cat did a Rubik's cube, Adam had agreed to stay with her brother, to keep him safe. Not because Nacho meant much to him but because Nacho meant so much to her.

What did that mean?

It means he's a nice guy. You've known that since the first time you met him.

Maybe so, but he'd done all that for *her*.

The door to the stadium opened, breaking her train of thought.

"Sandy!"

She saw when he recognized her. His lips tightened and his brows came down over sharp-edged eyes. And he kept walking.

"Sandy, you need to come to California. Not for your grandfather. For yourself."

When he hesitated, the stream of players flowed around them. God, she didn't want to do this. Especially not in public. But it might help—all of them.

"Trust me, I know how this works. I left my mother and all her drama behind and never looked back. I found out later that she died poor and all alone." She heard the pain that dripped from her

words but she had to keep going, because he was
listening.

His face was cold and closed, but still, he listened.

"No one should have to live with the guilt I
feel...the guilt I will feel for the rest of my life.
You need to—"

He held up a hand. "Look, lady, I'm sorry for
your problems. But trust me, I'm going to sleep just
fine at night." He shook his head. "However long
that old man suffers, it's a lot less than my grandma
did." He turned to walk away.

Oh, no, you don't. Not till I've had my say.

Adrenaline pumped into her blood. He'd only
taken one step away when she grabbed his bicep
and pulled him around. Her heartbeat drummed
in her ears and she shouted over it. "He's in Valley
Hospital in Santa Maria."

A rent-a-cop security guard stepped between
them. "Lady, let him go."

She tightened her grip. "You don't want to do
this, dude. You'll regret it for the rest of your life!"

Otto jerked his arm away. The guard put his
hands against Priss's shoulders and pushed her
back. Cotton tore.

Otto stumbled back, looking down at his ruined
shirt.

"Hey!" A cop in uniform ran up, grabbed her
hand and whipped it behind her back.

"Don't. Dammit, I'm just talking to him!" She twisted away, wincing when she felt a muscle pull in her shoulder. But the cop still had her by the wrist and the security guard blocked her view. She yelled over his shoulder. "Barney is sorry—sorry for it all. Do it for *you!*" She stood on her tiptoes trying to see around the guard.

When the cop behind tried to grab her other hand she flailed and felt her knuckles smack flesh. "Stop it! Sandy—wait. Let me go!"

Both arms were jerked behind her and her shoulder sockets screamed. At the cop's growl, she turned her head.

Fury in his eyes, his lips pulled back from teeth red with the blood spurting from his nose. Something kicked the back of her knees and she went down. When her head hit the pavement, the world winked out.

THE HOLDING CELL was cold. Or maybe it was shock that made her teeth chatter in spite of her clamped jaws. Her head throbbed with the bongo beat of her heart, and she raised a hand again to touch the goose egg at her temple. She'd only been out for a minute so the EMT had cleared her to the cop's custody.

The booking was as efficient as a meat-packing plant and she was spit out at the end feeling as processed as a cellophane package of hamburger.

Why do they have to crank the air conditioning so hard?

She shivered in vain. The six-by-ten cell contained only the cement bench on which she sat, a metal seatless toilet and metal bars. No cot, no blanket. She hugged herself and sat straight, having learned that leaning on the cinder-block wall leeched what little heat she had.

The cop may not have been gentle but she could hardly blame him. She hadn't recognized that wild woman at the stadium this morning.

Assault and battery on Sandy Otto. Resisting arrest. Assault on a police officer.

Holy shit, how had she let things get so out of control?

Just forget what can't be fixed. The important question is what are you going to do now?

Since she had no record, they were only going for misdemeanors. But since she didn't live here, she was considered a flight risk. Bail was not only more than she had on her, it was more than she had in the bank.

And Adam and Nacho thought she was on a plane right about now. She glanced around, but there was no clock on the wall outside the bars. After all, why taunt prisoners with passing time? She didn't need it anyway because she heard the minutes ticking away in her head.

How long before Adam started worrying?

If she were on her own, she'd work it out somehow even if it meant sitting her time out in jail. But because of Nacho, she didn't have a choice. She slumped on the bench, elbows on her knees, fingers dangling. She had to figure out how to best deal with this and get back to Nacho as soon as possible.

You're a great role model. She'd tried to convince Nacho to be an upstanding citizen and here she sat, in jail.

And how could she possibly ask Adam's help again? He'd been above and beyond wonderful up to now, but calling from jail for bail money? She imagined the disapproval in Adam's voice if and when she got the guts to call. Pictured him looking down his nose at her, the way he had Nacho that day he was caught stealing.

Shame coated the inside of her chest in a thick, caustic paste, burning through her illusions. She could go to community college. She could work in an office. She could act like she belonged in a book club. But at the bottom of it, Priss Hart was a still a mutt. Always a mutt.

Widow's Grove and the people in it had somehow gotten inside her, stripping her of her walls and weapons. She felt naked, bared to the skin and vulnerable to the braided leather whip of judgment.

But how could judgment hurt a woman who prided herself on not caring what others thought? She shifted her weight to the other deadened cheek.

It couldn't. Unless she was no longer that woman.

But if she wasn't, then who was she?

The clang of metal brought her head up. At the sound of footsteps on tile, she stood.

A police officer walked up to the bars, his hand around the upper arm of a woman. While he unlocked the door, Priss looked past the curtain of long black hair and heavy makeup.

She's so young!

"In you go."

The girl walked past the police officer, stilettos clicking, her bare shapely legs shown to best advantage in a tight butt-skimming skirt. Her lace spandex top left little to the imagination.

Overwhelmed by a miasma of cheap perfume, Priss stepped back as the girl plopped onto the cement bench and crossed her legs.

The cop locked the door and walked away.

The girl's eyes challenged, as if daring Priss to start something. "What'd *you* do?"

"Assault."

"What, did you get into it with another soccer mom?"

"Huh?"

"No, wait. There was a really good sale at Nordie's and you fought it out over last year's designer blouse."

Priss ran a hand down her faded Hurley T-shirt and holey-kneed skinny jeans. "Are you kidding me?"

"Dress down all you want." She tossed a hank of hair over her shoulder with a flick of her long fake nails. "I know middle class when I see it."

Priss snorted. "You don't know how wrong you are."

"Whatever." The girl turned to look out the bars, the clearest dismissal possible, given the tight quarters.

No longer able to even pace the three steps to the bars and back, Priss leaned against the wall. Hadn't this young woman only confirmed what she'd known since she walked into that dumpy hotel room?

You don't belong in this world anymore.

But she'd just admitted that she'd only been posing in her Widow's Grove world.

So where did that leave her? She felt like someone standing with one foot on a dock, the other on an unmoored boat, and if she didn't make a decision fast, her ass was sure as hell going to get wet.

But Nacho would get a dunking right along with her.

Oh, that's bullshit. You've been using Nacho as an excuse for too long. You're the one who always insists on the truth. So why don't you just face it?

Where she came from wasn't as important as where she wanted to be. Wasn't that why she'd flown from place to place since she left Vegas? She may not have known it at the time, but looking back she could see she'd been looking for a place to settle.

And these past months, she'd found it.

But it was more than that.

Her short fingernails bit into her palms.

If she really looked past that blind spot…

She wanted it all. The small-town life. The brick house with the rounded wooden door that looked like a Hobbit lived there. The small-town pharmacist who mistakenly believed she *was* all that.

The cold that chilled her blood wasn't due to the air-conditioning.

If something matters, you start to count on it. When it's taken away it leaves a hole in you.

But the old words that used to chew through her no longer had teeth. She wanted to grab at the chance the universe had mistakenly thrown her way.

The question was, did she have the guts to grab it?

"What have I got to lose?" A flash of heat bloomed in her chest.

She realized she'd said it out loud when the prostitute looked up.

Priss just smiled.

She already had way more than she'd flown into town with. She had Nacho. His behavior was improving. He was reading, and his grades were coming up. He'd found Bear, and maybe someday that relationship would lead Nacho to a career.

She'd stumbled onto a home and a family. No way she was leaving.

But what if Adam does finally see through the middle-class disguise to the mutt underneath?

Still pictures of Adam flashed through her mind. Him wearing that silly double-breasted white pharmacist jacket, smiling across the table at her. His hand, warm over hers, in the darkened car the night they searched for Nacho. The soft look in his eyes when he held her after sex.

Could he love her? Was that what was at stake here?

Yeah. I think it is.

He was the only man who saw past her bullshit and for whatever misguided reason, seemed to care about the woman underneath it. He was kind and giving, and she had done nothing but bring chaos to his orderly life.

And if she got up the guts, she was about to do it again.

She crossed her arms over her midsection to ease the burn. Bullets fired from her own gun always did the most damage.

Well, screw that.

She pushed away from the wall. She wasn't going groveling, looking for a handout. She was going to call the man she loved and ask him for help. She was who she was—rough edges and all. If Adam decided after this momentous disaster that he didn't want her, she'd survive that somehow. Avoiding pain by flying from it didn't leave it behind. Hadn't she found that out with her mother? Hadn't that been what she'd been trying to tell Sandy Otto?

Surety mingled with the heat in her chest, spreading outward, warming her.

Priss Hart had been many things, but never a coward.

She stepped around her celmate's stilettos. "Hey!" She yelled through the bars. "Don't I get a phone call?"

CHAPTER NINETEEN

"YOU'RE WHERE?" When several shoppers looked up from the aisles, Adam walked into the drug room and closed the door.

Priss's voice sounded continents away. "Are you and Nacho okay?"

"You're in *jail* and you're asking if we're okay? Are you drunk?"

"You know I don't drink. And you need to calm down."

He scrubbed his hand through his hair. "Just tell me what happened."

"Sandy Otto wouldn't listen. I got mad, and things got a little out of control."

"What are they holding you for?" His brain cranked in the background, working through how one went about wiring bail money.

"A couple of things. But the one I probably won't be able to plead out is the assault on a police officer."

"Jesus, Priss. When I get out of control, I disagree strenuously with an umpire. This is all new to me. Let me think. Will they let you out on bail?"

"Yeah, but—" she hesitated a heartbeat "—it's a lot."

"That's okay, hang on…" He reached for a scratch pad and pulled a pen from the breast pocket of his jacket. "Tell me how much and where I wire it."

She told him.

"It's going to be okay. Now, you hang loose. Help is on the way."

"Adam, I want you to know, I'm going to pay you back. Every penny."

"We'll worry about that later, Hart. Are you safe where they're keeping you?"

"Yes. But—no, dammit. That's not what I want you to know."

When he heard her sniff, his heart thumped, hard. He wanted to crawl through the phone and break her out of that damned jail. Why couldn't the Tigers have been playing in Phoenix?

"I want you to know. No matter what happens after this, I love you."

Click.

He stood staring at the display on his phone. "Did you just say what I think you said?" His voice came out all wavery, his throat clogged with emotions too big to get through.

He knew the guts it had taken for her to pick up the phone and call him for help.

He couldn't imagine the courage it took for her

to admit, at what he was sure she considered her weakest moment, that she loved him.

She loves me.

Joy threaded up through his chest like bubbles from the bottom of a champagne flute.

If his little scrapper had the guts to do that, what excuse did he have not to face what he feared most?

"Oh, hell, no. You're not telling me you love me and then hanging up." He dropped the phone in his pocket and fired up the computer to check flights to Tampa.

It was time to ring that damned bell.

"WHAT'S WRONG?" Nacho stood frowning in the doorway of the school office.

"Everything's fine. We almost forgot your dentist appointment today." The last thing he wanted was to explain within earshot of the secretary that Nacho's guardian was in jail.

Nacho scanned Adam's face. "Oh. Yeah."

"Let's go. We don't want to be late." He put a hand on Nacho's shoulder and steered him out of the office.

When they pushed out the glass door into the sunshine, Nacho shook off his hand. "What happened?"

"I've got to fly to Tampa. My mom has agreed to watch you until—"

"What's wrong with Priss?"

He glanced at the tats on the backs of the kid's fingers, imagining the life he'd lived so far. He could handle the truth. "Come on. I'll tell you on the way."

Nacho planted his feet. "Tell me now."

"I do not have time for this. I need to be at LAX in two hours." Adam glanced around the thankfully empty lot.

Nacho crossed his arms. "She's my sister."

"Okay. She got arrested, trying to talk to that ball player. I'm going to bail her out and bring her home."

A smile spread over Nacho's face. "Wow. Go, Priss."

"Now can we go? I've got to drop you off and get to the airport."

"I'm going, too."

"No." Adam strode for Mona, lounging topless beside the SUVs like a bad girl at a football camp.

Nacho followed, sliding over the door and plopping into the seat. "Seriously. Can I go?"

"No."

"Come on, Adam. I won't be any trouble, promise. I've never been on a plane before."

"Kid, this is not a vacation. It's not a joy ride. Your sister is in trouble."

"I know."

Adam turned when Nacho touched his arm.

The tough mask was gone. The kid looked scared. "Please let me go. She's all I've got."

He squinted at the kid. "Are you working me?"

Nacho held his gaze, tracing a cross over his heart. "Swear."

If the county got wind of her arrest, Priss would lose custody of Nacho in a heartbeat. He'd be sent back to the group home. Adam's chest tightened. God, he'd hate to see that happen.

The kid's got at least as much at stake as you do.

"Okay. If you promise *not* to be a problem." He clicked his seat belt. "*And* providing I can get you a seat."

"Yay!" Nacho held up a fist to bump. "We're gonna rescue Priss from The Man."

"You've been reading too much fantasy, kid." He bumped, hoping he wouldn't live to regret this.

Thanks to the gods of old cars, once they stopped in for a change of clothes and to tell Adam's mother the latest development, Mona started right up. The ride down to LAX was uneventful. That is, except for the fear that built in Adam like an approaching storm. It gathered in his muscles, slowly tightening them as if in preparation to withstand a gale force wind.

And when they walked into the terminal, it began to blow.

Beside him, Nacho looked everywhere at once, chittering like an agitated squirrel.

Adam tried to block it out, listening instead to the thunder rolling through his mind.

Nacho stopped at a huge floor-to-ceiling window. "How cool is that?"

A 747 lifted off the runway a few hundred feet away. Though the noise was dampened by the thick glass, the air vibrated with the power. Fear shot along Adam's nerves, and when it hit the ends, they cracked and sizzled like cut live wires.

Like the ones their plane had snagged on, all those years ago.

They found their gate and sat. Well, he sat. Nacho stood at the window watching the busy ground crews.

Shit. Who am I kidding? I can't do this. Hell, I can't even stand to look at the brochures I bring home; I just go get more. I've never gotten higher than twelve feet up the rock wall at the gym.

You are going to do this.

Walk down that tube? Into that aluminium casket? Then sit there for hours and act normal while you wait for it to go down?

You need to get to Priss.

You know you were meant to die in that crash.

If you can't do this, you're not man enough for a strong woman like Priss Hart. She'll eventually figure out that you're a coward and you'll lose the only thing that—

"Tower to Adam." Nacho stood front and center, waving a hand in Adam's face.

He swiped his fingers through the sweat at his hairline. "What?"

"If it'll take your mind off it, I could go steal something from the newsstand." Nacho plopped into the next plastic chair in line.

Adam shot a look around, thankful that not many people flew on Sunday. "Did your sister tell you?"

"Come on." Nacho did his whole-body sigh thing. "Like anybody can't tell you're scared. Kids are small, not stupid." He pointed. "You're shredding your luggage tag."

He looked down at the backpack he'd thrown their change of clothes into, just in case this took longer than he hoped. "Can you go up to the counter and get another one for me?"

Great. He pulled a pen from the pocket of the backpack. Now he was going to have the little hardass on his butt, cataloging his every move.

Nacho returned. "Here, give me the pen. You're not gonna be able to write so anyone can read it."

Adam handed over the pen.

Head down, writing, Nacho asked, "So what happened?"

Adam's hands twitched. He tightened his grip on his thighs. "You don't want to know. It'll make you nervous on the flight."

"Dude. This is your issue, not mine." He looked

up, straight into Adam's eyes. "Not to sound like Oprah, but it helps to say it out loud sometimes."

"How do you know?"

Nacho just shrugged and went back to writing.

So he told him. The sanitized SparkNotes version.

Nacho listened, rapt. "Damn. You're brave to do this."

One bubble of fear escaped with his snort. "I'm not on the thing, yet."

A woman's voice announced, "Delta flight 255 to Tampa, leaving out of terminal eight, Gate 22."

Nacho stood.

Heart hammering, Adam didn't. There was something wrong with his knees.

I can't do this.

"Hey, Adam."

"What?" He ground the words from between locked jaws.

"The Duke said that courage is being afraid and saddling up anyhow. Besides, just because that happened in one plane, doesn't mean all planes are bad."

The echo of what he'd told Priss about "nice guys" all those weeks ago made him look up into the eyes that were so like hers. "You know, if you keep taking after your sister, there may be hope for you yet."

"Call for all rows to board Flight 255 to Tampa out of Gate 22."

Adam flinched. *How am I going to do this?* His fingers shook even though they had a death grip on the seat of his chair.

"Hey." Nacho stood, hand extended. "Come on. We gotta go save Priss, remember?"

"Yeah, I remember." His words came out jittery but he managed to stand.

Nacho's hand slipped into his. "If you tell my homies I held hands with a guy, I'll make your life hell. You know that, right?"

"You're assuming we're going to live through this."

They boarded the plane together.

Nacho had asked for a window seat. Adam took the middle, figuring if he was sandwiched in it would make it harder to run.

At the stewardess's suggestion, he pulled his belt tight. Then pulled it tighter.

"Wow, is this amazing or what? I never thought I'd get to go anywhere on a plane."

"How could you expect so little of life?" Adam slid his hands under his legs to hide the shake.

Mouth tight, Nacho stared out the window.

Way to go, ace. Where this kid came from, a plane ride was as likely as you becoming an astronaut.

Shame loosened his terror.

"That's another good reason to choose your career wisely. You want to have the funds for the good stuff." When the engine drone rose, Adam grimaced. "Not that any part of this is the good stuff."

"How much do you think I'd make as a custom painter?"

Revenue expectations and retirement plan explanations carried Adam through takeoff with only one minor panic attack when the captain powered back at cruising altitude.

"See? That wasn't so bad." Nacho stared out the window. "Oh, cool, I've never seen the tops of clouds before."

Adam had to look. And he found he could, just, because the ride was so smooth.

Nacho pointed. "It looks like you could bounce on them. But—" his smile dissolved "—I knew that was bull."

"What?"

"Ah, nothin'."

"Tell me, Nacho."

He scanned the clouds. "Once, in the kid warehouse, a minister came to talk to me. He said that my mom was an angel living in the clouds with Jesus." He wiped a finger down the window. "I knew that was just a story to make me feel better."

Adam's heart squeezed but not from fear. "You believe this plane is going to stay up in the air, right?"

"Course I do."

"Why?"

"I learned that in school. It's 'cause of the way they shape the wings." He cupped his hand to demonstrate. "The air goes over it, and makes lift."

"How do you know? Look out there. I can't see it."

"Because you can't see air. But that's what—oh." One corner of Nacho's mouth lifted and he glanced over. "You're different than I thought."

"Ditto, dude."

Nacho smirked and rolled his eyes. "Don't say 'dude.' It is so not you."

"All right, deal." Adam reached out his hand and they shook on it. "You know, I have kind of a plan for when we see Priss. But it won't work without you. You want to hear it?"

"Does a bear shi—um. Yeah."

Just then Adam did something he never thought he'd do on a plane again.

He smiled.

CHAPTER TWENTY

WHAT THE HECK is taking so long?

Even the prostitute had made bail hours ago. Priss paced her three steps to the bars. Now she knew how a stray mutt at the pound felt. Except people came to see them. No one had come back here in a long time. Her gut twisted, only partly due to hunger.

What if Adam had to borrow the money?

You've asked too much. You should have worked this out on your own.

Yeah, but how? Stage a breakout? The forty dollars she had on her was a fart in the wind to that bail. And Nacho had to go to school tomorrow. If the county found out she was in jail, they'd take him from her.

She wrapped her arms around her burning stomach. "God, how did I honk this up so bad?"

You didn't think, that's how.

She was used to reacting, dancing and juking her way out of trouble when it found her. But that only worked solo. Besides, she'd vowed to leave all that shit behind.

But she hadn't left her temper behind and look where that had led.

Okay, so you're going to have to change. Again. She'd try to blend in, to toe the middle-class line from now on. It wasn't her. She'd hate it. But if it would give Nacho a safe, even-keeled home life, it would be worth it.

Her main focus had to be Nacho.

She straightened her shoulders and finger-combed her hair. She'd let it grow out. She'd wear ironed cotton clothes and proper loafers. She'd trade Mona in for a mommy-mobile.

No more temper. No more mutt.

She stopped, hands on the bars, peering down the hallway.

How long does it take to wire money? Maybe after he hung up, he got fed up and decided to let you cool your heels.

How would she know?

The money wouldn't show up, that's how.

Her stomach continued its attempt to consume itself.

She remembered Adam, standing behind the drug counter in that sexy white coat, smiling while an octogenarian told him about her great-grandbaby. She remembered him out in front of the drugstore, apologizing to Nacho.

Adam was a true-blue nice guy. If he said he'd

bail her out, he would—even if he wanted nothing to do with her after this.

Two hours later, despair had set in.

Set in, hell, it had camped out, lit a fire and commenced a drunken party.

She sat on the cold cement bench, knees pulled up, resting her aching forehead on them.

Clang!

The metal door at the end of the hall slid open, and she bolted upright. Footsteps, then a cop stepped to her cell. "You made bail."

Thank you, God...and Adam Preston.

There was an open-ended ticket home in her backpack at the hotel and the forty bucks she still had would buy her a cab ride to the airport. Luckily, the police station was only two miles from the hotel. Shouldn't take long to walk.

She bounced on her toes, waiting for the cop to quit fumbling and get the door open. Her stomach rumbled but it was just going to have to wait until she got home.

Home. Warmth spread through her. *You're going home soon.*

No matter what awaited her in Widow's Grove, it couldn't ruin the perfect feeling of having a home to go to. She followed the cop down the hall to a window where another police officer handed over her fanny pack and her baseball cap.

"Thanks." She flipped it and put it on backwards,

then remembering her vow, took it off and put it on right.

No more mutt.

When the cop unlocked the last door, she walked into the lobby of the police station, eyes on the door to the outside. If she jogged—

"Hey, where you going?"

Nacho?

He ran over, threw his arms around her and hugged her hard. "You saved me from the kid warehouse. So we came to save you back."

Closing her eyes, she put her nose to his hair and pulled in the scent of kid. Her kid.

She glanced up, and when Nacho let her go, guts jumping, she took the few steps to where Adam stood, hands in the back pockets of his jeans, his expression unreadable.

Nacho followed her, not touching, but close.

"You flew?"

"What else could I do? You hung up on me."

"Wow. That's amazing."

"Couldn't have done it without Nacho's help."

Nacho beamed.

"Priss—"

"Please, just let me get this out first." If she waited she wouldn't have the guts to say it. "It goes without saying—I'm going to pay you back as soon as humanly possible."

When he opened his mouth to speak, she held up a hand and addressed Nacho.

"I did a lot of thinking today. I put some things into perspective. First, we're staying in Widow's Grove."

Nacho pumped a fist. "Yes."

"It's past time I grew up. My focus from now on is you and making the best home that I'm capable of. If it means becoming a soccer mom, I'm going to—"

"Hang on. I'm not signing up for that crap."

"Dude, it's just a euphemism, relax." She turned to Adam. "And I want you to know that things are going to change. No more stray mutt. I'm going to—"

"But I like mutts." He spread his hands. "They're loving, fiercely loyal, and they're brave." One side of his mouth tipped up. "My life was way too boring before you two burst into it. You both helped me discover my own courage by witnessing yours." Adam's eyes bored into her. "You don't have to give up your priorities in order for us to have a relationship.

"Okay. But I think we all have things we can learn from each other. What do you say we call a truce in keeping score and just see where this leads?"

Watching them both, Adam waited.

"I'm in," Nacho said.

She'd have never believed there was a place for her to call home. And yet, in Widow's Grove, she'd found it. She'd never imagined having her own family, but then her brother dropped into her life. She'd never believed in wanting such a thing because it didn't result in having. But could it be that having *was* possible?

She wasn't sure. But one thing was certain; if she didn't reach out and grab the chance, she'd never find out. And with this man, it felt safe to reach.

A calm happiness welled in her as she took Adam's hand. "Oh, yeah, sign me up, too."

A smile transformed his face, softening the tight lines. His eyes promised things. Good things. He squeezed her hand. "Okay, then. Let's go home."

They walked to the door. Adam held it open, slipped an arm around her waist and whispered in her ear. "By the way, you hung up before I could tell you. I love you, Priss Hart."

CHAPTER TWENTY-ONE

A month later

NACHO PEDALED THROUGH the neighborhood, cool and slow, scoping it out. The trees hanging over the road rustled in the wind making sliding shadows on his bike look like ghost flames.

Hey, maybe Bear will let me practice by painting my bike.

He'd probably have to ask Adam first, though.

He rolled past a house. A basketball hoop on the garage roof, a Big Wheel overturned in the driveway. No dog in sight. Maybe he'd come back one day after school....

But the bouncy tickle he usually got in his chest thinking about it, didn't come.

He pulled a U-ie and cruised by again.

Crazier than that. The thought of going in one of those windows felt...weird now. Wrong. Not "gee, I shouldn't do that" wrong, but wrong inside.

Why, all of a sudden?

Pulling another U-turn, he looked close at the

little home. It was perfect. Hell, he could even see a window at the side they'd left cracked.

So why not?

Because that tickle was gone. And that wasn't all. Somehow, over the past weeks, that hollow roar like a big wind inside him had calmed and he'd been so busy he hadn't even noticed.

Things had changed since they flew back from Tampa. Priss seemed more settled. Happier, maybe. Probably because Adam was hanging around more. A lot more.

Well, Nacho could get behind that. Having another guy around was pretty cool, actually. It took two guys to balance out Priss's bossiness.

The door to the house opened and a man came out. A lady followed him, carrying a little girl, her legs wrapped around her mom's waist.

Nacho rode on.

He felt around inside his head.

Quiet. Calm.

No wind, no vacuum, pulling him in all different directions at once.

So what is this?

Maybe it was him. Maybe under all that wanting was *him*. Not the Nacho he was supposed to be, but who he really was. Maybe he didn't need those houses anymore because he'd found one of his own.

Maybe—

Beep!

Mona pulled alongside him, top down. Adam drove leaning back with just his fingers on the wheel, his other arm stretched over the back of the seat.

"Hey, Nacho, where've you been? I've been looking for you." He pulled over and threw the car in Park. "Come on, we're going to be late."

Nacho hopped off his bike. "Late for what?"

Adam got out of the car, walked around it and picked up the bike. "Barney's getting out of the hospital today. Sandy Otto called. He needs help moving his grandpa into his new apartment." He lifted the bike into the backseat.

"Can we get our old TV back now?"

Adam opened the passenger-side door, and Nacho got in. "You got my vote, but you'll have to ask your sister." He slammed the door and jogged around Mona's hood. "Anyway, we're going to swing by there before we go to dinner."

"So where's Priss?"

"She's talking to your mom. At the cemetery." He checked the mirror, then pulled out.

Nacho snorted. He thought a minute. "Do you think Mom can hear her?" he said softly, because he wasn't sure he wanted Adam to hear his question.

"Absolutely."

I'm going to do that. I want to tell Mom about Bear. He shot a look at Adam. *And stuff.*

They drove through town, the sidewalks crowded

with tourists. "Hey, Adam. Would it be okay if I paint your bike? Maybe purple. With ghost flames. It won't look ugly, I promise. Bear said—"

"It's your bike, guy. Do what you want with it."

That tickle in his chest was back. But this time it was happy excited, not scary excited. He smiled. He liked this tickle better. Leaning back, he draped his arm outside the car so people could get a good look at his natural coolness.

They rolled out of town.

"Hey, dude," Nacho said over the wind.

"Yeah?"

"When you gonna man up and ask my sister to marry you already?"

The car shimmied when Adam whipped his head around, his eyebrows raised above his sunglasses. Then he looked back at the road, his mouth in a straight line. "How'd you get so smart all of a sudden?"

THE NEW GRASS had grown over the grave, greener than the rest. They'd put a little marker at the head with her mom's name, and the dates that bracketed her life like parenthesis. Forty-seven was really young to die.

Priss glanced around to be sure she was alone, not sure how to begin. The sun was warm on her shoulders and a breeze played with her hair. The only sound was the far-off noise of traffic from the highway and the sparrows chirping in the shrubs a few rows over.

"Hi, Mom." She cleared her throat. "I'm back. Late, I know." She shifted her weight to the other leg. "Nacho's safe. I've got him now, and he's doing good. I think he may end up painting cars for a living. Can you believe that?" She slipped her hands into her back pockets. "I just wanted to tell you that I get it now. It's not easy raising a kid. I've already screwed up so many times. First I was too lenient, then I was too tough. I still don't know if I have it right, but I'm going to make the best home for him that I know how. So he won't have to…"

This didn't feel right.

She lowered herself to sit beside the grave and wrapped her arms around her knees. "See, I figured it out. You and me, we were birds of a feather." She smiled. "How could we not be?" Her mother's pretty face appeared in her mind. "You flew from man to man, looking for someone to love you. I flew from place to place, looking for somewhere to belong." She rested her head on her knees. "But you didn't need to go looking, Mom. I loved you. I always loved you." The wind sighed around her. "I know. It's not like having a man hold your heart safe in his hands. But it's something, you know? Nacho taught me that it's something pretty special.

"So maybe it's enough. Enough for you to rest easy." She tucked her nose in the crook of her elbow. "I'm sorry, Mom. So sorry that I didn't get it sooner. I should have been here. Should have…"

She waited until she could go on. It didn't matter; her mom had all the time in the world. "Thank you for telling Gaby that you didn't blame me. I'm going to pay you back, anyway, though. I'm going to put all my love into Nacho. He's not going to be weighted down by the shit you and I were held back by. He's going to fly free."

She wiped her eyes on the sleeve of her shirt.

"And, Mom? Thanks for bringing me here, to Widow's Grove. Because it turns out, here is the home I was flying around looking for."

She stood. "I gotta go now. But I'll come see you sometimes. Bring you updates, okay?"

She kissed her fingers, then turned to see her guys walking up the hill to her.

* * * * *

LARGER-PRINT BOOKS!

GET 2 FREE LARGER-PRINT NOVELS PLUS

2 FREE GIFTS!

HARLEQUIN®

Romance

From the Heart, For the Heart

YES! Please send me 2 FREE LARGER-PRINT Harlequin® Romance novels and my 2 FREE gifts (gifts are worth about $10). After receiving them, if I don't wish to receive any more books, I can return the shipping statement marked "cancel." If I don't cancel, I will receive 4 brand-new novels every month and be billed just $4.84 per book in the U.S. or $5.24 per book in Canada. That's a savings of at least 19% off the cover price! It's quite a bargain! Shipping and handling is just 50¢ per book in the U.S. and 75¢ per book in Canada.* I understand that accepting the 2 free books and gifts places me under no obligation to buy anything. I can always return a shipment and cancel at any time. Even if I never buy another book, the two free books and gifts are mine to keep forever.

119/319 HDN F43Y

Name _____ (PLEASE PRINT) _____

Address _____ Apt. # _____

City _____ State/Prov. _____ Zip/Postal Code _____

Signature (if under 18, a parent or guardian must sign) _____

Mail to the **Harlequin® Reader Service:**
IN U.S.A.: P.O. Box 1867, Buffalo, NY 14240-1867
IN CANADA: P.O. Box 609, Fort Erie, Ontario L2A 5X3

Want to try two free books from another line?
Call 1-800-873-8635 or visit www.ReaderService.com.

* Terms and prices subject to change without notice. Prices do not include applicable taxes. Sales tax applicable in N.Y. Canadian residents will be charged applicable taxes. Offer not valid in Quebec. This offer is limited to one order per household. Not valid for current subscribers to Harlequin Romance Larger-Print books. All orders subject to credit approval. Credit or debit balances in a customer's account(s) may be offset by any other outstanding balance owed by or to the customer. Please allow 4 to 6 weeks for delivery. Offer available while quantities last.

Your Privacy—The Harlequin® Reader Service is committed to protecting your privacy. Our Privacy Policy is available online at www.ReaderService.com or upon request from the Harlequin Reader Service.

We make a portion of our mailing list available to reputable third parties that offer products we believe may interest you. If you prefer that we not exchange your name with third parties, or if you wish to clarify or modify your communication preferences, please visit us at www.ReaderService.com/consumerschoice or write to us at Harlequin Reader Service Preference Service, P.O. Box 9062, Buffalo, NY 14269. Include your complete name and address.

HRLP13R

LARGER-PRINT BOOKS!

HARLEQUIN *Presents*

PASSION GUARANTEED SEDUCTION

GET 2 FREE LARGER-PRINT NOVELS PLUS 2 FREE GIFTS!

YES! Please send me 2 FREE LARGER-PRINT Harlequin Presents® novels and my 2 FREE gifts (gifts are worth about $10). After receiving them, if I don't wish to receive any more books, I can return the shipping statement marked "cancel." If I don't cancel, I will receive 6 brand-new novels every month and be billed just $5.05 per book in the U.S. or $5.49 per book in Canada. That's a saving of at least 16% off the cover price! It's quite a bargain! Shipping and handling is just 50¢ per book in the U.S. and 75¢ per book in Canada.* I understand that accepting the 2 free books and gifts places me under no obligation to buy anything. I can always return a shipment and cancel at any time. Even if I never buy another book, the two free books and gifts are mine to keep forever.

176/376 HDN F43N

Name	(PLEASE PRINT)
Address	Apt. #
City	State/Prov.　　Zip/Postal Code

Signature (if under 18, a parent or guardian must sign)

Mail to the **Harlequin® Reader Service**:
IN U.S.A.: P.O. Box 1867, Buffalo, NY 14240-1867
IN CANADA: P.O. Box 609, Fort Erie, Ontario L2A 5X3

**Are you a subscriber to Harlequin Presents books and want to receive the larger-print edition?
Call 1-800-873-8635 today or visit us at www.ReaderService.com.**

* Terms and prices subject to change without notice. Prices do not include applicable taxes. Sales tax applicable in N.Y. Canadian residents will be charged applicable taxes. Offer not valid in Quebec. This offer is limited to one order per household. Not valid for current subscribers to Harlequin Presents Larger-Print books. All orders subject to credit approval. Credit or debit balances in a customer's account(s) may be offset by any other outstanding balance owed by or to the customer. Please allow 4 to 6 weeks for delivery. Offer available while quantities last.

Your Privacy—The Harlequin® Reader Service is committed to protecting your privacy. Our Privacy Policy is available online at www.ReaderService.com or upon request from the Harlequin Reader Service.

We make a portion of our mailing list available to reputable third parties that offer products we believe may interest you. If you prefer that we not exchange your name with third parties, or if you wish to clarify or modify your communication preferences, please visit us at www.ReaderService.com/consumerschoice or write to us at Harlequin Reader Service Preference Service, P.O. Box 9062, Buffalo, NY 14269. Include your complete name and address.

HPLP13R

11/29/14